Praise for *Centerville*:

"Karen Osborn's deeply af.⁣_____ ___terville keeps the incomprehensibility of evil always in focus, as her characters—young, old, brave, cowardly, driven by doubt, and committed to faith—struggle to find a way back to the innocence they once took for granted. In this subtle, beautifully written novel, the reader can almost hear the gates of paradise slamming closed on the American dream."

—Valerie Martin, author of *Trespass, Mary Reilly, Italian Fever, Property,* and *Salvation*

"Most writers would stumble over the top describing a blast that literally explodes the personality of a small town. In the hands of a master of craft, like Karen Osborn, devastation is rendered with devastating restraint. You may try to forget *Centerville,* but you never will."

—Jacquelyn Mitchard, author of *The Deep End of the Ocean*

"A novel that seems as if its subject isn't past at all but rather pulled right from America's latest cycle of mass murder and senseless carnage, a novel of brilliant prose and deep insight into the dark alleys of our twisted nature. . . . As with *In Cold Blood* or *The Sweet Hereafter,* Karen Osborn's beautifully written *Centerville* uses a single, horrific, smalltown act of violence to dissect the values and morals of an entire culture—a culture that is at once violent and brutal, materialistic and superficial, yet capable of moments of heroism, compassion, and redemption."

—Michael White, author of *Beautiful Assassin* and *Soul Catcher*

Karen Osborn

Centerville

a novel

Vandalia Press • Morgantown 2012

Vandalia Press, Morgantown 26506

Copyright 2012 Karen Osborn

All rights reserved

First edition published 2012 by Vandalia Press

Printed in the United States of America

20 19 18 17 16 15 14 13 12 9 8 7 6 5 4 3 2 1

PB 978-1-935978-64-0

EPUB 978-1-935978-65-7

PDF 978-1-935978-66-4

The quotations from the Bible are taken from the following versions: the King James Version (Cambridge and Oxford), the New American Standard Version, and the New Oxford Annotated Bible.

Library of Congress Cataloging-in-Publication Data

Osborn, Karen.

Centerville, a novel / Karen Osborn. -- 1st ed.

p.   cm.

ISBN 978-1-935978-64-0 (pbk. : alk. paper) -- ISBN 1-935978-64-0 (pbk. : alk. paper) -- ISBN 978-1-935978-65-7 (e-book) -- ISBN 1-935978-65-9 (e-book) -- ISBN 978-1-935978-66-4 (pdf) -- ISBN 1-935978-66-7 (pdf)

I. Title.

PS3565.S385C46 2012

813'.54--dc23

2012013716

Praise for *Patchwork*:

"A psychologically sophisticated tale. . . . Ms. Osborn, herself a poet, often renders rural dialect into something close to poetry." —*New York Times Book Review*

"A haunting and purely told drama of kinship, womanhood and the long aftermath of tragedy . . . this is fine new fiction, deserving a place on the shelf and in the heart." —*Booklist* (starred)

"An admirable example of the trueborn storyteller's art. . . . This is an exciting novel, powerful and memorable." —George Garrett

"Karen Osborn has many gifts, not least among them a talent for dialogue that impels her story forward with hard power." —Fred Chappell

Praise for *Between Earth and Sky*:

"Osborn has the rare ability to encompass a grand time span . . . lyrical, focused, and enchanting." —*Booklist*

"The landscape itself becomes the central character in Karen Osborn's novel, placing its mark on all those who are ensnared in its power." —*New York Times Book Review*

Praise for *The River Road*:

"An extraordinary effort to engage the American condition as we find it now, write down what happens in a given situation, or what might happen, and adroitly slip away, leaving the reader to decide the meaning—which has nothing to do with arcane literary allusions, but everything to do with the state of the human soul. . . . Karen Osborn should be proud of what she has done here." —*The Washington Post*

"Hypnotically and seductively fluid . . . beautifully told. . . . Osborn immerses us from the beginning in hot and cold currents of love and hate that sustain, divide and inexorably pull us all toward an uncertain fate." —*USA Today*

"Bursts with sensuality and the recklessness of youth." —*Booklist*

"With grace and poetry, Osborn explores how the biggest emotions are sometimes found in the smallest seconds—and how a single moment might be the switchback that changes our lives." —Jodi Picoult

For my father, Kenton Osborn
1929–2006

On Main Street sunlight fell through the four large windows that made up the storefront of Greenly's Drugstore. A golden haze moved through the store, spreading like liquid poured from a gigantic cup, as George Fowler carried a brown paper sack inside and stood next to a display of birthday cards. The display was set up on a tall, narrow rack that could be rotated to view the different choices. His wife, Joyce Fowler, a cashier, had just finished straightening it.

At the back of the store, Carlton Greenly, the store's owner, sorted through cardboard boxes. He'd just sent Al Freeman, the store's pharmacist, across the street to get some lunch, which meant the pharmacy was temporarily closed, and he was working at the back alone.

George Fowler leaned down, and a flash of light from the windows slid across his shirt as he placed the paper sack on the floor. It was an innocuous-looking brown bag, the sort a customer might have left behind. There was a new crease at the top, where he had pressed the two sides of the bag together and folded them over so they would stay shut. The bag sat on the gray linoleum, slightly rumpled in the afternoon light. He straightened, looking oddly calm, and left the bag on the floor.

It took a few minutes for the paper bag to be discovered. Stella McNeese had come into the store on a sudden impulse that struck her as she left the bank. As she walked toward a display of journals and notebooks, she paused, staring at the sack. "What's this?" she said, bending down to pick it up. "Someone's left this."

Bruce Watson had come into the store on his work break because he needed cigarettes. He had decided to get a candy bar as well. When he heard Stella, he was standing in front of the candy shelf vacillating between a Baby Ruth and a Three Musketeers bar.

"What is this?" Stella McNeese asked, a little louder.

He glanced up then and saw her lifting the paper bag. He heard the sound that seemed to be coming from inside the bag, a slight sound that blended with the other sounds inside the store so that it was hardly noticeable. "Don't," he said instinctively. "Put it down. Don't touch it."

She bent over and placed it back on the floor, afraid now.

"Where did it come from?" he asked. "Who set it there?"

An employee, Billy Sandler, rounded the aisle, on his way to the back of the store to see if the delivery truck had come yet. Behind him was Davy Sandler, Billy's cousin, who was a year younger and had been working at the store for only a few weeks.

"Mrs. Fowler's husband was carrying a bag like that," Billy said.

"He was here?" Joyce straightened up from a shelf, and walked around to the aisle where the others stood. "When?"

"Just a few minutes ago," Billy told her, nervous at the accusation in her voice. "I didn't say anything. I mean I figured he has a right."

"What was he doing here?" She spoke the question as a demand, and Billy stepped back, not answering her. Joyce had left George a month before. A few weeks ago, a box had arrived at her sister's duplex where she was staying. When she'd ripped away the packing tape and pried open the cardboard, she'd found strips of cut material. Passing her fingers through them, she'd realized the pieces of rayon and cotton were from the dresses she'd left hanging in her closet.

Bruce Watson knelt down on the floor, listening. The sunlight seemed to gather around him and he felt suddenly warm. "It sounds like a bomb," he said, his voice strangely matter-of-fact. He pressed the edge of the paper bag between his thumb and forefinger, gingerly opening it. "It's a bomb!" he said, louder.

Debra Gregory looked up from the soda fountain where she worked. Her younger brother sat at the fountain with his two friends, drinking Cokes while their mother got her hair done across the street.

Carlton Greenly looked up from a box he'd just opened, uncertain of what he'd heard. "A what?" he called.

"A bomb!" Joyce Fowler and Bruce Watson yelled at once.

"Oh Lord," Joyce added. "George has brought in a bomb!"

Carlton set down the box. It was filled with aspirin bottles, and as it tipped on its side, several bottles rolled out onto the floor. He stood, watching them. Then as the final bottle came to a stop, he was filled with a sudden decisiveness.

"It could explode!" Bruce shouted.

"Throw it to me!" Carlton yelled. He reached up his hands with an instinctive gesture. He wanted to get the bomb as far away from the store and the people as possible. "I'll throw it into the alleyway." A vacant lot stretched behind the drugstore and the business next door. If he pitched the bag hard enough, he could clear a sizable distance between the bomb and any of the nearby buildings.

Bruce curled his fingers around the top of the bag and slowly straightened, lifting it from the floor. Stella McNeese moved quickly toward the door, but Joyce Fowler froze watching him. She expected the bag to be heavy, and the effortless motion of Bruce Watson's back as he raised it from the floor surprised her.

Bruce stretched his arms overhead and snapped back his wrists, as his hands released their grip and the paper bag sailed through the air. It was an excellent throw, made with the over-handed ease of an outfielder. The bag cleared heads and the racks of merchandise, narrowly missing one of the light fixtures. Because Bruce had secured the top of the bag with two additional folds, none of its contents dropped as it skimmed along the ceiling.

Carlton Greenly held his hands up. There was a millisecond as the bag seemed to hang suspended in the sunlit air above him, and then he caught it. He tightened his hands around it, feeling the crinkle of paper between his fingers as he brought it down, cradling the bag against his chest, his body pivoting toward the rear of the store. He did all this automatically, a surge of power filling him.

"Yes," Bruce breathed out, raising his arms in an involuntary sign of victory. And then the bomb exploded.

Behind the soda counter, Debra saw the explosion, but her mind didn't keep pace, so she didn't know what had happened. What she saw was actually two explosions happening within seconds of each other—the sudden bright flash of the bomb followed by the burst of flames as the gas line at the back of the store ignited. She stood staring in surprise as her brother and his two friends turned into three columns of fire. Inside the flames, she could still trace the outlines of their faces and bodies. This seemed a strange thing, and then she looked down and saw that her own body lay on the floor covered with flames. Glass from the Coke bottles littered the floor. She wanted to go and search out the broom and dustpan to sweep it up. The linoleum countertop curled as it melted.

Joyce Fowler was staring at Bruce Watson when the bomb exploded. Somewhere in her mind, she knew the danger of throwing an explosive, but between the discovery and the pitch, she hadn't thought about that. Instead she'd been filled with an odd sense of hope and even assurance that Carlton could throw the bag into the alley before it detonated. Now both she and Bruce were quickly engulfed by the fire that followed. Bruce turned and looked at her, first with alarm, then with a look of kindness. "Sorry," he seemed to be saying with the shrug of his shoulders, and she felt her own apology well up inside her. George had meant the explosion for her, but now it would kill all of them.

Stella McNeese, at the front of the store, heard the explosion behind her and felt the great suck of air as her body was thrown from the building. Billy and Davy had begun to run through the front door as the paper bag sailed over the aisles, and they heard the smashing of glass as the large windows exploded. It seemed to them that this was the main sound, and they weren't aware of the sound of the bomb going off or the roar of the fire. The explosion lifted them, carrying them toward the sidewalk, but before Davy reached it a section of the ceiling crashed down, hitting the back of his head, and he lost consciousness.

The light seemed to move through the store more swiftly now, as if the flames fed it. Joyce Fowler saw it spreading like a giant web. "Hold on to me," the web seemed to call, as she reached up out of herself.

Carlton Greenly hadn't heard or seen or felt anything. Bruce Watson had seen him make the catch and turn his back. He had watched Carlton turn into the blinding light of the blast, a glow that hovered afterward like billions of iridescent particles.

Within seconds, the building swelled with flames. They hissed down the aisles, lapping against the walls and shelves. In the center, the flames burned white. Along the edges they flickered yellow and red. The flames rose higher, ingesting oxygen, feeding on anything in their path. The light spread over them, and in the roar and crashing as the second floor dropped through the ceiling, there was the radiance of that light, like a chorus or the singing of angels.

Two miles away, Reverend Edwards, the minister of Centerville's Methodist church, heard a sound like that of thunder. He glanced up from his desk. He'd been working on the next day's sermon. What he knew was this—Centerville lay tucked away in the heart of the country bordered by the plains of the west on one side and the cities of the east on the other. In his twelve years at the church, the congregation had grown from forty members to more than one hundred, and tomorrow morning they would fill the pews. When he heard the chords of the processional, he would walk up to the front of the sanctuary and stand before them. He would read the words from the Old Testament and the Gospel, followed by his sermon.

His service would celebrate the evidence of God on earth, and he had just finished reading a verse he would use from Isaiah: "In the year that King Uzziah died I saw also the Lord sitting upon a throne, high and lifted up, and his train filled the temple. Above it stood the seraphims: each one had six wings; with twain he covered his face, and with twain he covered his feet, and with twain he did fly. And one cried unto another, and said, 'Holy, Holy, Holy is the Lord of hosts: the whole earth is full of his glory.'"

Now he sat listening. The room was quiet. The only sound was the rattle of an electric fan and the whisper of tires against the pavement on the street beyond the window. Tiny seedpods had formed on the maple tree, and if he looked closely, he could spot one drifting toward the lawn—pale green and transparent in the light. Sunlight still danced across his desk, shifting into patterns of shade on the floor and walls. The minister shut his eyes, and when he opened them again, the paper in front of him seemed glaring white in the haze of the afternoon sun.

A strange silence, afterward shouts and the sound of something else, like a blast of wind. Even one block away, there is the smell of smoke. An ignition stutters, then an engine catches, coming to life, and a vehicle rolls forward.

Chapter 1

en thousand years ago, glaciers receded across the Midwest of America, leaving the land flatter and laced with streams, lakes, and rivers. Thousands of years ago, on that same land, an ancient people constructed large, earthen mounds. On the flattened earth, they could be seen from miles away. Viewed from above, they resembled cones, circles, squares, octagons, and giant loaves of bread. Centuries later, when the European settlers arrived, the earthen mounds were still present, and they scattered their homesteads, towns, and cities among them.

Centerville was typical of these towns, and in 1967, Sandi Edwards lived there with her parents in a modest, white brick colonial, in the neighborhood behind the church where her father was the minister. Upstairs, she had her own bedroom with two windows. One looked onto the backyard, and from it she could see the red-roofed rim of the town's hospital and the woods next to it that lay between her neighborhood and the church. The other window looked out onto the sidewalk, which connected the neighborhood to the nearby streets leading downtown. For a fourteen-year-old, the house was perfectly positioned, because you could walk out the back door and along the nearby sidewalk and be downtown in thirty minutes.

In the summer of 1967, in a small town like Centerville, it was still possible to drift from one day to the next. Days were defined by what happened during them, and very little happened. Monday became Tuesday, which turned into Wednesday—each one slipping through the fingers like knots tied on a thread. Almost two years earlier, before his death, Malcolm X had referred to the "American nightmare," but in Centerville, people were still experiencing the American dream, which was sleepy and slow, filled with decisions about the latest models of a Ford or a Chevrolet and maybe a new frostless Frigidaire. Places such as Detroit and Newark, where the racial riots were happening that summer, felt far away. The events at My Lai and Kent State hadn't occurred, nor the assassinations of Martin Luther King and Robert Kennedy.

Early in the afternoon on Saturday, Sandi and her friend Bert walked downtown to Bert's father's drugstore. Sandi had dark hair, which she was attempting to grow out. Recently, her mother had tried to trim the bangs, and they'd argued, as Sandi had wanted them longer so that she could sweep them off her forehead as Bert did with her longer, blond hair. Bert was the kind of girl who could turn a liability like being christened Bertha after a great-grandmother into an asset. For a few years now she'd insisted on Bert, and the name invested her with a kind of power. The nickname Sandi, on the other hand, popular due to a generation of mothers absorbed with Sandra Dee, made Sandi nearly anonymous. Even her decision to spell it with an "i" instead of a "y" hadn't distinguished her. Bert and Sandi had just started high school, and after just a few days, it seemed that Bert already knew everyone, while Sandi disappeared when she walked down the crowded hallways, and if she couldn't find Bert when she stepped into the lunchroom, she wasn't sure where to sit.

The two girls had been close friends since the age of five, and for a couple of years now they'd been walking to the drugstore a few times a week to sit at the soda fountain and paw through magazines or wander up and down the makeup aisle with its shelves of lipsticks, pressed powder, and tubes of mascara. The models pictured in the magazines that year all wore pale colors of lipstick—muted pinks and milky lavenders with hints of silver and names taken from the ocean like Soft Coral or Pink Shell. Their pictures showed long, straight, blond hair and skin that had been darkened with a new product said to produce a tan without the sun. Joyce Fowler, who worked at the drugstore, saved Bert and Sandi samples of lipstick, nail polish, and perfume. Recently Joyce had shown Sandi how to test a lipstick's color by rubbing a little of it on the inside of her arm.

It was the end of August, but the past few days the temperature had reached nearly one hundred, and it was clear that this was still the season for tornados. Yesterday the students had been let out early since the buildings weren't air-conditioned. Today it was even hotter. Nothing moved—the dogwood and mimosa trees that lined the sidewalks, the awnings on the buildings, and the two stoplights, each one block apart, dangling over the intersections. White clouds rimmed the horizon, and the asphalt pavement, which had just been torn up and rolled out new again, gleamed like a black river.

In the sunlight, the drugstore's large front windows glared. Sandi put her hand on the door, but then instead of opening it, she stepped away. Bits of dust floated through the air like slivers of mica as heat poured off the building in waves. It was as if something as ordinary as a wall had descended, forcing her to turn away.

"Why are you stopping?" Bert asked as Sandi let go of the door's handle.

"Let's go down to the bowling alley first," Sandi said, walking away from the store. Her flip-flops slapped against the sidewalk as she shook her dark hair back from her face.

"We said we were going to the drugstore," Bert told her as she turned to follow. "I don't want to go to the bowling alley."

Sandi kept walking. She didn't know why she had changed her mind, but now she told herself that the bowling alley, with its central air conditioning, would be cooler. She had a self-conscious slouch, and her orange-and-white short set that had fit her at the beginning of the summer now looked too small on her. Bert wore a pair of cut-offs and a red halter-top her mother didn't know about.

"The bowling alley won't be as hot," Sandi said.

"My father probably has that air conditioner turned on. And there's all those fans. The drugstore wouldn't have been that hot," Bert argued as she traipsed behind.

"Maybe Carl and Harry are at the bowling alley," Sandi told her, referring to Bert's sixteen-year-old brother and his best friend, a boy Sandi had a crush on. "Isn't that where they said they were going?"

"Great. You just want to see Harry, and I already get enough of Carl at home. Way enough."

Sandi wasn't sure what to say back. The idea that the boys would be there had been an afterthought, but she felt herself blush just the same. The bowling alley, located a few buildings down from the drugstore, had a brick front with no windows and a door of darkened glass. "I hate bowling," Bert said, pushing past Sandi as they reached the door.

They slid inside quickly, and everything went briefly dark. It was something Sandi loved about the bowling alley, the inside was like a cave. Beside her, Bert let out a groan. "We don't have to bowl," she told Bert, standing next to the counter waiting for her eyes to adjust. "We can just hang out for a few minutes."

"I wanted to get a magazine," Bert said. "And a root beer float."

The bowling alley was one of the few buildings downtown with central air conditioning, and today it was turned up high. Sandi shivered as Mr. Jameson folded up his newspaper, slipping it under the counter.

"How about a game, girls? You want to rent some shoes?"

"No, thanks," Sandi told him.

"No way," Bert muttered.

As Sandi's eyes adjusted to the lighting, she glanced over at the eight bowling lanes. All of them were empty except for the last one where Carl and Harry were playing. As Sandi and Bert stood watching, Carl rolled one of the balls, and it thunked against the floor and spun into the gutter. Then Harry turned around, pivoting as he scooped a ball from the trough, his movements smooth and fluid. Sandi had heard he was helping to run the school newspaper, which she was thinking of signing up for.

"Hey, Bert and Sandi," he called out, noticing them as he moved to the top of the lane. "You want to take us on?"

Sandi followed Bert over to where they were standing. "If you think I'm going to play against my brother, you're crazy," Bert told them.

Carl glanced up. "Scared?"

"No one cares." Bert brushed her hair back from her forehead, tilting one hip higher than the other, the foot forward. She shaved her legs every morning, and they looked polished and darkened from tanning lotion and the sun.

"When I get my driver's license, you'll be begging for rides," Carl told her. He bent over and lifted another ball. He was wearing jeans and a T-shirt with his baseball team's name, Centerville Pioneers, in blue letters. His dark blond hair was cut short and acne mottled his forehead. He glanced up at Harry, who stood at the top of the lane holding his ball. "What are you waiting for?"

Harry hesitated, turning around as if he wanted to say something. Then he smoothly swung the ball back behind him, dropping down into a lunge. The ball hit the floor. It rolled toward the pins and cracked as it arrived at the end of the lane. Then a boom like thunder sounded from outside, and the lights of the bowling alley turned off.

"Shit," Carl muttered.

"That was a strike," Harry said. "I bet it was."

The blackness of the room was sudden and complete. Sandi couldn't see a thing. "Stay where you are, I'm getting a flashlight," Mr. Jameson called out.

"Maybe lightning hit the building," Sandi said.

"As soon as the lights come back on, I'm getting out of here," Bert told her.

"I've got a flashlight," Mr. Jameson shouted. A small, precise circle of light formed at the other end of the room. They felt something pounding outside, as if a train were about to come straight through the door.

"Jesus. Is that a tornado?" Harry asked.

Just then, the door to the bowling alley cracked open, and Sandi knew. She didn't understand what was happening, but she knew it was terrible, and she knew it was not a storm or a tornado.

"Get out of the building," someone yelled from outside. "Get everyone out!"

The flashlight's beam circled toward the entrance. As the door swung open, they could see Mr. Jameson stepping through it.

"Holy Christ!" Mr. Jameson's voice echoed from across the room as the beam from his flashlight scuttled back across the floor. "Get out of here! All you kids, get the hell out!"

Feeling their way, they tried to move as fast as they could, squeezing around the edges of ball racks and lane markers, bumping into benches. A metal waste can tipped over, crashing to the floor.

"Sorry, Mr. Jameson," Sandi called out, falling against Harry in a fit of embarrassment as she bent to pick it up.

"Leave it," Mr. Jameson yelled. The narrow beam of light swept across the floor as Bert tripped on a step. "Watch yourselves."

They stumbled to the entrance, where Mr. Jameson grabbed each one of them in turn by the shoulder, shoving them toward the door. "Quick. There's a fire."

"Why didn't the alarm go off?" Harry asked.

"The electrical outage must have disabled it."

What Sandi saw as she was pushed through the door made no sense. A wall of fire stood several hundred feet away from her. The flames swallowed the three stories of the building that was the drugstore. Then, Bert was sprinting toward it, screaming, "My father's in there!"

Small pieces of the fire dotted the sidewalk and street, and smoke filled the air. Above them, long plumes twisted like kites. Bert ran through a burst of fire, and it didn't seem to touch her. "Dad!" she yelled.

Sandi wasn't aware of her legs as she zigzagged across the pavement around spots of flames, lunging to miss the larger ones. The only fires she had seen before were the ones her father sometimes built behind the metal screen of their fireplace in the depths of winter. Once a small kitchen fire in her house scorched the walls, coating them with black soot. She had been in the front of the house cutting out ballet costumes from a booklet of paper dolls, and her father came as the fire alarm sounded and hurried her out the door before she even smelled the smoke. Later she'd found her cutouts scattered and trodden upon from where her father had rushed back inside to use the fire extinguisher. Afterward, instead of feeling frightened, she had felt a new sense of safety, as if anytime something dangerous happened, she would be rushed away while the danger was snuffed out.

By the time she reached Bert, they were so close to the fire Sandi felt as if they were inside it. The building no longer looked like a building. A three-story wall of flame blasted heat and the air throbbed. "Bert!" she screamed as loud as she could over the roar. She reached out and grabbed Bert's hand.

"My dad's in there!" Bert screamed back. She turned for a second and looked at Sandi, her face bright red with the heat.

More flames sprang up around them, the roar from the fire pounding like a hammer. It was so loud Sandi couldn't hear anything else, so hot she couldn't feel anything. "We have to get back!" Sandi screamed, jerking hard on Bert's hand.

"Let go!" Bert yelled, glaring at Sandi as she shoved her away.

Sandi stumbled backwards as Bert turned and ran, her red halter-top a smear of color against the smoke.

"Bert!" Sandi screamed. Bert's hair was white next to the fire. It stood out from her head as if she had stuck her finger in an electrical socket. She took several long running steps, and when she stopped, she was so close to the fire that she seemed to be inside it. She raised her arms to the sky, her hands spread wide. Sandi could see the pink nail polish Bert had applied the night before with careful strokes.

"Beauty is a product-based phenomenon," Bert had told her, holding the tiny brush between two fingers. Sandi had sat on the floor of Bert's room thinking about that statement for a long time.

The sound that came out of Bert now couldn't be defined. She screamed over and over. Her hair gleamed as if lit with sudden combustion. "Noooo!" She collapsed onto the pavement, as a burst of flames dropped from the sky next to her. "Nooooo," she wailed inside a ring of fire.

All around them now, fire dropped out of the sky. A woman who looked strangely familiar to Sandi sat nearby on the pavement in a flowered sundress. Several feet away, a white straw handbag lay with its contents spewed onto the pavement. Sandi spotted a tube of lipstick made by Revlon. The drugstore had been running a sale on them, and earlier Bert had talked about buying one.

"Get back!" someone yelled. Suddenly, a policeman grabbed Sandi by the shoulders and shook her. She noted that his skin was dark and there was an ashen smear across his face. His shirtsleeve was ripped. "Move back!" he yelled.

A few minutes later, he ran past, half dragging, half carrying Bert. "You! Get back!" he screamed at Sandi again. There was another man helping him, a man wearing a white jacket slashed with blackened ash. For a second, he stood so close to Sandi that she saw a clip with the man's name on it. With a start, she realized he was Mr. Freeman, the drugstore's pharmacist. "Get as far away from the fire as you can!" the policeman yelled at them. Somewhere a siren beat red, piercing the sound of the fire.

Sandi moved toward the curb, but she couldn't feel her feet. She couldn't connect the pieces of what she saw. The drugstore was a tower of flames, and there were small fires on the pavement in front of her and behind her. Smoke passed through her like air, and the places that had melted on the pavement glittered with an oily sheen. On the sidewalk where Bert sat, hunched over, others gathered, coughing. She recognized several of them, but in this context none of them felt familiar. A woman shouted, and a man raised his arm, pointing. Bert had stopped screaming. The street filled with fire, flames skimming the surface of the pavement. The policeman and Mr. Freeman were gone.

"Only one fire engine?" the man who was pointing yelled. "Where is the rest of the goddamn fire department?"

Sandi closed her eyes. Nothing about the scene felt real, and she couldn't imagine yet that anyone she knew was actually in the fire. If Mr. Freeman was still alive then Bert's father must be also, she told herself. Joyce must be alive, too. Just a few days ago, Joyce had given her a bottle of perfume with a Yardley's label on it and offered to curl her hair for her sometime. She had said Sandi could come over to Joyce's sister's house where Joyce was living now. Her sister worked downtown as a hairdresser, and Joyce was going to ask her to help them. Ever since Joyce had mentioned it, Sandi had been imagining the kind of hairstyle they would give her. She wanted it to look puffed out at the sides and flipped up on the ends, the way Joyce wore hers.

Sandi heard more sirens. The sound seemed to come from high above, as if it were dropping down on them with the pieces of fire. When she opened her eyes and looked up, all she could see was smoke. One of the fire engines was parked not far from where she stood. She watched the firemen in their dark coats and hats. Under the smoke they looked diminished, like a small colony of ants scrambling to protect their hill. One of them held a hose, and another one was waving his arms around, shouting orders.

Next to her, Bert knelt on the ground, her blond hair tangled and the red halter top coming undone, hanging down so that the top of her bra showed white against her tanned skin. A few days ago, she had lain sunning, topless, in her backyard. Before they walked downtown, Bert had shown Sandi the absence of her tan line. Sandi had tried to tan all summer long, but her skin just turned pink, then flaked and peeled. Even now, looking down at Bert's back, she felt the prick of jealousy, and it made her shudder. Nothing matched up.

The sirens grew louder, until she couldn't hear anything else. Two more fire engines came screaming around the corner. One passed them, its siren shrieking, while the other pulled up in front of them, the firefighters in their coats and hats vaulting from the truck, shouting at each other, and dragging a second hose across the pavement to a hydrant, where Sandi and the others stood. A fireman turned the wheel on the hydrant, and water arced through the air.

"Hell of a lot of good a few hoses are going to do," a man next to Sandi said. The woman beside him was crying.

A group of firemen gathered in front of the first truck. Then one of them ran to the edge of the fire and seemed to pluck something out. He lifted it over his shoulder, carried it back toward the curb, then laid it on the ground and wrapped it in another firefighter's coat.

"Could be Davy or Billy Sandler," someone said.

"Or maybe Carlton. He's about that height."

Bert stood up and Sandi put her arms around her. She felt Bert's heart beating fast and hard under the halter top.

"Let go!" Bert snarled, shoving her away.

"We have to stay here," Sandi said. "We can't move any closer. It's too dangerous."

"Who cares about dangerous?"

The firefighters carried the body to the sidewalk where everyone was standing. "It's Billy Sandler," someone yelled. "Where's the ambulance?"

"They've got farther to come," one of the firefighters told him.

"It's hard to get through all the traffic."

Sandi heard the shriek of more sirens. Bert fell forward coughing over and over again, a hard, retching cough until she vomited on the sidewalk.

"Oh Christ," the man next to them said. "Are you all right?"

Bert tried to speak, but nothing intelligible came out.

"What is it, dear? What do you need?" the woman asked her.

"We were with her brother," Sandi said. "I have no clue where he is."

"Maybe he went around to the other side of the building," someone said. "There's fire engines back there also."

Suddenly, a firefighter was in front of them. "Move back! Get away from the fire! Go down to the courthouse!"

An ambulance careened to a stop next to the fire trucks, its doors swinging open at the back, as medics jumped out and carried a stretcher to the body of the boy lying nearby. "This girl over here may have inhaled too much smoke," the man next to Sandi and Bert yelled. No one seemed to hear him.

"I don't know where her brother is," Sandi said again.

The man and woman helped her pull Bert up. Then Bert started coughing again, and the halter-top came undone, the front falling to her waist, revealing her bra, which looked too white above the tanned skin on her stomach.

"Retie her blouse," the woman told Sandi.

Sandi reached down and tried to pull the material up over Bert's chest, but Bert rammed her hard with her elbow and Sandi pulled away.

"It's all right, honey," the woman said. "Just leave it."

They lumbered several feet together, then stopped again. Someone shouted. The wall of fire beat red and yellow, and the flames that dropped behind them onto the road were strangely alive and beautiful, like bright birds.

"It was a bomb," someone said.

"How do you know?"

"It had to be."

Bert sat down on the sidewalk. A woman ran into the street, screaming, and grabbed hold of one of the firefighters. "Both my children were in the drugstore!"

The firefighter yelled something back, and seconds later another firefighter grabbed her arm. "Get back on the sidewalk!"

"You have to find them!" She passed a blue cloth bag from one hand to the other. Her head was covered with hair rollers. The firefighters struggled with the hose, and the blast of water from it seemed to feed the flames. Everything seemed to feed the flames.

Then Sandi saw another policeman. He was stepping into a pair of boots and pulling a dark firefighter's coat on over his uniform. A firefighter put something on his back and handed him a hat. They stood together facing the fire, and then Sandi watched as the policeman walked straight into the flames.

"Everybody, move away!" the other policeman yelled at them. "Get back to the courthouse."

Some of them turned and started to run toward the courthouse, but Sandi stood watching. She felt as if she were already inside the fire, as if she were part of it somehow, or part of what was feeding it.

"John went over to the drugstore just thirty minutes ago," someone said.

"I think Lucy was over there also."

"I have no idea where my kids are."

"What happened?" a man asked. "Are we sure it was a bomb?"

"Had to be. What else could it be?"

"Who would set off a bomb?"

Bert still sat curled over on the sidewalk. Sandi could look down and see the clasp of her bra. She thought about it coming undone the way the halter top had. "This tan took me all summer. I have to show it off," Bert had said earlier when she took the halter top out of her drawer. "I bought it yesterday."

"Did your mother see it?"

"Would I still own it if she knew about it?"

"Your dad will see it if we go in the drugstore."

"He doesn't notice anything when he's working. Plus, he's not like my mom. Thank God he's not like my mom."

Sandi crouched over her. "Bert, we have to move away," she told her, but Bert curled up tighter, her head firmly against her knees. Sandi heard the dark, deep sound of a sob move through her.

"Get back!" the policeman yelled. "That hardware store might explode!"

"Bert!" she screamed, not knowing what else to do. Then the policeman bent and lifted Bert up again in his arms. As he began to run with her, Sandi ran after him. She kept his uniform and his dark head in her sight. The man and woman who had been next to them were gone. It seemed as if the only person in the world besides herself and Bert was the black officer.

They ran for about half a block, away from the fire. The officer set Bert down and turned to Sandi. "You kids, keep running! Don't stop until you reach the courthouse! Do you hear me? Do you get it?"

Sandi nodded. She turned and felt herself beginning to run. Beside her, Bert stumbled, coughing. The air was on fire.

Then, suddenly, Harry appeared in front of them, and she saw the steps of the courthouse. "What are you guys doing?" he screamed, grabbing hold of her. "Why were you so close?"

"Where's Carl?" she yelled back.

"I don't know," he said as he helped her with Bert. "I've been looking all over. I can't find him anywhere. I don't goddamn know."

Chapter 2

Standing in front of the fire, Jack Turnbow struggled into his firefighting gear. His hands fumbled as he pulled the protective pants over the slacks of his police uniform and fastened them around his waist. Fire Chief Morgan strapped an air tank to his back as Jack fit the mask across his nose and mouth. Everything he touched or looked at was gray, already coated with ash. His eyes teared from the smoke and his skin felt raw. Turnbow was a policeman who was also a volunteer fire fighter, and while he'd assisted with a number of fires, none of them had been this large. The only living thing he'd ever gone in to rescue was a terrier. Now Jack was going in to find another firefighter after he and the boy he'd been sent in to rescue hadn't come out. Morgan hadn't wanted to risk anyone else, but Jack had argued that he would go in and get out quickly.

"As best I can tell they're in that corner where the wall fell. That's about where they were before the radio went dead." Morgan pointed to the right side of the fire, near the corner of the drugstore. "If you don't find them right away, get out. We can't risk losing anyone else."

Jack nodded. He took the fireman's hat from the chief and fit it onto his head. Jack was a large man who had started to bald. The firefighter's coat fit snuggly across his shoulders, and the helmet scraped his scalp as he adjusted the chinstrap. When the bomb went off, he'd been in his patrol car with his police partner, Martin Beckley, less than a block away. Stopped at a red light, they'd seen the building explode. In the silence that followed, he'd heard Beckley, a young, black officer Jack had been assigned to train, whisper, "He will destroy the covering that is cast over all peoples; He will swallow up death forever." As Jack ran toward the fire, his partner had started clearing people from the area.

"If you don't find them, come out," Morgan repeated now. "Don't spend too much time in there."

Jack nodded. He was staring down at the pavement in front of him, which was dark with water from the hydrant. His gloves felt too large, his boots like weighted casts. The other firefighters were focusing on containing the fire to the building where the drugstore had been and the one next to it, a two-story brick building that housed professional offices. Insulation, blown between its walls a few years ago, allowed the flames to spread without being seen. Because they couldn't reach the flames behind the bricks, the fire would feed on the insulation, raging inside the narrow space between the walls. The entire building could suddenly flare up, igniting the hardware store next to it, which housed over a hundred gallons of paint.

"If the hardware store goes, we won't have much warning," Morgan added. "When you hear me tell you to get out, do it fast."

Jack nodded and as he moved toward the flames, everything slowed, as if time itself was slowing down, when in fact events were tumbling one on top of another. The feeling numbed him, so that when he should have been most afraid, he wasn't. He saw the colors of the fire—the bright reds and strange oranges and yellows, the pure white with a sharp blue at the edges. He had loved fire when he was younger, had always asked to lay the wood down in the hearth when the house felt cold and damp. He would strike the match and sit watching the paper catch suddenly in its hidden place under the wood, the flame sputtering and then burning steady and bright. It felt as though he'd brought something to life.

Now the fire flamed above him, falling from the sky, pockets of it blossoming on the ground. He heard his breath inside the mask, and he felt his heart as if it held him instead of beating inside his chest. The skeleton of the drugstore branched in front of him, and he watched as one of its limbs flamed suddenly and came crashing down several feet away. For a moment he stood still, just looking, surveying the area. Then he perceived a small movement to his left, twenty feet or more away in the liquid flickering.

"I see them," he said into the radio, stepping around a patch of fire. The shape of a human limb lay on the ground next to the outline of a firefighter's helmet.

"Hurry up." Morgan's voice came through, full of static.

Jack's breath filled his mask, and his mind went blank. "Did you hear me?" Morgan's voice crackled through the radio.

"Yeah," he breathed out. "Heard you."

He was moving swiftly, even though it didn't feel that way, and within seconds he crouched over the firefighter, a man by the name of Glynn Sheer. Davy, the young stock boy, lay next to him. A wooden beam lay across the firefighter's legs, and both he and the boy appeared unconscious.

Jack bent over and grabbed the beam, straining to try to lift it, hearing the rush of heat inside his body. "What's going on?" Morgan's voice came through the radio, disjointed like sounds from another world. "Are they accessible?"

"Yeah," Jack told him.

"What's their condition? Can you get to them quickly?"

Leaving Glynn for a second, Jack knelt by the boy. The boy was still breathing, his shirt stuck to his back with a dark red stain. The voice of the chief came again from the radio.

"Jesus Christ, what's going on in there? You carrying them out? Access them quickly or leave them. That hardware store is unstable. It could go at any minute."

Jack hesitated, feeling the shrug of his shoulders under the heavy coat.

"Damn you, Turnbow. Give me an answer," the fire chief said, his voice gravelly with static.

"I'm carrying them out," Jack said, and then he turned off the radio.

Bending over, he lifted Davy. It was a struggle, getting his arms under the boy's shoulders and knees, but after he straightened, the boy's weight felt as light as a blanket. Taking several steps, he heard his own breathing, short and shallow in the mask. He turned to avoid a wall of flames and ran through the smaller clumps of fire that covered the ground.

Dan Lieberman, Jack's mentor when he started but now retired, was waiting at the fire's perimeter, having run across the fire-dotted pavement to meet them. Dressed in gear, he took Davy into his arms.

Jack spun around before the older man had a chance to say anything to him. Outside the fire's roar, a siren keened, and the foghorn blasted Morgan's voice. "Get back! And that means everyone!" The area where Jack had left the firefighter had filled with flames. He stamped out as many as he could, then bent over and grabbed hold of Glynn's arms. The firefighter's coat was slippery under his gloves, and it took him a moment to find a grip. Steadying himself, he placed one foot on the beam and pushed hard with it while he pulled with all his strength. When the man broke free, it was so sudden, Jack fell backwards onto the pavement.

"Shit!" He breathed out as he hit the asphalt. He wanted to laugh and scream. Pain radiated across his back. Not allowing himself to feel it, he forced himself up off the pavement, sliding one arm under Glynn's legs and the other under his torso. The man was limp, and Jack couldn't tell if he was breathing. Flashes of color from the flames rippled over them. He heard a ringing sound, and then there was a second of silence where everything was still, even the wall of fire. Next the ground shook as a burst of wind knocked him over. A string of explosions ripped the air, and in what felt like slow motion, he was thrown forward, landing on top of the man he'd been carrying.

Once he had a book about King Arthur and the sword Excalibur. There was a picture of the sword rising out of a lake, the sword silver and gleaming, the lake turquoise blue. He liked the rituals in the book, the ways in which knights were dubbed and the journeys they were sent on. Later he learned about other rituals, the ones followed by the Indians when they hunted.

Chapter 3

A block from the drugstore, Elizabeth Greenly was lifting her three-year-old daughter, Izzy, into the backseat of her car. The car was a new, dark-blue Oldsmobile station wagon with a silver luggage rack on top and an optional third seat in the back that her husband, Carlton, had recently bought for her. For several years after he'd taken the drugstore over from his father, the business had struggled, but now it was doing well enough that they could afford a second car. She had picked the station wagon out off the showroom floor, and Carlton had signed the papers agreeing to the terms of the loan. Then she had driven it home, and he had followed behind in their old sedan.

Now she didn't have to drive him to the drugstore early in the morning just so that she could have a car, and they had a larger vehicle to take on vacations. She wanted to drive south this year during the kids' spring break and stay in one of those small cottages on the coast of Florida, the kind tucked among a few palm trees next to the water, so that she could walk out the door and look at the ocean and feel as though she was at the edge of something enormous. Years earlier, before any of their children were born, she and Carlton had made that trip to Florida. It had reminded her of the northern coast where she'd grown up, except that Florida was a softer, warmer version. After just a few hours, the sound of the waves breaking against the sandy shore had become the only thing inside her head.

"Nine days, that's all it would take," she'd told Carlton a few nights ago after supper when they were sitting alone at the table. "Two days to drive there, two days to drive back, and five days that we could spend on the beach. You can be away from the store for nine days. Your father could look in on things, and Al Freeman could take over as general manager. We haven't taken a vacation in six years."

"Responsibility comes with ownership," he'd replied doubtfully, as if owning something made you less able to do what you wanted.

Now, as she slid into place behind the steering wheel, she inhaled the smell of the new upholstery and heard the crackle of the vinyl. Her hair was pulled back with an elastic band, and she wore comfortable shorts and a sleeveless shirt. She'd gained weight since this last pregnancy, and the seat belt rode up against her abdomen. Behind her, Izzy leaned forward over the back seat and slipped her hands around her mother's shoulders. "Mommy, I'm a kitty," she purred into her mother's ear.

Elizabeth reached back and rubbed her daughter's soft head. The blond hair that fell to Izzy's shoulders was straight and as easy to tangle as the silk on a corncob.

"All right, kitty, sit back in the seat and buckle your seat belt. Do kitties know how to do that?" she said.

"Hmm hmm," her daughter hummed into her ear. Then she felt Izzy slide away and heard the reassuring click of the seat belt. It was another reason she had wanted the new car. Their other car only had seat belts in the front seat. Now, if there was an accident, the entire family had protection.

"Meow," Izzy murmured. "Pet me."

"Not right now, Izzy. Mommy has to drive." Elizabeth peered

through the windshield as she started the car, squinting from the glare. The station wagon hadn't come with air-conditioning, but the dealer had said he could install it under the dashboard. She'd told Carlton she didn't need the air-conditioning, but now in the sweltering heat, she was reconsidering.

Earlier, when she was inside the post office talking with Janice Fitzpatrick, she'd heard what she thought was thunder. Two of the boxes stacked behind Janice awaiting pick-up had fallen, and the overhead lights had blinked and trembled. Since then, there had been the sound of sirens.

"We're supposed to get a doozy of a storm," Janice Fitzpatrick had said. "I heard about it on the radio. They said we could get as much as six inches of rain. And hail, they're predicting hail."

A dark cloud rested low in the sky in the direction of downtown. Elizabeth hoped to finish her errands before the rain started. She planned on stopping at the hardware store next to pick up more tiles for a birdbath she was covering as a crafts project. Now, as she prepared to leave the parking lot, she turned on the radio, anxious to get news about the storm. Two years ago a tornado had touched down in one area of the town, damaging half a block of buildings.

Slipping the new car into drive, she felt the sure shift of the gears. The hardware store was located two buildings down from Carlton's drugstore, and she told herself she would stop in to see him after buying the tiles. She drove to the exit, prepared to turn onto Main Street, but the steady stream of traffic meant she had to stop, waiting for an opening. Bits of powder drifted down from the sky, swirling toward earth, looking oddly like scattered flakes of snow. For a moment, she simply watched them. Then one of the flakes landed on her windshield, and she saw that it had a ragged, unsymmetrical shape. And then she realized the flake was ash.

Chapter 4

Reverend Edwards sat writing his sermon in his church office. Because the church itself was small, the brick house next to it that had once served as a parsonage was used to hold church meetings and the minister's office. When Reverend Edwards had first arrived in Centerville as the newly appointed minister of the Methodist church, the congregation hadn't filled the pews, but now some mornings they had to set up metal folding chairs at the back and along the sides to fit everyone. The growth of the congregation was his pride, and even if pride was a sin, he allowed himself the surge of it each Sunday morning as he looked out over the sanctuary. Recently the church members had discussed fundraising for the main building's expansion. These facts were part of what brought the minister such ease as he sat in the square of light writing the final notes for the sermon he would deliver the next morning.

His calling had arrived when he was a sophomore at a small religious college intending to major in chemistry. That fall he'd enrolled in a required religion course with the Reverend Dr. Fleming, and in the high-ceilinged room where the class met two afternoons each week, Dr. Fleming's words had moved him. Other students had complained about the professor who recited long passages of Scripture from memory, but the words had caught inside Reverend Edwards and he'd looked forward to those afternoons. Later he wasn't sure whether it had been those recitations that had convinced him to become a minister, or the debates held on topics like good and evil in the modern world, or the time he'd spent in Dr. Fleming's office. Dr. Fleming had alternately made him question his beliefs, then filled him with a certainty in both God and himself. Suddenly that year, the struggle of his parents to make ends meet during his years of growing up in the Depression had come into focus. His parents had let that struggle define their lives, when what mattered was not the daily toil but that one's life found meaning from within, despite the hardships the world sent. His decision to enter the seminary at the college had brought with it an immense relief, so much so that when his mother had worried that a minister's salary would be considerably less than a scientist's, he'd brushed her aside. The Korean War was being fought, and his decision meant he could end up without a draft deferment after college, but that hadn't deterred him either. Even before he'd learned he wouldn't have to go and fight, he hadn't felt any fear or hesitation. Instead, he'd been filled with the solid sense of having found his way.

After graduation, he'd married his college sweetheart, and everything had fallen into place. The draft for the war had ended, and a few years later, after serving under another minister, he'd been sent to Centerville to pastor his own church. The small town felt idyllic after the city where he'd grown up. In the relative peace and prosperity of the nineteen fifties and early sixties, his optimism had evolved naturally. Compared to previous wars, the Cold War was a quiet, faraway threat. Neighborhoods expanded, and all across town his parishioners sat around the supper table each night in their houses to say grace. When his daughter was born and his congregation began to grow, the minister felt he'd been handed the world.

Nothing had threatened his sense of easy optimism, not the recent racial discontentment in the large cities, nor even the more particular but possibly ubiquitous threat portrayed in the widely publicized, upcoming movie release of Truman Capote's *In Cold Blood*. Reverend Edwards was a quiet man who enjoyed equally sitting alone in his sunny office writing or holding meetings with his parishioners. A good listener, he found the right words that would direct, or reveal, or cause someone to see the other side of an argument or situation without his seeming too preacherly. Standing at the pulpit had been the only part of his office that had initially felt strained. He'd stepped up behind it, looking out through the thick lenses of his glasses at the sparsely populated church for signs of boredom or disagreement. But eventually, he'd eased into his vocation, and standing at the front of the sanctuary, he'd discovered the depth and volume of his voice.

Everything he saw was focused through the lens of liberal optimism. He'd read Martin Luther King's book *Strength to Love* and quoted from it in his sermons. He believed in integration, in the Voting Rights Act, and in the fight against poverty, but the problems of segregation and the poor seemed far away to him—in places such as Birmingham and Atlanta or Newark and Detroit.

Recently, when Charlie Bourne, a younger member of his congregation, came to his office after receiving his induction notice, the minister told him about his own experiences with nearly being drafted to fight in Korea. If the war hadn't ended, he would have served, he explained.

"Some are burning their draft cards," Charlie argued. "They say the Vietnamese don't even want us there."

"You can't believe the views of those who break the law," the minister told him.

"No one knows what the fight is for. And it's unfair—there's those that get exempt with a doctor's note or deferred because of an entrance exam, and then the rest of us."

"There are plenty who are fighting, and freedom is worth defending. Reporting is both a legal and moral obligation." The minister had spoken forcefully, because he believed in a world where responsibilities were clear-cut and morality meant possessing the courage to follow convictions governed by allegiance.

Charlie had lowered his head. "I should have enlisted two months ago, the week I graduated. I could have joined the navy or something. Now I have no choice. I'll end up in a rice paddy."

He'd left the minister's office, resigned to follow the right course. A few days later, the minister learned he had reported.

The sermon he was writing now came from his reflections on a passage in Mark: "Then Peter began to say unto him, 'Lo, we have left all and have followed thee.' And Jesus answered and said, 'Verily I say unto you, there is no man that hath left house, or brethren, or sisters, or father, or mother, or wife, or children, or lands, for my sake, and the Gospel's, but he shall receive an hundredfold now in this time, houses, and brethren, and sisters, and mothers, and children, and lands, with persecutions; and in the world to come eternal life. But many that are first shall be last; and the last first.'"

He scrawled the word *democratic* on a blank sheet of paper. Suddenly he glanced up from his writing. A shriek of sirens had invaded the small room. He stood and looked out the window. The church was blinding white in the afternoon sun, the colors of its stained glass windows drenched in light. The maple tree spread like a huge skirt between the two buildings. He identified two separate sirens and then a third. Because the church sat near the main artery that ran between the hospital and the downtown, sirens were not uncommon. Probably a traffic accident, he reasoned. But as his eyes adjusted to the light, he understood what he was looking at—not a few simple rain clouds pressing together at the horizon line, but cloud after impossible cloud of smoke.

He backed away from the window and began to dig in his desk drawer for his keys. Coming from the direction of the downtown area, the smoke, he reasoned, was not far away. The church was safe, but only a fire enormous in size could produce that amount of smoke. Some of his congregation would be down there, and possibly his wife or daughter. Then, as he grasped his keys, the telephone rang.

"The radio is saying there's a fire downtown. The drugstore is completely in flames," his wife said as he answered it. "Sandi and Bert left here to walk there over an hour ago."

He looked out his window again at the clouds of smoke, which bubbled toward the sky. "Just stay where you are in case they come back to the house," he told her. "I'll leave right now. I'll drive down and look for them. As soon as I find them, I'll bring them back."

He hung up not waiting for her response, and shoving his keys into his pocket, walked swiftly down the hall and out the front door. As another siren screeched to a terrible pitch, he ran to his car.

Chapter 5

Sandi had been sitting against the wall of the courthouse with Bert for more than an hour by the time the minister found them. "Sandi!" She heard her name being called and saw him moving toward her as she stood up and was pulled into a tight hug. There was a solidity to being held that made her feel even more fragile than she had felt sitting against the brick wall next to Bert watching the buildings across the street burn. She felt suddenly faint and her limbs began to shake.

"Are you hurt? Are you okay?" Reverend Edwards pulled back and held his daughter by the arms looking down at her face. He'd parked his car three blocks away because of the traffic, and he had run most of the way. "Are you injured?" he asked her.

Sandi managed to shake her head no.

He glanced behind her at Bert. "Were you two in the fire at all?"

Sandi shook her head again. "We were in the bowling alley when it happened," she told him.

The minister pressed her face against his shirt again, hugging her so hard it hurt her arms. When he let go, she wished he hadn't, but he had turned to Bert who was sitting against the wall of the courthouse. "Are you all right?" he asked her. When she didn't answer, he took Sandi by the hand as if she were a little girl and walked her over to the wall. Sandi slid down next to Bert again, and he crouched in front of them.

"Bert, are you all right?" he repeated, laying a hand on Bert's shoulder. Bert didn't resist the way she had when Sandi tried to comfort her. Instead she seemed to move closer, folding her body toward him.

Sandi leaned back against the wall. Earlier when someone who knew them from the church had stood with them trying to talk about the fire and see if they were okay, Sandi had found it difficult to respond. The woman had helped Bert retie her halter-top and had offered to try to find out something about Bert's father. "Will you two be okay until I come back?" she'd asked Sandi, and Sandi had nodded without answering. Now she reached down and touched the edge of her shirt. When she was younger, she used to get comfort from running a finger along the folded edge of a piece of fabric.

"It's all right," her father was saying. Bert had begun to cry. Sandi heard the soft muffled sobs. "Have you heard anything about the people who were working in the drugstore?" her father asked Sandi, and she shook her head. She'd always admired his ability to comfort people, but now she felt a stab of jealousy. She wasn't sure what she was jealous of—the fact that he was attending to Bert and not to her, or that Bert was letting him comfort her when she'd refused to let Sandi.

"Were you two close to the fire?" her father asked her.

Sandi nodded. "A policeman helped us get away. He told us to stay by the courthouse."

Less than a block away, the fire raged on. The crowd around the courthouse had grown in the past hour, and Sandi had recently overheard someone commenting that a nearby town was sending additional firefighters.

"We just weren't prepared for something of this size," the man had explained to the people standing next to her. "How could a small town like ours be prepared to take on something like this?"

No one had argued with him or said anything in response, and now as she stared at the fire, those words repeated themselves in her head. How could you fight something like this? How could you possibly be prepared? She couldn't finish any of her thoughts. Earlier she'd felt like she couldn't say anything that made sense. Ever since they reached the courthouse, Bert had been coughing off and on, long strings of wrenching coughs that made her double over onto the sidewalk. At one point, before they'd moved back to the wall and sat down, she'd thrown up again—a thick string of mucus that smelled like bile. Sandi had only coughed a few times, but the smoke stung her eyes so much that she couldn't stop them from tearing.

Now she sat next to her father and Bert, listening to her tell him that she knew her dad was in the fire. Earlier she'd felt as if she couldn't see anything she was looking at, but now, as Sandi sat listening to Bert's voice, the images worked their way into her—the height of the flames, the great clouds of smoke, the red fire truck where three of the firefighters stood facing the burning buildings. The images started to sink in and imprint themselves. A bomb had gone off. Mr. Jameson stood not far from them. His bowling alley was next to a building that housed a barbershop and several offices, which the firefighters had been struggling to save ever since the hardware store next to it had exploded.

"Are they going to let the whole block burn down?" she heard Mr. Jameson say to the group of men standing with him watching the firefighters.

"It won't go any farther, Stan," the man who owned the barbershop told him. "You're safe."

"Do you have insurance?" someone else asked the owner of the barbershop.

"Yeah. I haven't looked at the policy in years, but I've got it."

"That'll help."

The barbershop owner nodded. Sandi's father was still talking softly to Bert, his voice steady and sure. "Whatever's happened, God will help you. He'll help all of us." Sandi shut her eyes for a minute and listened to the sound of his voice. She wanted to cling to her father's hand, but instead she leaned against him and felt a familiar sense of calm rising up. Then, out of the piece of silence inside her, she had a realization—I didn't go into the drugstore.

It was a speck of a thought, a tiny sliver of something she knew was larger. I could have, she thought. I almost. She opened her eyes and looked at the fire again.

I started to go into the drugstore. She could feel the heat from the flames and smell the smoke and hear the shouts of the firefighters. Occasionally Bert let out a sob, and the sounds of her father's voice and the voices from others on the sidewalk drifted over her. Sandi watched the fire burn, and after awhile it felt as if she were inside the flames. She noticed the way they moved and bent effortlessly, like a stream of water might flow over and around rocks, and she felt a strange kinship to the fire, as if deep at her core she also held the power to burn away whatever was inside her.

Others were gathering near them—friends from their church and neighbors. Harry came over to tell them he had found Bert's brother, Carl, who had gone around to the other side of the fire to try to find out what had happened to his father. So far, no one knew. Harry had a burn on his arm, and Sandi's father said they should try to find a medic who could look at it, but Harry left again before they could.

Eventually Sandi's father stood up and began to walk around, talking with the others. He moved through the different groups, stopping to listen to someone or pat a shoulder. People were drawn to him, and after several minutes, he was surrounded by a tight cluster. They turned and listened when he spoke and moved closer if he touched their arms. They seemed to disappear for a few seconds if he reached out and held them.

When she was younger, Sandi had loved her father more than anyone else in the world. She had felt like she loved him more than she loved God, which she knew wasn't right, but she couldn't imagine loving anyone or anything more. Now that she was older, she didn't think about him that way, but on nights when he was home, she liked to sit at the kitchen table with him after the supper dishes were cleared and have him help her with her homework. Sometimes she pretended not to know how to do her assignments, so he would sit next to her and work through them with her. She liked the sound of his voice, which was gentle yet firm. She liked to sit in the pew on Sunday mornings and shut her eyes and listen. His voice sounded deeply familiar at those moments, yet also distant and strange. It had the cadence of compassion, forthrightness, and wonder—all at once. She liked his voice's certainty and the thought that everyone else in the church believed what he said. "The words from the Gospel lead us to this," he might begin.

Now he came over to the wall where they were sitting and told them that he was taking them home. "We'll have to walk to the car," he said. "I'm parked a few blocks away."

Sandi didn't want to leave. She couldn't explain why, but she knew she wanted to stay here with her father, watching the firefighters and waiting to learn what had happened. She knew also it would be useless to argue. Reluctantly, she bent down and told Bert that they were leaving. Bert got up without saying anything. As they followed her father down the street, Sandi watched him stop to talk again with other members of his congregation.

"I'm driving these girls to the house, and then I'm coming right back," he said, reassuring someone.

Often he drove over to the church in the evening for meetings or Bible study groups, and some weeks he was so busy Sandi hardly saw him. Now Sandi wanted his attention, but he seemed mainly concerned about the others.

She and Bert followed him down the street, past the people who had gathered. He stopped every now and then to talk to someone else, and it took a long time to reach the car. By the time they got there, Bert had started crying again. Silently, Sandi watched as her father helped Bert into the car. As soon as he was finished, she shoved past him toward the open door.

"Sandi, what's the matter?" Her father tried to grasp her arm, but Sandi pitched herself into the back seat, then stared straight ahead.

One emotion lay on top of another, like the layers of flames— her fear, covered with outrage and anger, then her embarrassment which flickered across both of them. Her father stayed bent over, looking in at her through the open car door. Then he straightened and swung the door shut.

Sandi swallowed hard as he walked around and got into the front seat, surprised and a little scared by her own behavior. Without turning to glance at them in the back, her father started the car's engine and began to drive. It seemed as if every car in the town was on the roads because of the fire, and even though they were in the lane driving away from town, cars were still moving slowly, bumper to bumper. In front of them, Reverend Edwards focused on driving, not speaking. Bert slumped over beside Sandi with her eyes closed, as if she was sleeping. Sandi didn't feel any more anger. She wished she could cry, which would be a release, but she couldn't. She closed her eyes and realized her head was throbbing.

Finally, the car turned off Main Street, but not before an ambulance had forced them to the side of the road, its siren blaring. Sandi stared out the window. The air was clearing of smoke now that they were farther from the fire, and the deep blue sky came in pieces through the car's windows. She wondered what had happened to the storm that was supposed to come.

As the car pulled into her driveway, she felt momentary relief. Her father got out, leaving her and Bert alone, sitting side by side on the back seat.

"Do you want to come up to my room?" Sandi asked, as if they had just gotten back from a regular trip downtown. Often they sat on the floor of Sandi's room and looked at the magazines they'd bought or played 45s on her portable record player.

Bert turned and looked at her for a full minute without speaking. "Why would I?" she said finally.

Sandi shrugged. Then her parents both came from the house, and her mother opened the car door. She bent down and reached inside, grasping Sandi by the shoulders. "Thank God you're both okay," she said. "I wanted to drive down there, but I knew your father was looking for you. I must have telephoned the hospital at least a dozen times asking about you." She pulled back and Sandi saw tears welling up in her mother's eyes, but somehow they didn't touch her.

She got out of the car and watched as her mother went to the other door and put an arm around her friend and led her around the back of the car. "Sandi, come on inside. I'll help you both clean up," she called out as she made her way across the lawn with Bert.

Sullenly, Sandi pushed the car door shut. Her father was already getting back into the driver's seat. "Be sure to take care of Bert," he said before he closed his door.

Sandi stepped away from the car, as he pulled out of the driveway. After her father's car disappeared down the road, she dragged her feet against the walk, and one of her flip-flops, already damaged by the last few hours, came apart, causing her to trip.

"Damn," she said. She had never said a word like that before, and it felt hot and heavy in her mouth. "Damn," she said again, wondering what her father would think of that, the minister's daughter using profanity. She bent down and picked up the broken flip-flop. Her big toe hurt and was already turning red. There was also the red streak of a burn on her calf, and her feet and legs were dirty, smeared with remnants of ash.

Suddenly she felt dirty and broken all over, as if she were full of the smoke and flames. She went inside the door, left open by her mom, and walked to the kitchen. Bert was standing by the sink where her mother was running water. "I thought you two could wash up here," her mother said, glancing at her.

Sandi pushed against the floor with her hurt toe, a needle of pain running through her foot. After another minute, she got up and began to walk out of the room.

"Where are you going?" her mother asked. Sandi didn't answer. Her mother turned off the water and left the sink for a moment following her to the hallway.

"Are you all right?" she asked, her voice a little louder.

Sandi hunched her shoulders and kept walking. She thought about her father and the fire and Bert, and she could feel the explosion building inside her, white and hot.

"Sandi." Her mother put her hand on Sandi's shoulder and tried to turn her around.

"Don't." Sandi knocked her hand away. She expected her mother to reel away with the shove or take her roughly by the shoulder and tell her to go upstairs to her room, but instead her mother grabbed hold of her.

"Leave me alone!" She was crying now, pummeling her mother's shoulders, and she didn't know at all what she wanted, to be left alone or to be smothered inside of her mother's body. The drugstore raged inside her. Her mother didn't move. She drew Sandi closer and held on.

Joyce and he had gotten married because Joyce thought she was pregnant, a false alarm. He hadn't realized how marriage would affect him. It made him hold onto her like a child who closes a butterfly in his fist to keep it from flying away. If she looked at someone else or didn't come home when she said she would, he felt threatened. He hated anyone who came in contact with her, and after a while, it seemed like that was everyone.

Chapter 6

Elizabeth Greenly glanced up at the clock on the mantle above the fireplace in the Edwards's living room. It had just turned six o'clock. She wasn't sure how long she'd been sitting on their couch, and she couldn't remember all the steps that had led to her being there. Reverend Edwards had come up to her, seemingly out of nowhere, when she was standing with Izzy on the sidewalk downtown. They had spoken and maybe he had gone away and come back again, or maybe he had stayed with her, but at some point he had picked up Izzy and carried her to Elizabeth's car and persuaded Elizabeth to follow him over to his house.

She remembered walking around the edge of the area that had been sectioned off from the fire and asking questions. She had talked with a police officer who had tried to get information about Carlton for her, but had been unable to learn anything. At some point Louise Bradley, who had come downtown concerned about her own husband who owned the bakery, had spotted her and tried to help her get information. Thomas Masey, who managed the hardware store, had told them the story that was circulating, that a bomb had exploded in the back of the drugstore.

"Do we know this for a fact?" she'd asked, the words like a tight cage around something fragile that was opening inside her.

Thomas had shaken his head, taken aback by the brittleness of her question. "We don't know anything for a fact," he'd said.

She had been hopeful, the way a mind can latch onto something until it grows bigger and bigger. This was something she still remembered, sitting in the Edwards's living room. For the first few hours, she had been sure that Carlton was safe and would end up being rescued.

"I'd know if he was dead," she'd told Louise Bradley and Janet Darcy who stood waiting with her. "We have a strong connection. I would sense it if he wasn't alive."

She had been so convinced, that watching the fire, she hadn't felt afraid. Instead she had felt larger than herself. She had known other things in her life also, for example, that Carlton and she would end up getting married, something she had felt with certainty several weeks after they started dating when she was in college. She'd known also that they would have three children, and that no matter what happened, the children would grow up to be all right. Standing in front of the fire, she was filled with that same clarity—everything will work out—so that when Janet Darcy asked if she was all right, she had answered that she was fine.

Now, sitting in Reverend Edwards and Nancy's living room, listening to the radio reports, she didn't know anymore what would happen or if anything would ever be all right again. She felt as if the ground underneath her had dropped away.

"I have a long way to fall," she told herself. She wasn't sure where that thought had come from.

Nancy Edwards sat down next to her on the couch and laid a hand on her knee. Nancy was always neatly dressed, and Elizabeth felt large and messy next to her. While Nancy kept busy cooking and doing volunteer work for the church, Elizabeth preferred to sit reading or drawing. She loved to go for long car drives.

Now Nancy said, "Would you like a sandwich or something to eat? I have a plate I could bring you of crackers and cheese, a little fruit."

She shook her head. "No. No, thank you," she said, thinking that eating was the furthest thing from what she could imagine doing.

"Have some more iced tea." Nancy handed her the glass, and she noticed that the ice in it had melted while sitting on the coffee table, the cold condensing in beads of sweat that ran down the outside of the glass and made a ring on the polished wood of the table.

She held it to her mouth and began to drink, and once she started she couldn't stop. She heard herself swallow again and again, turning the glass up as she kept drinking until she'd emptied it. When she set it back on the table, she felt her stomach tighten and had to bend over with her head lowered for a moment.

"Are you okay?" Nancy patted her back.

"Yes." Slowly, she sat back up. "Thank you."

When she was younger, she had been taught to be patient and polite. These were the two "P virtues." Good things come to those who wait. Now she was doing that, falling back onto what she knew.

"Where's Bert?" she asked, thinking suddenly of her older daughter who had refused to go upstairs with Sandi and change out of the red halter top that was so dirty and had a rip along the seam.

"Bert, just put on something of Sandi's for now," she'd told her older daughter when they were standing in the kitchen.

She couldn't remember what Bert had said back, but whatever it was, she had given in quickly, feeling a sort of collapse.

"They're in the kitchen. They just got back from walking over to the hospital. And Carl is out in the driveway talking to Harry Conner."

She nodded, glancing at Izzy who was curled up in an armchair, asleep. All of them were accounted for.

"Should I turn the radio off?" Nancy asked her.

"No." She shook her head, reaching out to squeeze Nancy's hand. "I need to listen to it."

Just then a reporter came on with more news, stating that a bomb of some sort had caused an explosion in the drugstore and the fire that had followed, destroying three other buildings, including the hardware store. It was estimated that eleven people had been killed, including most of those in the drugstore. Only Davy and Billy Sandler had been rescued. Both of them had been close enough to the store's entrance that they had been thrown into the street by the initial force of the explosion. Davy was said to be in critical condition, but Billy, who had been thrown farther from the flames, was conscious, and had spoken with authorities at the hospital.

The reporter relayed the story Billy Sandler had told. George Fowler, the husband of an employee at the store, had entered the building a few minutes past two o'clock, carrying a bomb inside a paper bag. Someone had picked up the bag, and realizing what was inside, had thrown it to the back of the store, where Carlton Greenly had caught it, planning to carry the bag to the back alley. Before he could take it there, the bomb had exploded. Billy Sandler had seen George Fowler inside the store just moments before the bomb went off. The count of those presumed dead had been assembled in part from the list Billy had given authorities of those who were in the drugstore when it happened. George Fowler was counted among the probable victims.

Nancy got to her feet. "I'm turning that off," she said.

Elizabeth nodded, only partly comprehending what she'd heard. Carlton rarely left the store while it was open, even at lunchtime. And it made sense that he would have been at the back, signing for a delivery or working in his office. If he had been trying to carry the bomb from the store when it exploded, he would have been killed. And the man who had brought the bomb into the store was George Fowler. She had seen George Fowler sometimes in the evenings when she'd driven to the store to pick up Carlton and George had been there waiting for Joyce. Once, she remembered, he'd given Carlton a ride home.

She glanced up and met the eyes of the minister, who had sat down in the chair next to the couch. "I'm so sorry," he said.

She nodded. Somewhere in the landscape of herself she knew there was a reason for his sympathy, but she couldn't connect with it. "Joyce Fowler's husband carried the bomb into the store," she said slowly, still trying to take it in.

"I know." He shook his head. "I can't believe it either."

"He attended the church." She could picture Joyce and her husband, sitting in a pew toward the back on an occasional Sunday a year or two ago. Joyce had not worn a hat, even though one of those Sundays had been Easter Sunday, and her dresses had seemed a little too short, her eye makeup too heavy. After the service, Carlton had stopped and said a few words to them. "What's Joyce's husband do?" she'd asked once as they'd left the church.

"I believe he's in construction," Carlton had said.

Outside, the air was cooling off. She could see the deeper blue of the sky gathering. There was a stillness in her that could settle easily into that color, and it felt as if once there she would never feel anything again. "I should be going home," she said.

"You're welcome to stay the night here," Nancy offered. "Bert and Izzy can sleep in Sandi's bedroom, and we have the couch in here and the guest room."

"We can go with you tomorrow and help you figure out what to do next," the minister told her.

"Nothing's certain yet," Nancy added. "You shouldn't be alone right now."

Slowly, she got up and thanked them. Reverend Edwards offered to walk her back and carry Izzy, but when she bent over Izzy to rub her back, Izzy woke up and said she would walk home. Elizabeth called to Bert and Carl, and the two of them went on ahead of her.

"Are you sure you'll be all right at your house?" Nancy asked her as they were leaving.

Elizabeth nodded.

"I'll call you tomorrow morning."

"Thank you," Elizabeth said, taking Izzy by the hand.

"Can I run back, Mommy?" Izzy asked her.

"Let's just walk," she said as they neared the sidewalk. But then, several feet later, she let go of Izzy's squirming hand and told her, "All right. Run ahead. Just be careful."

"I will, Mommy," Izzy sang out, full of cheer at the unexpectedness of an evening outing.

By the time Elizabeth reached her house, the stillness inside her had concentrated so that it was a solid, heavy thing. It made every movement difficult. Numbly, she performed routine motions, foregoing Izzy's bath and tucking her, filthy, between the cool sheets. Bert and Carl sat in the living room staring at the television set, but after Izzy was in bed, instead of trying to talk with them, Elizabeth walked outside to the backyard and stood by the grill where Carlton cooked every Saturday night in the summer. Barbecuing was the one thing other than his work that Carlton was passionate about.

He had invented his own sauces for chicken, pork, and ribs and slow cooked the meat, so that when they sat down to eat, it fell off the bones in tender pieces that had soaked up hours of flavor. She touched the grill now, a rectangular stone structure Carlton had had made several years ago, spending an extravagant amount of money, convincing her that a good grill made all the difference.

The birdbath she'd begun to decorate with the pieces of tile was near the grill, and after a few minutes she went and got a lawn chair and sat down next to it. She sat alone in her darkening yard, not thinking about the explosion, or George Fowler, or her two older children who had said so little all evening. When she was growing up, she had lived near the ocean, and she'd learned to swim at an early age, often swimming alone far out into the frigid waves of the mostly protected inlet near her home. Her parents didn't worry about their children swimming, it was as natural to them as walking or breathing, but once she had gotten too far from the shore, pulled by the current of a rare rip tide. She hadn't noticed it immediately, had felt only the slight tug of the water, making the swimming unusually easy. As she moved effortlessly through the waves, she tracked her progress occasionally by glancing at the coast. When she realized how strong the current was, she was already far from the shore.

Her sister had run and gotten their father, and he had raced to the beach and started up their small motorboat. By then she was just a pinprick in the waves, barely visible from the shore. It had been the only frightening experience of her childhood. She could remember the waves lapping against her head and ears, the tug of the current underneath her, and an infinite amount of water. She had been frozen by the time her father reached her, so cold that he had rushed her to the house where her mother had stripped off her wet swimsuit and wrapped her in warm blankets.

She thought about that experience now, the nearly missed tragedy, and it seemed linked, somehow, to the fire. "You kept your head about you," her father had commented that evening, complimenting her on not panicking. Some children would have become fearful after an experience like hers, but she had become braver because of it, pushing herself daily to swim farther. It was that bravery which years later had prompted Carlton to fall in love with her.

"You're not afraid of much, are you?" he'd asked on their third date, as he gripped the console of the car his friend had loaned them, while she took a tight turn too fast. He had fallen for her quickly, and she had thought him so sweet and good. But she hadn't been in love with him, even after she'd known that she would marry him. That had come more slowly.

"I want to go up to your room. I want to have sex with you." When had she said that to him? It had been early on, when they'd only known each other a month or so. Carlton had been made nervous by her assertiveness, but he'd agreed to take her to his room, and when she'd removed her clothes and walked over to him, he had kissed her neck and her breasts.

"Keep going," she'd said, and he had, moving slowly down the length of her body.

Now she sat in the yard, and the images of the fire and smoke mixed with her memories of making love with him and of the ocean. They all felt the same. The water had gone on forever, underneath her and on all sides. She had kept swimming as hard as she could against the current, but she'd been swept farther and farther out to sea. There was a sense of inevitability that filled her now as it had then, as if the world had been set in motion, and if she tried to resist its current, she would be carried away even faster.

She reached out and touched the birdbath, running her finger along the surface where she had started to cover it with tiles. The grout around the tiles had hardened, and the surface was a mixture of smooth and rough. She'd been careful to cover any of the sharp edges, and that had been part of the pleasure, the mingling of textures, the softening and taming of the jagged edges. The pattern had been the other pleasure. In the darkness, under the dim light from the moon and the house, she could still make out the mixture of whites and greens and blues. It had been the ocean she was calling back she realized now, the swirl of water mixing with the nearby fields, the white foam riding the crests of the waves. She got up and lifted the shallow bowl from its pedestal and dropped it onto the concrete. Then she threw the broken sections down again and again, splitting them into smaller and smaller pieces. Carlton had probably died by being shattered like this, she thought, only faster and more absolutely.

"I can't agree to a trip to Florida," he'd told her a couple of nights ago when it was late and they were both overtired. "The thought of leaving the store for that long makes me too nervous."

"Everything makes you nervous," she'd replied. "You worked all those extra hours, afraid that the store wouldn't survive when Rexall opened. Now that your store is doing well, you're still afraid of taking a trip. I just want to be by the ocean for a few days where it's warm in the spring. Maybe I'll drive down myself and take the kids if you can't go."

She'd gone to bed then, and he had stayed up so late she'd been asleep when he pulled the covers back to lie down next to her. The thought of her driving alone to Florida with the children had, she knew, made him even more anxious.

What had initially caused him to fall in love with her had become his nemesis. Now as she stood over the broken pieces from the birdbath, bits of tile gleaming in the thin wedge of light from the kitchen window, she couldn't make sense of anything. Somewhere inside of her, she felt outrage welling up, and underneath it a darkness that spread immense as the ocean, a fear that had no bottom. The store had been blown up because the husband of a woman Carlton had hired carried a bomb into the store. Al Freeman, the store's pharmacist, had left the drugstore minutes before it happened. She'd heard several people comment that they had planned to go to the drugstore that afternoon, but one thing or another had delayed them. If the explosion had happened twenty minutes later, she and Izzy could have been inside it, too.

She turned away from the broken pieces and went into the house. Carl and Bert had both gone upstairs, and she sat in the kitchen telling herself she needed to try to sleep also. Then a few minutes later, she was back outside, gathering up the tiles that had split away from the birdbath and carrying them into her kitchen. She lugged the bag of grout from the mudroom and set the materials next to the wall beside her kitchen table. She started by using the tiles, adhering them to the wall with an adhesive. Later that night, when the tiles were gone, she took an empty, green beer bottle of Carlton's and broke it. Next she lifted a cup and saucer from her kitchen cabinet and dropped them into the porcelain sink. In the early hours of morning, she picked out two dinner plates, wrapped them in newspaper and struck them with a hammer. By the time the sun came up, she had set in a number of pieces and smoothed the grout between them, turning portions of her wall into a splintered mosaic.

A scattering of stars toward the east, a chunk of the moon at the horizon. Lights from the search lamps waver, disappearing then reappearing. An occasional figure looms in the light of the lamps.

Chapter 7

On Saturday night, Jack Turnbow was still lying on a bed in the hospital's emergency room. After being thrown when the hardware store exploded, he had been carried out of the fire by two other firefighters. His oxygen tank had fallen off, and he'd inhaled too much smoke. The ambulance ride had been sickening, and he had the dim recollection of vomiting as it pitched from one side to the other.

Once they reached the hospital, Glynn Sheer, the firefighter he'd carried out, had been taken to the intensive care unit, while Jack had been placed on a bed next to a wall in the general emergency room. He had no clue now what time it was or how long he'd been lying there. They'd given him a painkiller and he'd slept for a while, then woken, then slept again. Through the curtains that were pulled around him, he could hear beds being wheeled past and the voices of nurses and doctors. Someone on a bed near his kept coughing, and farther away a child cried.

"Officer Turnbow, would you like a drink of water?" someone said. A female voice, belonging to his nurse. He opened his eyes and tried to raise himself onto his elbows. "Lie still," she said, and he felt her hand against his chest. "We still need to get you to X-ray to make sure you didn't break anything. Take this straw and sip a little."

He felt the pressure of the straw against his lips, then the coolness of the water along his tongue and teeth. Immediately, he became aware of a burning sensation in his mouth and throat, as if he had swallowed ash.

"That's good. Don't take too much at once," the nurse said, pulling away the straw. "I'm going to raise the top half of your bed a little more in case you start coughing." As soon as she said this, he felt the urge to cough deep in his belly. At the same time, he felt himself clamping down as if trying to hold himself together so that a cough wouldn't jar his body. His back hurt. He was becoming completely aware of this fact, and of the need to hold himself as still as possible. If he moved at all, pain pierced him.

"Lie still and try to relax," the nurse told him. "The restraints are to keep you from hurting anything, and you've still got the oxygen tube in your nose to help you breathe and an IV to keep you hydrated." Jack looked at his arm and saw the tube feeding into it and a new fear spiraled through him. "I'll be back in a few minutes. I have to check on other patients. I think they're going to take you up for the X-ray in a few minutes."

He shut his eyes when she had gone away. Bright overhead lights permeated his closed eyelids. The milky whiteness from them moved as if alive, swirling and undulating. Tiny lines of light stretched through the whiteness, and as he sank down away from himself, he became absorbed in tracing them. The more he focused on them, the more the fear of where he was and what had happened receded, and he was able to block out the sound of crying that came from a place he couldn't identify.

The only other time he'd been in a hospital was years ago, shortly after his graduation from high school, when his mother was in a car accident. She'd been taken to this same hospital, but it had looked different, seen from the vantage point of the waiting room. He could still remember the torn-up Pontiac, tipped over at an odd angle at the side of the road with a swarm of emergency lights blinking around it, and then the red ambulance light, seen through the windshield of his father's car as they followed behind it. He'd sat alone in a chair outside the emergency room while his father went back to talk to the doctor. Later a nurse had walked with him to his mother's bedside, where the doctor and his father explained that his mother had died.

His mother rarely drove, and earlier that evening, Jack had kidded her about her nervousness behind the wheel and convinced her to drive herself to her bridge game. When the accident happened, she'd been cautiously attempting to pull out onto the main road, and the other driver, who had been speeding, had come suddenly over a rise a couple hundred feet away. Because of a small town relationship between the attending police officer and the other driver, he was never ticketed. Jack's outrage over what had happened prompted him to become a police officer, and after the sudden loss of his mother, he'd gradually kept more and more to himself. He'd never married.

After a while, the nurse came back and fit the straw between his lips again, and he felt the water pool in his mouth before it slid down his throat. "You're next to go down to X-ray," she told him. "Someone will come in a minute and take you."

He tried to ask her what was wrong with him, but his throat closed up again, burning. "Don't try to talk," she told him. "Try to relax."

As his eyes shut, he felt the slight pressure against his nostrils from the oxygen tube, but his main sensation was the pain radiating from his back. Any other sensation seemed to float inside it. He had no idea how badly he'd been hurt, but his back felt like it was on fire. Someone near him started moaning, and if he listened more intently, he heard the voices of the doctors and nurses and the clatter of equipment. When they'd taken him to see his mother, her body had been lying on a bed like the one he was lying on, and now it seemed like this was the same scene, only he was the one on the bed, and she was standing where he'd stood looking down at him.

"I'm going to put more pain medication in your IV before you go down," the nurse said, suddenly there again beside his bed. "I'm sorry it took so long to get the additional order, but we are completely backed up with all the injuries. The doctor said he'll examine you after we get the X-rays."

He nodded his thanks as a warm sensation similar to sleep began to move through him. At first he fought it, trying to keep his eyes open and pay attention to what was happening, nervous about giving up his awareness, but eventually he let go and shut his eyes again, sinking into the warmth. It seemed as though he could enter the channels of his blood through that warmth, and he found himself doing just that, slipping over the curves of his ribs and down the length of his painful back. After several minutes, he fell into a soft, light sleep.

When he woke, the bed he was lying on was moving. "It's okay, Officer. We're just taking you for some X-rays," a male voice told him. "We have to ride down in the elevator."

He opened his eyes, then quickly shut them again, feeling dizzy as soon as he saw the ceiling moving over him. The wheels underneath him rolled, and he heard the clatter of the bed. Don't go so fast, he wanted to say, a sudden nausea rising up in him. Then the bed came to an abrupt stop, and he heard the opening of the elevator doors. All these sounds seemed familiar, but they also seemed totally foreign. The elevator lurched, then moved downwards.

"How many in line before him?" someone asked a few minutes later, as he was rolled from the elevator into a hallway.

"I don't know. Three, I think."

His bed was pushed down the hallway, and then he felt it stop abruptly, bumping against a wall that ran along his right side.

"Officer, we're going to leave you here for a few minutes until X-ray is ready for you. Someone will be along to take you in."

X-ray. This time when he heard it, the word tumbled around in his head for a minute. The only other time he'd gotten an X-ray was when he was little and his mother had taken him to buy shoes where the store owner had X-rayed his feet. He remembered the picture in the machine—white bones floating in a sea of gray. The milky confusion inside him felt almost comforting, like being wrapped in a cocoon. Around him, he heard pieces of conversations.

"My leg . . . broke . . . they think."

"Fell . . . when the. . . ."

"He was downstairs. . . ."

"I heard . . . flying in a burn specialist. . . . "

"What time. . . ."

"Been here since four o'clock and. . . ."

The pulsating feeling from the medication came back, and he felt himself sinking into it again. There was a rhythm to the pulsing—short, then long. His rhythm, he told himself, the sound of his body. Sinking into it was like being cradled, the way an embryo is cradled inside its mother. He held the image in his mind of a tiny seed of a person, and he didn't wonder at the oddness of the image, or think how strange he was for thinking about embryos out of nowhere. He felt like he was the embryo.

For a while he dozed again. When he woke, he was being moved, and the jarring sense of it filled him. "We'll have to lift him onto the table," someone said. "Officer, are you awake? We need to get you onto the X-ray table."

He opened his eyes. "Yes," he said. The sound was a whisper. More than anything he wanted the straw again with the water.

"Officer, we're going to lift you very carefully and place you on the X-ray table. You don't need to do anything but lie still. Let us do the work." There was a pause, then more movement of the bed and the sound of the rails being lowered. He felt the sickening sense in his gut again. He had never had to give up control like this, allowing others to position him. Usually he made decisions about what would happen.

Someone released the belts that had been securing him, and he started to lift his arm to stop what was happening. "Don't move," he was told. "Let us do the positioning."

He wanted to argue, but the technicians above him performed their jobs with quick efficiency. "Possible fracture. We'll lift him onto the table at the count of four."

Hands squeezed under his shoulders, head, and legs. Someone counted. "One, two, three, four," and he was lifted into the air, carried, and lowered.

A belt came around his midsection, and his head was placed between two clamps as his legs were strapped down and someone positioned the oxygen and the IV next to the table. A tight fear unraveled in him. If his spine was injured, he might not walk again. He sometimes saw a guy downtown who had come back from Vietnam like that. The man rolled himself up and down the street in a wheelchair. Jack had put money in the can he carried.

"We're going to do a number of X-rays. We'll be getting pictures of your entire skeletal body to find any fractures from your fall.

We'll take the ones from the front first, then turn you and do them from the side and the back."

The door opened and shut again, and the technicians were gone, leaving him alone in the room. The table under him was cold, and for the first time, he realized that his clothing had been removed and replaced by a hospital Johnny. He couldn't remember when this had happened. The X-ray machine clanked as it took the pictures, and he started shivering.

After what seemed hours and at the same time a couple of minutes, two of the technicians reentered the room. They moved his body into another position on the hard, cold table, then left again. The clanking of the machine began, and the sounds traveled straight through him. A few minutes later the door opened, and the same sequence was repeated. "How many more of these?" he asked, trembling all over now.

"Lie still another few minutes," someone said. "We're almost done."

Finally, he heard them call for more help, and he was released and lifted from the table back onto the bed. The sheet was pulled back over him, and his restraints were refastened, his tubes connected. Then someone covered him with a thin blanket, and he felt a wave of relief. A few minutes later, when yet another blanket was tucked around him, he thought he might start to cry, his sense that he was being comforted was so great.

But as they wheeled him back downstairs, the panic returned. He didn't feel cold any longer, but he was shivering so hard his teeth and muscles hurt. The bed advanced too quickly, and it made him dizzy again and sick to his stomach. In the elevator, he had the sensation of falling.

Once again he was wheeled into the room with curtained partitions. Not all the curtains were pulled shut, and there were numerous beds with people in them. Other people stood or sat in chairs. He realized that most of them must have been hurt in the fire.

"Officer Turnbow, you're back," the nurse from earlier said. "Let's move you over into this corner while you wait for the doctor."

His bed was wheeled again, and he felt it bump up against something else.

"Hold on for a second, and I'll bring you some more water."

Her face was close to his. She had dark hair and pale, smooth skin. He felt her hand, the touch of her fingers. She was so kind, it seemed to him, in the midst of everything, that he felt his eyes tear up.

"What's the matter with my back?" he asked her.

"We have to wait and see what the doctor says after he's looked at your X-rays."

The nurse raised the top of his bed again so that he could drink. This time the water that ran into his mouth tasted sweet, and he swallowed again and again, feeling how large and dry his tongue was.

"Don't try too much at once," the nurse said, taking the straw from his mouth. "Can you remember what happened?"

Images of the fire fell through his head. He could see the flames and the two people he'd gone in to rescue, lying on the ground. He could remember pulling Glynn Sheer's legs out from under the wooden beam and struggling to carry him. There was also the image of the officer who was his younger partner, running along the rim of the fire, shouting at people to move back from it. Jack had no idea what had happened to any of them.

"I went into the fire to attempt a rescue and the hardware store exploded," he said.

The nurse lightly touched his hand. He shut his eyes, feeling the coolness of her fingers. His mother's hands had always been cool like that. "You're doing really well. Just rest for a few more minutes until the doctor comes." She brushed his forehead with her hand, smoothing it for a second, and then she was gone.

He could picture most everything that had happened—the boots he had worn and the pavement covered with areas of fire. He remembered how quickly the fire had spread, how he had argued with Chief Morgan about going in for the rescue, and later how he had turned off the two-way radio. He could touch each of these memories in his mind, but it was as if he didn't have a framework to put them in. Several minutes before the drugstore exploded, he and his partner had pulled someone over for driving through a stop sign. The driver had turned out to be a teenage boy with a new license, and Jack had given him a warning.

"Pay attention from now on," he'd told the kid. "Don't be playing that radio so loud." He and his partner, Beckley, had joked about it afterward. The memory of that more ordinary event now seemed less real than anything else.

Lying on the bed, he listened to the others around him, picking up pieces of what they were saying. The fire had been large, spreading to four different buildings. A back-up fire department had finally arrived from one of the bigger towns; otherwise they never might have put it out. Up to ten people were presumed dead. The explosion had come from a bomb, someone said, and the news reporters were saying it had been carried into the drugstore by a man named George Fowler. That detail swirled in Jack's head. He knew the name. Then suddenly, it connected, and he saw a photograph of the person taken from his high-school yearbook.

After a while, a doctor pulled a chair up next to his bed and introduced himself while he paged through some papers. He removed the restraints and walked around to the bottom of the bed. "Can you feel this?" he asked, touching Jack's foot with the end of his pen.

"Yes," Jack told him, feeling the slight pressure against his foot's arch.

"Try to move your toes."

He stretched and then curled his toes.

"Can you move your legs?"

Trying to ignore the pain in his back, he moved one leg, then the other off the bed.

"How about your arms?"

He bent his elbows and lifted his hands.

"Good." The doctor sat down next to him in the chair. "What's your name?"

"Jack Turnbow."

"What day is it?"

"Saturday."

"Do you remember what happened to you?"

Jack nodded and told him about going into the fire and the explosion.

The doctor spent a minute shining a penlight in his eyes, then he listened to Jack's chest with his stethoscope, ordering him to inhale and exhale and finally to cough. The cough caught in his throat and he had to clamp down, swallowing hard afterward so that he didn't keep coughing. He felt the deep ache in his belly.

"You're a lucky man. No broken bones, and your spine looks undamaged," the doctor told him. "I'm guessing most of the pain you're feeling is muscular. Your lungs sound clear, and you don't have a concussion. You might be feeling pretty confused or overwhelmed, but right now we're all feeling that way."

As the doctor wrote on his clipboard, Jack grasped at a sense of relief. "I'll be able to walk?" he asked.

The doctor glanced down at him. "You'll be fine. I'll prescribe some painkillers, and we'll get you out of bed and moving around in a few minutes. I think we can take out the IV and the oxygen. I don't see any lasting damage from the smoke inhalation, and you seem to be breathing and drinking fine on your own."

The doctor stepped away, and seconds later Jack repeated to himself what he'd heard, that he was fine and would soon be out of bed and moving around, but the truth didn't penetrate. He tried to keep his eyes open, but the lights above him were too bright. They glowed like the headlights of a car. This was the meaning of the phrase, *blinded by the headlights,* he told himself, thinking of deer that would startle, then freeze in the road in front of an oncoming car at night.

After several minutes, the nurse came back and told him that someone would soon be coming to help him up. They would release him once he was able to walk on his own.

"Wait," he said as she turned to walk away. Now that he'd been told he would be all right, the images from the fire and from the night of his mother's death tumbled together faster and faster through his head.

"Would you like more water?" The nurse picked up the cup again and set the straw between his lips.

He drank, this time taking longer sips and swallowing. "What happened to the others? There was another firefighter, Glynn Sheer, and a boy who worked at the drugstore that I went in to rescue. And my police partner was there, a younger officer. He's still in training. I have no idea what happened to any of them." He felt the nurse's hesitation as she steadied the cup.

"I believe the firefighter and the boy who worked in the drugstore are still somewhere in the hospital. I haven't heard of another officer being treated."

He wanted to ask more questions: Were the other two going to live? Were the X-rays they'd taken of his back for certain? Was there any chance still that he wouldn't be able to walk? He started to ask them, but he was too scared. Soon someone would come and help him out of bed, and by the time he left the hospital he would realize that he was going to be fine, but now he felt as if he would never be all right.

"Don't go," he said as the nurse lifted the cup.

Glancing away, she looked around the large room. "I guess I could stay for a few minutes."

She went and got a chair and pulled it up to his bed. He could feel her next to him even though she didn't touch him and they didn't say anything to each other. They waited like that until two orderlies came to move his bed to an area where they helped him to stand.

Chapter 8

What happened next didn't get printed in the newspapers, and even though a small town can be a mill for gossip, hardly anyone who learned of it later talked about it. Late that night, after the fire had been put out, a man came to the church office where Reverend Edwards had fallen asleep on his couch. All afternoon, the minister had wandered through the crowds on and around Main Street. The onlookers had pressed together on the sidewalks near the drugstore watching the fire. Mrs. Gregory, a woman the minister knew only vaguely as she attended a different church, was standing close to the flames. A police officer, who'd been trying to get her to move farther back, had asked the minister to help him. She had been in the beauty parlor when the explosion occurred, and her hair was still in rollers. She told the minister that her daughter worked at the drugstore, and her son had gone into it with two friends to get a Coke. She didn't want to move farther from the fire, and he finally had to take her by the hand and walk her down the street. Loose strands of hair and little tissue papers hung from the curlers that had been set in straight lines across her head, and her hand felt thick and soft, like rising dough.

"I think we should get you over to the hospital to see if they know anything about your children," he said, repeating the words several times before she heard him.

The whole time he was standing with her, he'd been aware of others—David Miller, Catherine Thompson, and many others who were worried about someone who might have been in the building. He'd felt torn between them, as he'd been torn when his daughter and Bert needed to be brought back home. Finally, someone else offered to take Mrs. Gregory to the hospital, and then the minister went over to Bob McNeese, who was standing next to one of the firefighters. Even from twenty or so feet away, he could tell that Bob was yelling, while his arms gestured wildly, causing his thin frame to look as if it were being jerked one way and then another.

"Let's stand back, Bob, and let this man do his work," Reverend Edwards told him, gripping his arm.

"Leave me alone! I'm trying to find out where my wife is," Bob said.

Later the minister couldn't remember what had happened with Bob, but somehow the fire had gradually lessened, and he'd found Elizabeth Greenly and driven her back to his house with him. After she and her children had gone home, it seemed to have turned dark outside quickly, and that darkness made everything feel more settled and safe, as if it were rolling up the day. He'd gone into the bedroom to change out of his clothes, which were very dirty, and Nancy had come up to him.

"Hold me," she said, and they got into bed together. "Hold me tighter," she told him, and they made love but it was frantic and quick. There was a sort of desperateness to it, as if they each needed to assert—you're still here; I didn't lose you.

Afterward, he wanted to go to sleep, but he forced himself to dress again. He made a few telephone calls, stopped by the hospital, and then drove to the church to look at the unfinished sermon he had to give the next morning. Sometime around midnight, he closed the door to his office feeling everything drop away. The notes he'd taken earlier for the sermon swam before him on his desk, one word following another for no reason. As he lay down on his couch, he told himself it was only for a few minutes, but then he sank into a dry, dreamless sleep.

"Reverend Edwards." The man knocked on the door, then cracked it open, peering inside and whispering his name as Reverend Edwards tried to rouse himself. He forced his eyes open for a second, then shut them again, and the fire from the afternoon flamed under his lids. The voice echoed, dream-like. On the wall, a clock read quarter past three. The light he'd left on blazed against the black windows, and he told himself that some parishioner, also unable to sleep, had sought him out for comfort.

"Reverend Edwards," the voice came again, a little louder and more insistent. Then the minister looked up and realized that the man was George Fowler.

"I had to talk to you." The man worked quickly, closing an opened window, pulling the curtains. The minister's head swam. He saw George both as a parishioner and as the man who set off the explosion. "I couldn't hold back. I had to talk to someone."

The minister pushed himself up to a vertical position, blinking slowly and deliberately as his eyes, sticky with the few hours of sleep, tried to adjust to the light. He nodded, and the movement felt wooden and mechanical. "The radio report said you were killed in the fire," he said, his voice sounding strange to his own ears.

"I know it," George told him hurriedly. "I needed to talk to somebody, and I saw your light on in the window."

Ever since the radio broadcast had identified George Fowler as the one who had brought the bomb into the drugstore, the minister had been haunted by the thought that he'd married George and Joyce Fowler several years ago. For a year or so after the wedding, George and his wife had come once and a while to a Sunday service. He'd stood in front of George when the man said his vows and shaken George's hand after Sunday services. George had seemed ordinary, no different than the others in his congregation—flawed but well intentioned. He always told himself he knew each member of his congregation, but maybe he didn't. There was a close circle of members who came regularly and attended prayer groups or sang in the choir. Maybe beyond this periphery, he didn't see anyone else.

George Fowler stopped pacing by the door, bent down and turned the lock. Then he switched off the overhead light. A minute later, there was the sound of George fumbling with the objects on the desk, then a small click as the desk lamp he'd placed on the floor came on.

"I have a sermon to give in the morning," the minister said, almost perfunctorily. The light from the desk lamp made everything seem real and deadly.

George sat down in the small armchair next to the couch, letting out a soft sound that was almost a groan. He was not a large man, but he came across as bulkier than he actually was and his movements had no grace. Settling into the chair, he looked collapsed, his back hunching over as if he'd just set down something heavy, and he breathed out loudly, recovering.

"I was up late trying to work on it, and I still have more to do before the service starts," the minister continued, uncertain what his point was in saying anything at all about his sermon. "Other people will see you," he added, still not thinking about what he was saying. "People could start arriving."

George nodded. "I know it." The words escaped him like a cut off sob. "I heard everything on the radio. I just need a little time." He glanced up and the minister saw his face up close for the first time since he'd come in. It was unshaven, rough looking with the growth of a new beard. His eyes and nose were red. Nothing about it matched the clean-shaven face he remembered seeing several years ago when he performed the marriage ceremony.

"You can't tell anything I say, right? You're a minister."

Reverend Edwards nodded. "Yes," he said, verifying whatever it was George wanted to hear. His fear kept expanding even while his mind went back to the necessity of the sermon, worrying over it.

George was nodding, looking at the floor again. He tapped his feet rhythmically, making a muted sound against the rug as he rocked back and forth in the chair. "I needed to talk this out, and I thought of you being a minister and all, and then the whole confidential, secrecy thing." He glanced up at the minister nervously.

There was a longer pause, for one or two minutes. George looked around the room. "I need something to eat," he said finally. "You got anything here? I haven't had anything since early yesterday morning."

Reverend Edwards thought about the small kitchen down the hall where the boxes of communion wafers and grape juice were kept. There was a cabinet of dishes and a drawer of silverware. Then he remembered the ham sandwich his wife had wrapped in wax paper for him before he'd driven over to the church on Saturday. He'd gone downtown without eating it when he'd heard about the fire.

"There's a sandwich in my desk drawer," he said.

"You get it for me." George motioned toward the desk. "But don't touch the telephone or anything else."

The minister got up, feeling unsteady. As he walked over to his desk, he heard George standing and felt him move behind him. He opened the bottom drawer and lifted the wrapped sandwich.

"Hand it to me," George said.

The minister turned, holding out the sandwich.

"What's that?" George pointed at a thick envelope in the drawer.

"Money we collected for a missionary."

"I'll take it too." George held out his hand, and the minister reached down and picked up the envelope. George took it from him, then reached over and lifted a letter opener that lay on the desk. He used it to quickly split the envelope's seal, and then, looking inside, he thumbed through the bills. The minister waited while he counted them. "Thank you," George said, glancing up at him when he'd finished. "Now you can go and sit back down."

The minister walked back the few steps to the couch and slid down onto it. George stood by the desk, eating the sandwich. He held the letter opener in his other hand, and he took large bites so that the sandwich was finished in what seemed like a few seconds.

"I got no need for this," he said, holding up the letter opener when he'd finished eating, but still, he kept it in his hand. He walked back over and sat down in the chair again, and the minister tried to think of what to say, but nothing came to him.

"I need to find somewhere to go while I get my bearings. I'm not sure if I'm coming or going." George choked a little over the last few words. He glanced at the minister again, his eyebrows raised, his eyes opening wider, like he was seeing the minister for the first time. "You married me and Joyce, Reverend, remember?"

The minister saw Joyce in his mind, looking pretty in a hand-sewn dress with two bridesmaids and her sister acting as maid of honor. George had had few relatives attend, and Joyce's brother had served as best man, causing George to look hemmed in by the future father-in-law on one side and brother-in-law on the other.

"Do you remember, Reverend?" George asked, more insistent.

The minister nodded. "You seemed in love," he said, not because he remembered this, but because it seemed the right thing to say.

"You asked about us having kids," George went on. "Joyce said she wanted two or three."

Reverend Edwards couldn't remember much about the conversation they'd had before the wedding, or if he'd ever heard anything about Joyce's wanting children. He thought about George standing in front of him repeating the words of the marriage ceremony and George seated next to Joyce in a pew toward the back of the church. The thought that George had carried a bomb into the drugstore came from some other universe.

"I don't know what happened," George said, as if he were reading the minister's mind. He looked up from the floor, his two thick hands framing his face. "I can't say."

"George, do you want to turn yourself over to the authorities?" Reverend Edwards looked at the man's face and saw how the light coming from the lamp on the floor created a small, gold-colored globe around it, a sort of mocking halo.

"No," George said flatly. Then they both sat not speaking, and Reverend Edwards's mind scrambled for what he could say next, but words came to him only partly, and each thought was a dead end. No one would come for a few more hours. In religion classes there had been lectures on the nature of man's relationship to God—the God who could forgive, the God who judged, the God who gave life and would take it away. But none of that felt of any help.

"I drove away after I put the bomb in the store. No one's seen me. You're the only one." George swept his hands up, and the blade of the letter opener caught the light from the lamp and flashed in the air.

The minister watched him nervously. He noticed a bulge in one of George's pockets, and it occurred to him that it was a gun. "But don't worry, Reverend," George went on, almost good-naturedly. "I wouldn't want to kill you or anything."

"The fire was huge," the minister told him. "It burned down four buildings."

George nodded again. "I know. They said a spark from the explosion ignited the gas lines. I didn't plan that. I didn't know about it ahead of time, or the paint in the hardware store nearby." He leaned forward and his knees were just inches from the minister's. "It was Joyce who wanted to get married," he went on, an edge of defensiveness in his voice.

The minister nodded, shifting uncomfortably on the couch. The Sunday ushers would arrive as early as seven. It was possible also that his wife would call or drive over before the service to see how he was, or that someone else might seek him out, as George had, to talk about the explosion.

"Three months ago she moves out," George said, cutting off his thoughts. When he spoke the next part, his voice rose to a higher-pitched imitation of Joyce's voice. "Said I was making her claustrophobic. I was always trying to control her. She needed time to think about things without me breathing down her neck."

"She moved out," the minister repeated numbly.

George's voice flattened, becoming strangely declarative. "She was the one pushed for marriage, then she moves in with her sister and starts seeing someone else. Said I was threatening her when I was just standing outside the drugstore waiting to talk to her."

George ran his thick hands through his hair. The minister stared at him, everything coming into clearer focus—George's reddened face and his dirtied work pants, the desk behind him that loomed overcrowded with papers, and the shelves against the wall with books of various sizes and framed photographs.

"She accused you," he said, trying to calm George, unsure of how to move the conversation toward the need for repentance.

"Told me that two weeks ago, after *she* had left me, when *she* had been the one to leave. Right before that, a guy at work said she was seeing somebody else. A guy at work tells me, can you believe it?"

The room fell silent. George had tightened his hands into fists, and now when he opened them the letter opener lay in one of his palms. A line of bright blood spread across it. "That's nothing," he said wiping his hand against his pants. He dropped the letter opener on the floor in front of him.

They both sat for another few seconds, not speaking, and the minister tried to think hard of what to say. "God hasn't deserted you," he said, speaking softly. "He's here for you."

George nodded, hearing that, and encouraged, the minister moved forward and touched his hands. They were cold and the fingers were wide and rough. Another line of blood welled up along the cut. "We could telephone the police. I'll go with you when they come. You made a mistake. The explosion was bigger than you thought it would be. It ended up killing a lot of people. But you can ask for forgiveness."

For a minute they sat in silence, the minister's hands curled around George's, George looking down at them. Then George glanced up. He smiled a small, far-off smile. "You got a church service in a couple hours, and people will be coming for it."

"That doesn't matter, George. I'll stay with you."

The minister tried to tighten his hold, but George pulled away. "Pick up the Bible." He gestured to the Bible the minister had set on the small table next to the couch hours ago.

Reverend Edwards reached down and lifted the book with its worn black cover. The edges of the pages flashed gold, and a single red marker fell out from between them. George bent down to the floor and turned out the small desk lamp. For a second, before he turned the switch, the light clung to him, as if he were the object with the power of illumination. Then the room darkened.

"You can change your mind," Reverend Edwards said. "You can be forgiven."

"Hold the Bible, put your hand on top of it," George told him, his voice flat with the directive. George stood behind him and placed his hands on the minister's shoulders.

"Swear you won't tell anyone I was here."

"I won't tell anyone," Reverend Edwards said, the words flowing out of him automatically with his fear. "I swear."

"All right." George backed away. He picked up the letter opener, and with a deft movement, slid it back into its sleeve, and dropped it onto the desk.

The minister's hands still held the Bible and they were trembling, but he wasn't aware that they were moving. He barely felt them.

"You never thought much about me, did you?" George asked. Then, not waiting for an answer, he opened the door, and seconds later, he was gone.

For a while the minister stayed seated on the couch, not moving, as if George were still there sitting across from him. Words from the Gospel of Luke came to him: "What man of you, having a hundred sheep, if he has lost one of them, does not leave the ninety-nine in the wilderness, and go after the one which is lost, until he finds it?" He watched the pale light in the opening between the curtains becoming more visible, and for several minutes, he stayed absolutely still as if everything were dependent on that. Then he got up and unsteadily walked to the center of the room. He picked up the lamp and put it on the desk, fitting it between two piles of papers and switching it on so that the room was washed with light. Finally, he turned to the window and lifted the curtains that George had drawn, looking out across the lawn that ran between his building and the church. The sun was rising and a pink streak singed the edge of the sky. A milky fog covered the grass. He made out the familiar shape of the maple tree and the dark strip of road behind it where George was nowhere in sight.

Suddenly it was as if he had come back to his senses, and he walked quickly to his office door and locked it. He went to his desk then and picked up his telephone and began to dial the operator to ask for the police, but before she could answer, he set the receiver down again. He felt as if George were still in the room. On his desk, spread out, were his notes for the sermon he had to give in a few hours. Now the fear inside him knew no bottom. It was like the fear he had had as a child when he experienced an asthma attack. His mother hadn't known what to do for the attacks except give him cough syrup. She would tell him to lie quietly on his bed, and he used to try to do as she had said, becoming as still as possible. If you stopped everything and didn't demand much of your body, your lungs would fill more easily—he knew that was how it worked. Gradually while lying there, willing himself into stillness, the attack would dissipate, and by the time he got up again, he would be breathing more easily.

Now as he sank down into his chair, he was doing the same thing without realizing it, his body reverting back to its pattern. For a long time, he sat in front of his desk and became more and more still inside. George was probably far from the church, he told himself. Possibly, he was even driving on the highway, headed east into the sun, or maybe north, or south, or west. The vehicle would be traveling fast. The minister pictured this. The windows would be rolled down so that the wind could blow straight through them.

It seemed as if he sat for a long time thinking these things. Other possibilities still felt inconceivable—that the man he had married and who had sat in his church had killed ten people, that this man was now at large and could kill someone else, that he had sat in the minister's office and threatened him. These things fell through the minister's head, circling like a great wheel.

At some point, he picked up a pen and began to write the words he would speak in a few hours: "There are no simple answers at a time such as this. God's presence seems far away and hidden, and in the middle of the night, we yearn to feel it inside us like the beating of our own heart."

Outside the fog was lifting, and a pale sun rose higher. The minister remembered how even before he had been forced by George to swear his confidentiality on the Bible, he had verified it. "Yes," he'd said, when George had asked him if whatever he told the minister was confidential. He'd answered quickly and without thinking.

Reverend Edwards glanced at the window again, then he looked at the letter opener that lay on a pile of papers on his desk, thinking that there might be blood on it from where George had cut his hand. He reached down and picked up the telephone receiver again, and this time he asked the operator to connect him with the police.

Chapter 9

After Reverend Edwards made the phone call to the police station, he sat at his desk staring at the sentences he had written for his sermon. Then, a few minutes later, when he heard the police cruiser drive into the parking lot, he got up, opened and then closed the curtains. He had thought the arrival of the police would make him feel safer, but seeing the cruiser he felt more anxious.

"Come in," he answered when he heard the knock, turning away from the window, still touching the edge of one of the curtains.

The chief of police, Chief Reynolds, opened the door and stepped inside. "Morning, Reverend," he said, glancing around the room. "Perhaps we could get more light in here—either turn on the overhead or open those curtains."

The minister stood behind his desk, not moving to do what the police chief had suggested, and the chief peered at him quizzically. "Are you all right, Reverend?" The chief shut the door behind him, and after turning on the overhead light, walked toward the center of the room. He was a heavyset man with a thick, meaty face, and as he spoke he raised his eyebrows, which made his whole face move.

Reverend Edwards nodded, a strangely automatic gesture that felt like it had nothing to do with him.

"We can leave the curtains closed, if you'd rather."

The minister glanced behind him at the window. He told himself that George Fowler was probably miles away, and that even if George was close by, the closed curtain would make no difference. George would see the cruiser in the church parking lot. But none of these facts penetrated, and the closed curtains were the only thing that made him feel safer, as if the closed-off room had nothing do with anything that was outside it.

"You're sure you're all right?"

He nodded and the chief glanced away. "You said he left about twenty minutes ago?"

"Yes," he answered. He reached down and touched one of the sheets of paper on his desk. The gesture felt ordinary, but it did nothing to steady him. "That dirt is from his boots," he added, pointing at the bits of dirt near the doorway.

The police chief wrote a note on the small pad of paper he'd taken from his pocket, then walked over and crouched down next to the footprints. "He said he was George Fowler? Talked to you about the bombing and all that?"

The minister nodded as Chief Reynolds stood up, grunting a little with the effort. "Reason I ask is sometimes a person will claim they committed a crime, but it turns out they've got some sort of illness." He gestured at his own head. "Turns out their confession means nothing. They may even claim they're someone else, insisting they committed it. They actually think they did it. Or wish they did it. Happens more often than you would think, especially if the actual criminal is already dead."

"This was George Fowler." Reverend Edwards glanced away, gathering himself. "He came to my church. I married him."

"Oh." The chief's eyebrows creased again. He made another notation. "When did you last see him?"

"I don't know, a year or so ago I guess." The one sheep, he told himself, who was in the darkness of the forest, where no one could go.

The police chief narrowed his gaze. "Are you sure you're okay?"

"Yes, I'm fine," he said. But he spoke the words quickly, shaking his head as if he were disagreeing with himself. "What about the roadblocks you mentioned when I called? Have they been set up yet?"

The chief nodded. "As we speak."

The minister shoved his hands into his pockets, but he wasn't someone who normally did this, and he pulled them out again and curled, then uncurled his fingers.

"How'd he seem?" the police chief asked. "You said on the phone he threatened you."

The minister nodded. "He didn't use a gun, but I think he had one in his pocket. I tried to get him to turn himself in. I thought I would be able to convince him, but he refused. Then he made me swear on the Bible I wouldn't tell anybody about him."

The chief wrote down what the minister was saying on his notepad. Reverend Edwards looked over at his Bible, which lay on the table next to the couch. "Will you be able to catch him easily?"

"I got three patrol cars out there looking, and the state troopers are setting up a roadblock on the highway. Twenty minutes is a pretty good-size lead, but we're checking the streets around here and his parents' house, just outside town." He paused, pointed at the window. "You said you didn't see what he was driving."

"I looked, but there was no vehicle. I didn't hear an engine start up or anything either. He must not have been parked close by."

The chief jotted down a note. "Our records show he drives a pick-up truck, tan, fairly nondescript. Did he say why he blew up the drugstore?"

The chief had stopped writing and stared at him, but Reverend Edwards couldn't meet his gaze. He looked at the floor, and the pattern on the frayed Oriental rug swam in front of him. That forest, where it was darkest, where evil dwelled.

"Not explicitly. He said his wife had betrayed him and moved out. She went to live at her sister's."

"What's her sister's name? Do you know?"

The minister thought for a second and shook his head. "I can't remember."

"Well, we can find out. I always said that most crimes fit into two categories—crimes of passion and crimes of greed." He raised his eyebrows. "Kind of like sin, right Reverend?"

The Reverend kept his eyes on the floor. "I suppose so."

"Then there are those sins that don't fit as crimes. I guess betrayal is one of them." He made another note.

The minister rested his fingertips on the desk. The police chief had been referring to George's wife's betrayal, but the minister knew George would see his talking with the police as a betrayal, and part of him felt like that betrayal was the worst thing he could do. He was like the Pharisees and scribes who had said, "This man receives sinners and eats with them," when they were denigrating Jesus. And yet . . .

"How soon will everything I told you get out?"

The chief walked over to the couch and crouched on the floor in front of it. "You mean when will this information be on the radio or in the newspapers?"

"Yes. How soon?"

"We can try to keep it under wraps for a few hours, give us the advantage of him thinking we still believe he's dead. But not for long. We have to warn the public."

The minister stared at his desk. On it was a section of a newspaper from earlier in the week. Yesterday morning he had been thinking about commenting on it in his sermon. Next to an article about the way in which the Vietnam War was progressing was one on East Germany's economic boom, called "the little miracle." Progress moved humanity forward, toward God's vision—that had been his thought. The letter opener that George had tossed onto his desk lay between the newspaper and his sermon notes.

"He used the letter opener on my desk to open an envelope with some money in it," he said as the chief straightened up from the floor. "Afterwards, he held onto it for awhile, and he cut his hand at one point on it."

"I'll take it with me when I go. Might prove useful for fingerprints. I assume he took the money?"

The minister nodded. He had a brief pang about the loss of the letter opener, a gift one Christmas from his daughter.

"How much was in it?"

"A little over a hundred dollars, I believe."

The chief made another note, then pocketed the letter opener and his notepad. "From what you told us on the phone, the chances are pretty good that George Fowler is no longer in the area. You said, best of your knowledge, he left about five-thirty. When you called it was already six. They probably just now finished getting the roadblocks set up on the highway. I'll argue to keep them in place as long as possible on the chance he might still be in the area, but it's likely he fled. That's why it's important to issue a broader warning. You said he gave no indication where he was headed?"

The minister shook his head. "Will they catch him?"

"Can't say."

There was a moment when their eyes met and the minister pictured George driving across the state line. The right words spoken might have been like a key applied to a lock. He picked up the papers with the notes for his sermon.

"I thought he might still be here when the others arrived or that he would force me to go with him," he told the chief.

The chief nodded. "Fortunate, that." He gestured toward the clock. "You better get ready for your service. I'll finish here. I can come back later if there's anything else."

The minister walked to the door, intending to use one of the meeting rooms down the hall. "Should I tell my congregation?"

"Wait a few days, see what happens. This may resolve quickly, and then you can tell them. Meanwhile, no reason to alarm everyone."

The minister stepped out into the hallway, but even when he'd left his office, he could still feel George's presence, and it didn't matter if George was miles away. As he walked into a small meeting room, he pictured George's face. "You never thought about me," George had said, and the minister realized that he hadn't.

Two hours later, Reverend Edwards stood before his congregation. His first name was William, but he rarely thought of himself as William anymore, except when he was with his wife, one of the few people who still called him by that name. Hearing it from her was something of a relief, as if the sound of his first name removed the mantle of his obligations. Listening to the choir now, he thought of that, and it made him feel much younger and somewhat naked under the black robe.

He had expected a smaller congregation after the long Saturday, but the pews were full, and a few folding chairs were in use at the back. Nancy was there with Sandi in the second row, but Bob Mc-Neese, whose wife had been in the drugstore when it exploded, was pointedly missing, as well as Elizabeth Greenly and her children.

Standing at the pulpit, he tried to shake the sense that nothing in front of him was real. He felt like he was both awake and asleep at the same time, so that his voice sounded far away, and his words spilled down a widening crack between him and his congregation. As he gave the invocation, he couldn't keep track of which words he'd said and which ones he still needed to say. There was a brief silence, and then he heard the other voices join his in answer.

As he squinted at his congregation, the church seemed too full of light. He followed the order of the service, reading the Scripture from Isaiah, relating Isaiah's vision. Then as he spoke the words describing the seraphim, each with its six wings, he peered across the pews, and there sitting in the back he saw George Fowler. He stared hard at the man, reciting: "Holy, Holy, Holy is the Lord of hosts, the whole earth is full of His glory." Nothing seemed unusual about George's posture. He was simply sitting in the pew with his head bowed, like much of the rest of the congregation, listening. Reverend Edwards turned to the Scripture from Mark. He heard the rustle of the pages between his fingers, and he coughed a little, clearing his throat. Then as he began to read again, citing the Gospel, he looked back out over the pews. Briefly, the man raised his head, meeting the minister's gaze, and only then did the minister see that the man wasn't George. He paused in the reading for a second, trying to comprehend what was happening. It took him a minute to place the name of the person—Thomas Burke, a man who had George Fowler's dark hair and slumped posture. Thomas had started attending services last year, and his wife, seated next to him, had inquired about joining the choir.

Reverend Edwards kept reading as best he could, but he had no idea how the service was proceeding. Later, he wouldn't be sure of anything he'd said during the sermon. His notes made connections between the two lessons from the Scriptures, but he wouldn't be able to remember how he'd explained that relationship. In his mind, the two wouldn't even seem connected anymore.

As the notes of the recessional sounded, he walked down the aisle, then stood in the doorway shaking the hands of those in his congregation. He knew he should say something comforting, but he held his hand out almost mechanically and few words came to him. In his avoidance of saying anything about George Fowler, he realized, he had hardly even mentioned the fire.

"Are you all right?" Nancy asked as she slipped into place beside him.

"Yes," he told her. "Just tired."

"I'm worried about you," she whispered. "You look exhausted."

As his congregation filed out of the church, he tried to look people in the eyes. He forced himself to remember that Carlton Greenly, Stella McNeese, and the others were gone; they wouldn't be coming back.

"I'm sorry you lost your shop, Henry," he told Henry Casey, who owned the barbershop that had mostly burned down.

"Are your children all right?" he asked Catherine Thompson.

"Yes," she answered him, smiling. "Just worn out. We let them sleep in this morning."

When most everyone had walked past him leaving the church, John Scott and few of the others stayed on, to talk with him about the idea of planning a group memorial service with another church. Louise Bradley and Janet Darcy met briefly with Nancy to arrange meals for Elizabeth Greenly's family and Bob McNeese and his son, who was on a bus headed back from college.

After the gatherings finished, Nancy tried to convince him to go back to the house, but he insisted he needed a few more minutes to put things in order. Once everyone was gone, he stepped back inside the empty church. The wooden pews lined up regularly on either side of the center aisle, anticipating the symmetry of the altar and the cross above it. He slid down onto one of the seats toward the back. George could have sat in this same pew at some point. He tried to picture that. Had the man met his gaze during the sermons, or had he closed his eyes? Had he sung when they stood for the hymns? Had he walked to the front of the sanctuary for communion? The images of his congregation spread in front of him, and he couldn't be sure of anything.

He shut his eyes and under him the building settled with a slight creaking sound. From outside a car's engine blended with the whir of the overhead fan. He breathed out and heard a thin whistle coming from his lungs. All around him in the near silence, his fear descended like a wall. His chest felt both hollow and thick. The muscles clenched then unclenched as if he'd just run up a long hill. He hadn't experienced an asthma attack in years, and the tightness in his chest made him feel small again.

He concentrated on slowing his breathing as he opened his eyes and stared at the cross above the altar, following the contours of its wood. He couldn't remember what he'd told the police chief and what he might have forgotten. He was a careful person who usually paid attention to details. Normally any omissions would have been deliberate, having to do with his role as a confidant, but now he wasn't sure what he'd said. He also had no idea why it had taken him so long after George had left to make the phone call, a delay that had probably meant George's escape. Had it been a deliberation with fear or conscience, or had it been due simply to a failure in his character, the sort of failure that only came to light in the midst of crisis?

The first time George had asked him if everything he said would be confidential, he should have said, no. The outcome might have been different. His response made him think of Charlie Bourne, the young man who had come to his office with his induction notice. The look on Charlie's face had been fear, and the minister had dismissed it, talking of duty.

From outside came the sound of another car on the road. A ripening sun sat square in the middle of the sky, and nearby people were getting ready for Sunday dinner. After a time, the minister stood up. As he walked to his car in the noonday heat, everything appeared normal, as if nothing had occurred under the bright sun that wasn't ordinary.

Bird calls frequent the trees—cardinal, thrush, nuthatch, jay, the quick hammer of a woodpecker. Years ago when the cottage was newly abandoned, he used a tire iron to break one of the windows. It was late summer and he'd taken Joyce there. She danced through the rooms, pretending out loud where to put furniture and the colors for curtains.

Later he brought a blanket from the car and spread it on the floor because Joyce was too modest to make love outside, even if there was no one around. Afterward, they walked down to the lake, and she ran out into the water, then dove under, skimming along the surface. As he swam out to her, the sunlight fractured on the water, like broken glass. He followed her farther out, then back to the shore where they lay together on the hot, white sand.

Chapter 10

At close to ten on Saturday night, Jack Turnbow was released from the emergency room. The nurse, who was across the room by then with another patient, glanced up and waved to him as one of the orderlies pushed him in a wheelchair to the entrance where his partner, Martin Beckley, was waiting with the squad car to drive him home.

"How did you know to come get me?" he asked Beckley.

"The hospital called the police station."

Beckley's uniform, similar to Jack's, was blackened from the ash and one of his sleeves was torn. "You were off duty hours ago," Jack commented.

As Beckley prepared to pull out of the hospital's exit, he turned and Jack saw the blackened ash on his face. "None of us are off duty."

On Sunday, Jack lay in bed, taking painkillers and reading newspaper accounts of the explosion and fire. Then on Monday morning, having swallowed the pills the doctor had given him, he drove to the station to report for work.

As he walked into the front office, Jack heard the desk officer, Ted Clearly, on the telephone, talking to the state police office. "What's going on?" he asked when Ted hung up.

"They're searching for George Fowler," Ted told him.

Jack slid down onto the chair next to Ted's desk. It was early enough that the air was still cool, but the day promised to be hot again and Jack's shirt was already damp with sweat. The top of his head felt slick as he took off his police hat. "I thought George Fowler was killed in the explosion. That's what the newspaper reported."

"I know. But the minister of that Methodist church on Maple Street called yesterday morning and said George Fowler came to his office." Ted paused. "It's confidential, that part about the minister. We released a statewide warning late yesterday afternoon. It was broadcast a few minutes ago on the local station. I just heard it. It's supposed to be in this evening's paper."

Jack felt his back tighten up, as a thread of pain spiraled through him. While the medication the hospital had given him for his back helped, when he moved too quickly, he sent his muscles into spasm. Despite the pain, he wished he'd called in yesterday. Most of his duties in the small town involved things like traffic control. An opportunity to bring someone like George Fowler to justice might not occur again for years. "What's going on with the search?"

Ted glanced at the log. "The state's involved, and yesterday the chief sent officers over to George's parents' house. He's got a brother who has some land down by the state border. The state police were hoping he would show up there yesterday, while he still thought he was believed dead, but no such luck."

"Which officers from here are working it?"

"Crowley and Garner are assigned to it once they report in, and Dick, Dick Barnett. Joe and Stanley are already out there. Beckley is off this morning. He's on again this afternoon and evening. Everybody's schedule got changed because of the fire. You're listed as inactive."

"Inactive?" Jack said, louder than he meant to. The pain in his back radiated down toward his legs.

"I meant to telephone you earlier and see how you were doing, but I've been on with the state and Mike telephoned before that," Ted apologized.

Jack glanced back at the hallway that led to several offices, including the police chief's. "I mean I could understand assuming I'd take a sick day or two, but inactive? I wasn't even really injured."

Ted shrugged. "We all thought you were."

"That's all right. I'll go back and talk to the chief." He stood up, but his back seized, forcing him to stay bent over for an extra second or two before straightening all the way. He grimaced, avoiding Ted's gaze. "I'm fine," he muttered.

A minute later, he stood in front of the police chief's door. Normally he was well coordinated, but now everything he did felt awkward. He knocked, and as he opened the door, Chief Reynolds glanced up from his desk.

"Thought you would be at home recovering," the chief said.

"I was released Saturday night," Jack told him, turning with care to shut the door. "Nothing but muscle pain."

"You could have been hurt a lot worse. I heard about the rescue you accomplished. Chief Morgan said he was afraid that second blast had killed you. Take a couple of days. Come back later in the week. You've got plenty of sick days—more than anyone else in the department."

Jack ignored the chair in front of the chief's desk. "Ted said there's a search for George Fowler. I didn't hear anything about it on the news."

The chief nodded. "We're getting help from the county and the state. Our best guess is that he's miles from here by now. We've been making phone calls, interviewing people, but the guy, except for his job at the construction site, kept to himself. Even his mother hasn't seen him in over a year." The chief glanced down at his desk. "Come back later in the week when you're feeling better and we'll see where we're at."

"You can't send me home. Not after that man blows up a building downtown and kills all those people," Jack told him, sounding more agitated than he wanted to. He wasn't thinking about what had happened years ago to his mother, but since his scare in the hospital, it lay inside him like a body of water that could keep growing. "I was there. I went into that fire."

Chief Reynolds peered up at him. "That might be enough of a reason for me not to put you on this."

"I'm fine, really," Jack said, consciously lowering his voice. "And besides, you're short-staffed."

The phone on the chief's desk started ringing, and the chief pushed a button Jack knew would transfer it to the front desk.

"How many are dead? What was the final count?" Jack asked.

"The count is at seven, but we think it'll reach ten. They're having a hard time identifying remains in a couple of cases."

The chief looked at the schedule posted on the wall next to his desk. "I've got Beckley working with Ted during the afternoon. I don't have anybody with him this evening, so I'll tell him to pick you up if you're recovered enough. How's that? You can ride around for a couple of hours if you think you're feeling up to it."

Jack nodded. Beckley, the officer he was training, was the first black police officer to be hired by the town. Chief Reynolds had accomplished the hiring several months ago, despite protests from within the department. Jack had heard about the protests, and he knew also about the chief's insistence that a man's race had no bearing and that Beckley had an impressive record with the military police while in Vietnam. The chief believed Jack was the right person to keep controversy at bay.

"That's fine," Jack told the chief. "Have him pick me up. Just give me something else I can do now."

The chief thumbed through some of the papers on his desk. He opened a box that lay on his desk. In it, were several objects recovered from the fire. He took out a wedding ring and placed it in an envelope, then handed it to Jack with a couple of sheets of paper that included an address.

"This was found in the debris of the drugstore. We think it may have belonged to Carlton Greenly. You can take it over to his wife and verify that it was his. If you get a positive ID on it, return it to her."

Reluctantly, Jack took the ring. "What about the search?"

"This is related. Look at it as clean-up."

Jack stood there staring at him for another moment. He hated this kind of police work. Not knowing what to say to the family of victims, he often ended up stating the facts with a directness that was unsettling. Two years ago, after informing a couple that their son had been killed, he'd watched the father go into a state of shock that mimicked a heart attack.

The chief's telephone started ringing again. "What are you waiting on?" he said before picking it up this time.

As the chief began to argue about discontinuing the roadblocks, Jack walked out of his office and down the hall. Ted glanced up at him as he came through the front office, but Jack didn't stop to talk. Out in the parking lot beside the building, he found the patrol car his partner had left there and got inside. He stared at the envelope in his hand. Then he shoved it along with the paperwork into his pocket, as he started the engine and prepared to drive to Elizabeth Greenly's house.

Chapter 11

Off and on all day Sunday and into the night, Elizabeth worked on her kitchen wall, fitting one piece of glass after another into a pattern, blue pieces from the plates she'd broken next to green pieces from the beer bottles—a field of green and an ocean of blue. The edges were important, the place where one world turned into another.

During the night, the quiet of the house swept through her. It was completely dark outside the opened windows. The only sound, the steady hum of insects. You could close your eyes and drift inside that quiet. The clock read two and then three. The mosaic had its own life, the pieces growing next to one another in long, snaking lines. Here was a spiral, there a triangle, in the corner a circle that turned into a vortex. *Let me row through my tears. Let me turn my oars through the water.* Most of the time she couldn't conceive of a shore, but when she allowed herself to close her eyes, she sensed the bottom inside her, the place where it would all stop.

At three-thirty in the morning, when Elizabeth assumed her children were asleep upstairs, Izzy came up behind her so quietly that, sitting on the floor facing the kitchen wall, Elizabeth didn't hear her.

"Mommy," Izzy murmured as she draped herself across the back of Elizabeth's shoulders.

"What are you doing up?" She turned around so Izzy could tumble into her lap.

"Is Daddy home?"

Elizabeth shook her head. "Remember the fire we saw?"

Izzy nodded, stuffing her thumb in her mouth.

"Daddy was in the drugstore, and the drugstore was part of the fire."

"But when is he coming home?"

"I don't know, Izzy. They're still searching the buildings where the fire was. You need to go back to bed. Mommy needs to go to bed too."

Izzy pushed her head into Elizabeth's chest, beginning to whimper. "I'm hungry. I want toast with sugar on it. I want breakfast." Her hands curled into fists, as her face streaked with tears, and it took Elizabeth several minutes to quiet her enough to carry her upstairs.

After placing Izzy in her bed, she stopped in Bert's bedroom and saw that the window was wide open and Bert wasn't there. Piles of clothes and magazines lay on the floor, and the bed sheets were pulled back and rumpled. As she reached down to see if they were still warm, she heard a movement by the window. Just outside it was Bert sitting on the roof of the garage. "What are you doing out there?" she demanded.

"I like it out here," Bert said. "I like being close to the sky. I like being away from the house."

Elizabeth gazed out at her. Framed by the window, her daughter's profile looked shockingly like Carlton's. "The house is hard for all of us right now," she said. "You need to come inside. It's after three in the morning. I have enough to deal with without having to worry about where you are."

"You know where I am," Bert said evenly. "I'm stargazing."

"Come inside and go to bed," Elizabeth told her with an edge in her voice.

"In a while. Leave me alone." Bert lay back with her hands folded behind her head. She looked like she was relaxing in a lounge chair. Elizabeth wanted to grab her by the arm and yank her through the window, but she walked out of the room and went to bed herself instead.

When she woke, she checked and Bert was asleep in her bed. At a little after ten, she heard a vehicle pull up into the driveway. She was dressed by then, wearing the same pair of shorts and top she'd worn the day before. Her hair was loose and uncombed. Watching from the window, she saw a police officer walk up the sidewalk that had beds of flowering zinnias beside it. The flowers blossomed like a crazy quilt—bright reds, oranges, and yellows mixed with pastel pinks, soft greens and majestic purples next to the raggedy looking Queen Anne's lace she hadn't bothered to weed, deciding earlier in the summer that they looked pretty. He stopped on the walkway for a minute, looking at the chaos of color, out of place next to the well-groomed lawns on either side of hers. She noticed the stiff way he carried himself and the grimace on his face as he stood on her doorstep waiting for her to answer his knock.

She didn't want to answer it. She could guess the finality that would come with the visit from a police officer. Yesterday, when Reverend Edwards had stopped over, they'd sat in her living room together. In the past, talking with him had made her feel lighter, less burdened, but this time the conversation had felt too quiet, and there had been a darkness inside the quiet that she couldn't name. When he left, she felt an unexplainable relief.

The officer knocked again, a little louder this time. While Carl and Bert were both upstairs sleeping, Izzy sat at the kitchen table finishing a bowl of cereal. Elizabeth moved slowly to the front door, opening it. Then, managing somehow to sound normal, even to her own ears, she said, "Hello."

The officer took off his cap. "I'm Officer Turnbow with the Centerville Police Department," he told her, pausing after the introduction as if waiting for her to say something. "Can I come in for a minute?" he added when she said nothing.

She felt like telling him no and shutting the door. The rooms inside her house threatened her, each of them holding something of Carlton's—a shirt left on a chair or a scrap of paper he had scribbled a note on—but right now she wanted to be alone with those threats.

"All right," she said, standing aside, not knowing how to refuse him.

Officer Turnbow stepped into the front hallway. He took his hat in one hand, then passed it back to the other one. "Maybe we could sit down."

She stood in front of him without moving. Just tell me what you have to say, she felt like blurting out. Get this over with. But she pushed the door shut and led him into the living room.

"Please." She offered him a chair, and when he sat down, folding his body by bending slowly, resting at the edge of the cushion, she took a seat on the couch opposite him. The house was quiet except for the sound of an occasional car on the street out front and the soothing rumble of a distant mower. When she'd opened the front door, she'd seen that the morning sky was a deep, royal blue.

"There's no good way to say this," the officer began. "We found something at the scene of the fire that might have belonged to your husband." He watched her, which unnerved her, but she didn't lower her gaze. "We'd just like to identify the owner and be able to give it to the surviving spouse or nearest relative."

He stopped speaking and glanced around the room at the toys on the floor and Carlton's shoes by the entryway. The sofa where Elizabeth sat was blue with a row of pleated fabric that hung along the front and sides. She had picked it out with Carlton three years ago in a furniture store and had had it delivered. Carlton's parents had given the couple the chair in which Officer Turnbow sat. His parents had telephoned twice since the call Elizabeth had made to them the night of the explosion, wanting to know if it was certain that he was dead and what would be done about a burial. Even if no remains were identified, they'd said they would still want a funeral. Elizabeth hadn't known what to tell them. She'd said she would talk to her minister and call them back, and then yesterday had gone by like a stone falling down into a well.

"I'll show you the object in question," Officer Turnbow said finally. He stuck his hand into his pocket and pulled out the envelope. "I'm afraid it's a wedding band."

She nodded almost imperceptibly. She thought of the symbolism of the ring, a circle that was never ending, uniting lovers and representing wholeness. *With this ring, I thee wed.* When they had slipped the rings onto one another's fingers during the wedding ceremony, Carlton's hands had been shaking, and she had had to hold his left hand with one of hers to steady it.

Officer Turnbow held the envelope out to her. "Why don't you look and see if it's his."

Elizabeth got up slowly from the couch and carried it back to her seat with her. She sat down and held it for another minute or so before she opened it. The envelope hadn't been sealed, and she only needed to remove the flap to see the ring. She felt the shape of the ring first underneath the paper, then slid it out into her hand. It was a man's ring, wider than hers. Someone had rubbed the blackened ash from the gold. She wondered how it had survived the explosion and then the fire. Slowly, she picked it up and turned it over in her hands. The date inscribed on the inside, April 12, 1948, matched the date on her own.

"It was found among the debris. It must have been flung far enough from the building that it survived the fire," the officer said, as if answering her question.

She nodded. Somehow it made sense that this piece of who they were together would have survived.

"Did it belong to your husband?" Officer Turnbow asked her.

"Yes," she said, and then there were another few minutes of silence between them as she took the ring and slid it onto her finger up against her own, the larger ring and the smaller one, band to band, the edges touching.

"If you'll sign this, I can leave it with you," Officer Turnbow told her, unfolding the form he took from his pocket and setting it with a pen on the coffee table between them. "I'm sorry for your loss, ma'am." There were another few beats of silence before he went on. "I didn't know your husband personally or anything, but I used to see him in the store sometimes. Once I stopped by and he had just closed, but he unlocked the door for me and waited while I found a few things, then rung them up himself."

Elizabeth nodded. She heard everything he was saying, but the words didn't mean anything to her. Then she heard the scrape of Izzy's chair against the floor in the other room and the soft patter of her feet. "Were you there at the fire?" she asked, addressing him for the first time.

He nodded, shifting uncomfortably in the chair. "I'm also a volunteer firefighter. I went in to try to save someone who was trapped. Then I fell when the hardware store exploded. I ended up over at the hospital, but my injuries were minor."

She looked at him closely now, noticing the tight expression on his face and the stiffness with which he held himself. There were others in the fire who had died besides Carlton. She'd heard this on the radio reports. "I heard that almost everyone who was in the drugstore when it happened was killed," she said. "Even Joyce's husband, George Fowler. I knew him. Sometimes when I went by to pick up Carlton, he was there. They came to our church once in a while."

Elizabeth paused, but the officer didn't say anything. "Did the people you were rescuing survive?" she asked him.

"One of them died. The other one is in critical condition. They're transferring him to a larger hospital. It's not certain if he'll have the use of his legs."

"The one who died was Davy Sandler, wasn't it?" she asked. She'd heard Davy had died early Sunday morning of smoke inhalation and burns.

The officer nodded.

"Well, I should sign that form."

She began to gather herself to reach for the pen, but then she heard Izzy cry out in the other room. "Mommy! I hurt my foot."

Jumping up, she ran to the kitchen. An odd relief swept through her with the burst of movement that had nothing to do with Carlton or the explosion. As she rushed through the door, Izzy sat crumpled on the floor, holding onto her foot.

"It hurts!" she cried out, beginning to whimper as soon as she saw her mother.

"You must have stepped on a piece of glass," Elizabeth heard herself say in a soothing voice that brought order with it. She glanced around the room, taking in the broken glass she'd left on the counter and the small pile on the floor by the kitchen table, where a pack of Carlton's cigarettes lay. She'd never taken up smoking, but last night she'd smoked two of them. A broken bowl lay in the sink with the dirty casserole dish that belonged to a neighbor, and more casserole dishes and baskets of food covered the counters, as well as a box of Frosted Flakes and the milk bottle, left out from Izzy's breakfast. Yesterday, a few of her neighbors and friends who had entered her kitchen had asked how the dishes had gotten broken. One of them had tried to insist on helping by cleaning up the glass.

What a mess things are in, she thought, lowering herself onto the floor now to examine the place on Izzy's foot where the blood was welling up. Then she heard the officer step into the room from behind her.

"Is everything all right, ma'am?" he asked.

Glancing up, she watched him take in the food, the dirty dishes, the broken glass, and the wall she'd been covering. "She stepped on a piece of glass," she told him, wiping the blood from the cut as Izzy cried out again.

He continued to survey the room. "I can see how that could happen," he commented.

"If you hand me that form, I'll sign it so you can go," she said briskly.

He walked over to the table, still staring at the wall. Then he looked down at the floor and his expression softened. Stiffly, he sat down on a kitchen chair. "I'd get down on the floor to look at her foot, but I might not get up again. If you'll set her up here, closer to me, I'll take a look. I'm not a doctor, but I have first aid training, and I can sometimes fix a cut."

Elizabeth hesitated. Was there a penalty for leaving a pile of broken glass on one's floor, endangerment of some sort? She'd never liked police officers.

"All right," she said hesitantly, gathering Izzy in her arms and struggling to pull herself to standing.

She carried the child to the kitchen table where she sat down in a chair next to him. The table was rectangular and large enough to seat six. "Big enough for one more," Carlton had liked to joke. He used to put his arm around her waist and kiss her when he commented on the extra place.

"Can you hold her foot up to the light?" the officer asked.

"It hurts," Izzy whimpered.

"I know," he told her. "We'll fix it up. What's your name?"

"Izzy," she said, so softly that only the hissing sound came across, and he had to ask her again.

"Her name is Elizabeth, like mine, only we call her Izzy," Elizabeth told him, arranging Izzy so he could hold her foot in the palm of his hand.

"I can't see much in this light. If you have a flashlight and a pair of tweezers, I'll try to take out any glass in the cut. It doesn't look deep enough for stitches, but you should wash it good afterwards and bandage it."

Elizabeth nodded, shifting Izzy off her lap. "Mommy!" Izzy cried immediately, protesting.

"I'll be right back." Elizabeth bent down and kissed the top of Izzy's head. "Sit here with the officer, and I'll find what he needs to fix your cut foot."

"I like kitties," Izzy said softly to the officer as her mother walked away.

Elizabeth got tweezers from the bathroom, then opened the cabinet in the mudroom where Carlton kept the flashlight. His tools and barbecue utensils were neatly arranged on the shelves, and she stood there for a minute, unable to touch them.

"Can you find one?" Officer Turnbow called out, and she came back to herself with a suddenness that made her head spin.

"Yes, it's here." She reached in and grasped the flashlight. Carlton always kept fresh batteries in it in case of a power outage. She walked across the room, handing it to him. "Here you are."

Izzy squirmed back into her lap as she slid onto the seat. "Are you going to fix my foot?" she asked Jack.

He nodded, turning on the flashlight, testing the tweezers. "Put your foot here on the table and hold it very still."

Izzy looked up at her mother, and Elizabeth nodded, placing her hand on Izzy's foot to keep it from moving. Officer Turnbow prodded with the tweezers, wiping the blood away with a napkin. "There's a small piece in the cut. You can see the glint when the light hits it."

"Ouch!" Izzy cried out.

Elizabeth saw him glance down at Izzy. Then, with steady hands, he bent over her foot again. A few seconds later, he held up the tweezers with a sliver of transparent green glass between them.

Elizabeth pulled Izzy close and rocked her while the officer pressed the napkin to her foot. "Thank you," she told him, truly grateful that someone else had taken over this small emergency.

"I would wash it good and put a Band-Aid on it." He rubbed Izzy's head. "You might have to stay off that foot for the rest of the day," he told her.

"Like a kitty with a hurt paw," she said.

He smiled. "Just like a hurt kitty."

Elizabeth carried Izzy to the sink and set her on the counter so that she could run water over the foot. "Stay right here," she told Izzy handing her a towel. "Hold this on your foot while I say goodbye to the police officer."

Izzy took the towel. "Bye!" she called out.

"Goodbye." Officer Turnbow turned to wave as he walked toward the front hall. "Just sign here and here," he told Elizabeth, stopping at the door to hand her the form.

Elizabeth bent over, signing her name. "I know I should pick up all that glass," she said as she handed back the sheet of paper. For the first time since he'd arrived, she looked him in the eyes.

"You will," he told her.

She wiped her wet hands against her shorts and noticed the presence of Carlton's ring riding loosely against her knuckles. She would have to take it off her finger, she told herself, before it slipped off and she lost it. "Well, thank you for everything."

He gestured toward her kitchen. "What are you using on that mosaic in there—old bottles?"

She nodded. "And I have to admit, some of our dishes as well. I guess it seems a little crazy."

He shrugged. "What's a few dishes?" She had opened the door, and he was stepping through it. "Take good care of that little girl."

As Elizabeth went back to Izzy and began to dry and bandage the foot, she heard his police car start up and roll out of her driveway. She thought of his injury and the sadness on his face when he handed her the ring. He was someone else who had been hurt by what had happened. There were so many who had been hurt. Al Freeman was the only person who worked regularly at the store who hadn't been in it. He had just walked into the diner when it happened.

"It was just luck that kept him out," his wife had told Elizabeth when she'd telephoned. Al had helped to pull Billy Sandler from the fire. She'd heard he had had to be treated for smoke inhalation later that afternoon.

She carried Izzy into the living room and set her on the rug to play while she went back into the kitchen to clean up the glass. The sun was a little higher in the sky. She closed her eyes and felt the heat from its light filling her kitchen.

Once he watched a buck almost drown. It was January, and a skin of ice rimmed the lake. The buck was stuck in the frigid water, too exhausted to reach the shore. His father took a length of rope and threw it out, lassoing the buck's antlers. For a long time he and his father struggled to pull the animal to shore. The buck made great snorting sounds, and plumes of smoke rose from its nostrils. When it reached the shore, it broke through the ice and rose out of the lake on its massive legs.

This happened during hunting season, but his father didn't shoot the buck. Instead, he cut the rope as the buck dug its hooves into the shore. "Anything struggles that hard deserves to live," he said.

Chapter 12

In the school cafeteria, Sandi sat with four girls she knew from last year. Usually she sat with Bert. She hated walking into the big cafeteria and seeing a sea of faces, and now without Bert there, it was worse. The four girls she was sitting with were mostly ignoring her. She tried to sit close enough to them so that it looked like she was part of their group, but she ate her bologna and pickle sandwich in silence. She had the weird feeling that she wasn't real. Words that were said had nothing to do with her, and if she shut her eyes, it felt as though she didn't have a body. Her head felt larger than it actually was, and a moment later it felt much smaller.

She could sense the link between how she felt and the explosion. Her teachers weren't discussing it, and even though the temperature was already in the upper nineties, there was no indication that like last week there would be an early dismissal. The explosion was the only thing the kids were talking about. She'd heard it mentioned in the hallways and whispered about in her classrooms. Bobby, the brother of one of the boys killed in the explosion, was in ninth grade, and many of the students knew him. Many of the students had also known Debra, who had just graduated last June.

"She was so pretty," one of the girls at Sandi's table said. "I thought she should have been prom queen."

Sitting quietly, Sandi listened as the conversation spun on all sides of her. Behind her was a group of boys. "The guy who did it is still alive," one of them said. "They announced it on the radio. That's what Mr. Adams told us. He got away and they're looking for him."

"Are you kidding?" another boy asked.

"I heard his wife moved out on him, and he wanted to kill her."

"I heard he was crazy."

"My mom said his wife was a whore. She was seeing some other guy."

A few of them laughed as they began to put their lunches away. "That's not funny," one of them said. "That guy is still out there somewhere."

The bell rang, announcing the end of lunch. Sandi got up, stuffing her lunch bag with the rest of her sandwich and a small bag of Fritos corn chips into the trash can as she left. When she'd heard the news Saturday night that the person who brought the bomb into the store was Joyce's husband, it had shocked her, and she'd lain awake in her bed for a long time thinking about it. She knew who George Fowler was. She had sometimes been in the drugstore in the evening when he came to get Joyce. She couldn't believe she would know someone who would carry a bomb into a store, or that that person would be married to Joyce. Now she felt what the boys said about him being alive and Joyce being a whore sink to the bottom of her stomach, like the balled up bread and bologna she had eaten. They were lying, she told herself, they must be.

But when she got to her biology class, everybody was talking about George Fowler. Somebody asked the teacher if he was still alive, and she told the class yes, that it had been on WVYB, the local radio station. Sandi sat on her stool and pretended to do the lab. She tried to remember everything Joyce had ever said about her husband and if she had seen Joyce talking to any other men at the store. Usually when Joyce's husband had come into the store to get her, he had stood by the door waiting. Once, Sandi remembered, she had been helping Joyce straighten a shelf of makeup when he got there, and Joyce had said, "Keep talking to me. Pretend like you don't see him."

Finally biology was over, and Sandi went to home ec., her last class of the day. It was a requirement she originally didn't want to take. "We have to learn how to cook and clean while the guys use power equipment in the shop," Bert had complained last spring when they were given their schedules. But Sandi was finding that home ec. was the one class she looked forward to. It was her smallest class—only fourteen girls because there were only fourteen sewing machines. Already, they'd begun to cut the fabric they'd brought in. She'd chosen a peach-colored knit for the simple A-line, short-sleeve dress pattern because Joyce had told her that color was a good match for her complexion. Joyce had also said that she should cut it shorter than the actual pattern, and she had, lopping off a section of the tissue paper before laying it on the fabric.

"You have long legs. You would look great in a shorter style," Joyce had told her.

As Sandi began to sew together the darts and the shoulder seams, the hum from the machine was loud enough that she didn't have to hear anything that anyone else said. Afterward, when the last bell rang, she waited until most of the other girls were gone, and then she took her time going to her locker. On her way out, she stopped in the restroom. While she was there she turned over the band on her skirt, the way Bert had shown her, hiking it up a little, but as she walked outside, she flipped it back down again.

It was a clear afternoon and hot again, up in the low nineties. As she crossed the parking lot and walked along the brightly lit sidewalk, Mr. Willis, her math teacher who was on parking lot duty, gave her a wave. He was young, just recently out of college, and she had heard the other girls arguing over whether he had a girlfriend. For a moment or two after his wave, she felt almost happy, a thread of excitement winding through her, but then, as she turned onto Jackson Street, her feelings rose up again.

Everything was sliding away from her. Joyce had been like a big sister. Last year, Sandi and Bert had gone over to the diner with her when she was on her break. They'd ordered a plate of french fries while Joyce ate a tuna sandwich for lunch. "So, tell us about sex," Bert had said. Sandi had to struggle not to laugh.

"What do you want to know?" Joyce had asked.

"Everything," Bert had said, grinning.

Joyce had asked them what they already knew, then straightened them out on the anatomical facts. She'd cautioned them that when a guy looked at a girl, sex was his main thought. "But when sex is good it's like magic," she'd added.

"What does the magic feel like?" Sandi had asked her.

Joyce had smiled. "Like everything is so wonderful that you're going to explode with it. Nothing that's wrong in your life matters."

Now Sandi kept thinking about that and about Joyce, and her husband, and the bomb. A few weeks ago when Sandi and Bert had gone over to the same diner with Joyce, Joyce had told them that men were completely different creatures from women. "But we need them," she'd said. "Even if they're messed up. They're the only thing that can make us whole."

Sandi wondered whom she had been thinking about when she'd said that—her husband or some other man. Up until last week, Sandi had never questioned the notion that each stage of life led to the next in an upward spiral that included falling in love and getting married, but now that sense was gone. Her heart beat too hard and fast inside her chest, filling her whole body. She could remember the feeling of the drugstore's door handle under her fingers, solid and hot with the afternoon sun, and the sense she'd had that she couldn't move any farther inside, as if there were an unseen wall in front of her. It was as if some part of her had known that something like a drugstore blowing up could suddenly happen, even though she herself couldn't have comprehended that.

She turned up Maple Street, which would take her past the church where her father spent his afternoons working on his sermons and church business or meeting with church members. Sometimes, she would stop there to get homework help or sit talking with him. He asked her questions and listened to her as if she were one of the church members who might come for a friendly talk or help and guidance.

Recently her father had argued against Sandi's social studies teacher, who had stated that the looting occurring in some of the cities proved those rioting wanted lawlessness.

"They want the causes of poverty and segregation addressed," her father had said. Later, Sandi had thought about this—the way that stealing, which was a sin, could be justified if it resulted from a larger wrong.

Now, as she walked into the building next to the church, it was quiet, and she was grateful since the absence of a voice meant her father would be alone. She knocked on his door before entering. The inside of the building was cool after being outside, like a true retreat. Already, she knew how it would feel once she was in her father's office, the dread she'd experienced all day lifting.

"Hi," she said, more brightly than she felt.

Seated at his desk, her father looked up. "Hey there, Sandi." He smiled, a tentative, tired-looking smile, and Sandi read the preoccupation in it. "What're you doing here?"

He asked the question politely, with a slight tone of surprise, but Sandi was taken aback. "I was just walking home from school."

"Oh." He nodded, setting down his pen and running his hand through his hair as she stepped inside, closing the door behind her.

"Are you working?"

He stood and stretched, then rested his hands on the back of his chair, leaning against it. "I'm putting together ideas for a memorial service for some of the people killed in the fire. A group is meeting this evening to plan a joint service. It'll be held this weekend."

"Oh," she said, standing awkwardly by the door.

He looked at her with a direct gaze waiting for her to say more.

"I just came to say hi. I've got to get home and do some homework," Sandi told him.

He nodded, smiling a little, and she sensed his relief that she wouldn't keep him too long. Then, as she turned to go, he stepped out from behind his desk. "Hold on a second, and I'll walk with you to the edge of the churchyard."

Sandi waited while he put a book back on his shelf, then followed him out into the hallway. Walking with her to the edge of the churchyard was something he used to do when she was younger and first started walking to the church by herself to see him during the day. When she got ready to leave, he would go that far with her and stand watching as she made her way down Maple Street, feeling independent. Once he told her that even after she was out of sight and he had gone back inside, he still held her in the safety of his heart.

She was probably eight then, and he hadn't walked out with her to the edge of the churchyard in a long time. Now she wished he wouldn't do it. On the other hand, she wanted him to stand watching her for a long time after she walked away. She wanted to feel held inside that safety.

They walked together under the large maple tree with its deep, speckled shade, and when they reached the place near the sidewalk and beyond the church where they used to say goodbye, her father stopped.

"How was it at school today? Are kids talking about the explosion?" He was standing next to her, looking from her face back down to the ground with his hands shoved awkwardly in his pockets.

"I don't know," she said, not wanting to talk to him about it.

"How is Bert? Didn't you go over to see her yesterday with your mother?"

She shrugged. They'd walked over in the afternoon, carrying dinner, and while Sandi's mother stood at the front door talking with Bert's mother, Bert's mother had called upstairs to see if Bert wanted to talk to her friend. "Not really," Bert had called back down.

"She's okay I guess," Sandi told her father.

"You can be a big support to her as a friend, you know."

"I guess."

"Are you okay?" he asked, peering at her now with a concerned gaze, and there was something else in his eyes, only she couldn't read what it was.

"Yeah," she said, swallowing hard.

Part of her wanted to say everything to him, but another part of her knew if she did, there was nothing he could say back to her that would be of any help. Her father was not capable of fixing whatever it was that was going on inside of her.

"I heard at school the guy who brought the bomb into the drugstore is still alive," she told him.

Her father nodded, not saying anything.

"Kids at lunch said Joyce was having an affair," Sandi went on.

She shifted her book bag to the other shoulder, and neither of them spoke for another minute. "What does that matter?" her father asked her quietly.

Sandi took a couple of steps away. "I used to see Joyce in the drugstore all the time. One of the guys at school said his mother called her a whore." She blurted this out, and afterward took a breath, realizing what she had said. "I'm not saying she was," she added.

"That's a cruel thing to repeat," her father said. They were silent, and the silence seemed so huge that Sandi couldn't imagine saying anything else. Then her father went on. "You know, Joyce and her husband attended this church a few years ago. I married them."

She felt her head jerk up as she looked at him, realizing that this was true. She had associated Joyce with the drugstore, but now she had the vague recollection of Joyce and her husband seated toward the back of the church. Once she'd wanted to go up to Joyce afterward and say hello, but by the time she'd made her way to the church's entrance, Joyce had been gone.

"You married them," she repeated, and the fact seemed both a simple truth and an impossibility. Her father nodded, and suddenly Sandi realized the significance of what he'd said. He had married them and not even guessed at any of what had ended up happening.

"I could have been in the drugstore," she told him before she knew what she was saying. "Joyce died in that fire. I could have also."

"Any of us could have," he said softly but with a quiet emphasis. "It's just a matter of grace that we weren't."

"It's not because of grace." She was close to crying, and she didn't know why. She remembered how the handle of the door to the drugstore had felt in her hand and the sense that came from nowhere that she had to stop or turn around.

"Someday you'll understand what I'm talking about," he said gravely. "Someday you'll look back on all this, and while it won't necessarily make sense, you'll understand it more."

That's crazy, she felt like telling him. "I have to get home," she said, shifting her book bag from shoulder to shoulder.

"Enjoy your walk." The phrase sounded like an automatic response. It was what he used to tell her when she was younger, and then she appreciated the good wish, but now she felt brushed aside.

Go on back into your office and pray, she thought as she stepped down onto the sidewalk, realizing for the first time how useless his profession was. There was nothing about prayer or a well-worded sermon that had made a difference to George Fowler.

Walking quickly, as if she couldn't get far away fast enough, she glanced back over her shoulder. Her father still stood in the same spot, his hands thrust deeply in his pockets. She walked more than a block before looking back again, and by then he was no longer there. Turning the corner quickly, she headed back toward town. Last night she'd looked up Joyce's sister's name in the telephone directory. The house was located on Taylor Street, just off of Fearing in a section of town she didn't know, south of the downtown streets. Most of the people who lived there worked in the nearby paint factory. She'd ridden through when her family drove out of town. When she was younger, she had loved those Saturday trips in the summer. They would pack a picnic lunch and spend the afternoon visiting state parks or the monuments where the Indian mounds were. Once they took a borrowed sailboat out onto a lake. Sandi had stood on one of the seats to catch the rope her father was tossing her just as the boom swung toward her, knocking her into the water. It had happened so suddenly she hadn't had a chance to become afraid, and she had actually laughed just after she hit the water.

"Hey, this feels great!" she'd called out, splashing about in her shorts, shirt, and white sneakers. The water was dark brown under the hot sky, and she could see two or three small clouds reflected in it. Bits of sunlight shone along its surface like needles of glass.

It had been her big adventure, the one time she'd done something that afterward felt brave in the telling of it. Maybe that was the only way bravery could work for her, she thought—if she didn't allow herself to think about what she was doing.

Skirting the downtown area to avoid Main Street, she turned down Fearing Street and then Taylor where the businesses quickly petered out. The sides of the street were lined with small brick row houses. She glanced in a few of the windows and wondered what it would be like to live in them. She could imagine walking down this sidewalk each day after school or sitting on one of the stoops on a warm summer evening.

On the next block a row of duplexes crowded together, the edges of their porches almost touching the curb. After checking the numbers on them, Sandi found a small green one with 390B on its porch, which matched the address she'd found in the phonebook. She stepped up to the door, her heart beating fast. She would do this quickly, she told herself, before she had the chance to think twice and turn away. The window in the door revealed a small entryway with a light visible toward the back of the house. She forced her hand up and pressed the doorbell.

The woman who answered wore a long, pink housecoat and fuzzy, pink slippers. Her hair was short and blond, teased into a beehive, which was completely smooth on the top layer, like a shiny helmet. The house smelled of cigarette smoke mixed with the sharp odor of nail polish. The woman's nails were freshly painted. Sandi glanced down at her own nails. Yesterday when she'd been sitting in her room trying not to think about everything, she'd painted them pale lavender, a color Joyce had recently picked out for her.

"What do you want?" the woman asked. Staring at the beehive, Sandi saw the teased hair under the smooth top layer. It reminded her of the stuff called "angel's hair," sticky, white fibers which Sandi had once used to make Christmas decorations. Joyce's hair had been darker, and she hadn't teased it. She'd worn it long with a little flip at the ends and a headband. Today Sandi was wearing the same sort of cloth headband, just above her hairline. They had come in a package of several colors, and she'd chosen the light blue one this morning.

"Mrs. Kramer?" Sandi said, forcing the words out. Marge Kramer's name had been in the newspaper, but Sandi had already known it from conversations with Joyce who had told her stories about how when she was younger, she and Marge had gotten into a world of trouble. That had all ended when Marge got married to Joe Kramer, and several years after that, Joyce had married George.

"Yeah, I'm Marge Kramer."

"I'm Sandi Edwards. My father is the minister of the church on Maple Street, and well, I used to go into the drugstore all the time because I'm good friends with Bert Greenly." She stopped abruptly, suddenly unsure of how to say what she wanted. "I knew Joyce. I'm not writing an article or anything."

"Well, that's a relief."

Sandi couldn't tell if her tone was sarcastic or sincere, but she plunged on. "I used to go in the drugstore and see her all the time, and she saved samples of makeup for us and perfume, and she used to tell me about things. She was going to curl my hair sometime." She stopped, feeling nervous and like she didn't know anymore why she'd walked out there. Marge's fluffy slippers looked huge, out of proportion to her petite body. They made Sandi think of Bugs Bunny.

"Don't just stand there on the front step if you're going to talk about Joyce," the woman told her. "Come in and close the door."

Feeling even more nervous, Sandi stepped inside and shut the door behind her. "I got to be at work in an hour. Don't ask me why I'm bothering on a day like today," the woman added, wiping at her nose with a balled-up tissue.

The front door opened into a small living room, and without asking Sandi to come inside any farther, Marge perched on the edge of a chair near the doorway. Joyce had told Sandi that Marge worked both as a hairdresser and as a hostess at a restaurant near the downtown area. Once Sandi had walked past the restaurant and noticed that from the outside it looked dark, candlelit, and romantic. The dinners there were fairly expensive, and the restaurant also served cocktails.

"I was in the bowling alley when the explosion happened," Sandi told her. "I came out right afterwards. I saw the whole thing."

A stack of magazines and newspapers lay on the table next to Marge's chair. On top was the local paper with a headline about the drugstore fire.

"Joyce was really nice," Sandi added.

Marge sniffed noisily. "She liked kids. She wanted to be a school-teacher, but she didn't make it to college. If you're wanting to get your hair done, you'll have to come over to the shop. I work at the one on Cray Street on Wednesdays and Thursdays until about five."

Sandi nodded. Maybe, she told herself, she would go there. "I miss Joyce," she said.

"I hope they catch her goddamn husband. I hated him. I could see this whole thing coming. You know what he did two weeks ago?"

Sandi shook her head.

"He called up here and asked for her, and when I said she wasn't able to come to the phone, he said it didn't matter. He said to let her know that. 'Tell her I said, no problem,' he says in a voice that's carefree, like he doesn't mind in the least. The guy is a real bastard."

Sandi stood there, not saying anything. She tried to think if she had ever heard anyone use the word *bastard* before.

"The police were out here yesterday. I told them, you better hope he died in that explosion or that he's far away from here."

Marge glanced toward the back of her house, then looked at Sandi. "Joyce had diabetes," she added. "She was sick all the time."

Sandi looked down at Marge, and she couldn't think of anything to reply. She didn't know exactly what diabetes was, but she knew it was serious and that people with diabetes could die without shots of insulin. Now Joyce *was* dead, but it had nothing to do with diabetes. Instead her husband had blown up the store and killed her.

Marge stood, reaching behind Sandi to open the door. She touched her hair, patting the helmet, and then she glared fiercely down at Sandi. "I knew from the day she started dating George that he was the worst thing that could have happened to her."

"I was almost in the drugstore when it happened. I was with Bert and we were about to go into the store, and then I didn't—we didn't—because we went into the bowling alley instead." Sandi said the words all in a rush. She stood in the doorway, staring at Marge but hardly seeing her. She didn't know why she had told her father and now Marge about this, only that the moment of almost entering the drugstore had hold of something inside her, so that it kept replaying.

"What are you saying? Are you saying you saw what George was doing?"

Sandi shook her head. "No, I didn't see him," she said hurriedly. "I don't even know if he was in the store yet. It had nothing to do with him."

Marge peered at her, waiting. Now that she'd said what had happened, Sandi had no idea how to explain it. "I don't know why we didn't go in. It's like everything would be different if one second was changed."

"Everything would be different if Joyce never met George in the first place. Everything could have changed for a thousand reasons."

Sandi heard the dismissive quality in Marge's voice, but still the hugeness of the truth of what she'd heard washed over her. Each second was tied to every other second, and one second's change in something as small as a glance or a word could change all the other seconds. It made her shiver a little despite the heat.

"Thanks for talking to me," she said as Marge shut the door.

Sandi stepped down off Marge's porch, almost tripping on the steps. Meeting Marge had unhinged something in her. She wasn't quite sure what, but as she walked toward town nothing she saw, including the row houses with their small windows and dingy front steps or the gray, cracked sidewalks, seemed quite real. A police car drove by, and she felt the officer look at her pointedly. She walked with her head down, staring at the sidewalk, realizing she had nearly twenty blocks to go before she reached her house.

When she and Bert were younger, Bert had liked to climb trees.

By the age of eight or nine, Bert had been adept at it, scaling tree trunks by digging in with the sides of her feet and hugging the trunk with her legs. Sandi used to stand underneath watching as Bert worked her way up, the bright colors of her shirt and shorts flashing through the branches.

"Come on up," Bert would call down. "You can get up really high in this one."

But Sandi hadn't followed her, not even when the tree had low hanging branches. "You go first," Bert might suggest. "I'll give you a boost." But Sandi stayed on the ground, her head tilting back, watching as Bert ascended.

Bert used to send down gifts—tricolored leaves, acorns, walnuts, buckeyes, a blue-jay feather, the orange wing of a butterfly, and once a swarm of bees from a nest she'd disturbed.

"Run!" she yelled that time as she half-jumped, half-fell from the tree.

Later Bert sat in her bedroom, while Sandi tried to pick stingers out of her back with a pair of tweezers. "Don't tell my mom. Promise."

Sandi had finished by swabbing the welts with calamine lotion and promised. She had wished she was more like Bert, in fact sometimes she had wanted to be Bert—to climb a tree the way Bert could or laugh even though her back was covered with stings.

On Saturday Bert had acted like somebody Sandi didn't recognize, and now Bert wasn't even talking to her. No one was turning out to be who she thought they were. She had never realized Joyce was sick or that it was possible for her to be married to someone who would carry a bomb into the drugstore. Also, she had always assumed her father knew everything, but he had married Joyce and her husband without realizing any of this could happen, while Marge had seen it all ahead of time.

The air was hot and still, and there hadn't been rain for a couple of weeks now. She walked past one of the neighborhoods near the hospital where the lawns were turning brown, burnt by the heat. If she and Bert had gone into the drugstore, they would have probably been standing in the aisle with the makeup when the bomb went off. She pictured the two of them afraid and holding onto each other after the contents of the bag had been discovered. What next, after the bag was thrown? She couldn't imagine that, but she could still picture the drugstore windows glaring in the sun, and she could remember the feeling of the door handle under her fingers.

She didn't know why she had changed her mind about going into the drugstore, and the more she tried to recall that moment, the further it retreated from her. It was like trying to remember a dream. The feeling of the dream was still there, but she couldn't call back the reality of it.

Sandi glanced around. She had never paid enough attention to George Fowler to remember what he looked like. She wanted to get home and see if the evening paper had arrived. Maybe it would run a photograph of him. She planned to cut out any articles about him and the fire and save them. Picking up her pace, she hurried a little as she rounded the corner to the hospital. Her lavender fingernails glinted like jewels in the afternoon sun.

Fall will come soon. The maple trees will turn red and yellow, then drop their leaves. The ground will soften with pine needles. Then the wind will pick up and blow snow or sleet or freezing rain. Months later, the melting will begin. The crickets, katydids, and peepers will all wake up.

Whenever the radio broadcast comes on, the volume seems to automatically rise. "The police need your help. The man suspected of carrying a bomb into Greenly's Drugstore on Saturday afternoon in Centerville is believed to still be at large. He is described as a white male; thirty-seven years old; five feet, ten inches tall; weighing one hundred and eighty pounds. He has dark hair and may be driving a tan-colored, Ford pickup. He should be considered armed and dangerous. Anyone with information should call their local or state police."

Chapter 13

By Monday evening most everyone in the town had heard the warning about George Fowler, and they talked about him at their supper tables.

"I knew him because my brother-in-law worked with him," one person said.

"He used to come into the hardware store," another one commented.

"I knew something wasn't right. I could look at him and see that."

It was seven-thirty that night when the minister walked into his office after the meeting at the larger church to plan a group memorial service. At the meeting, he had been asked to deliver the sermon. He knew everyone who had died. Carlton Greenly had invited the minister and his family over for barbecue each summer. Stella McNeese and her family were longtime church members. While the others didn't attend his church, he knew who they were. It was hard to believe they were suddenly gone.

After the meeting, the minister got a sandwich with John Scott, and when John dropped him off in the church parking lot, he went to get his things and call Nancy to say he was on his way home. The parking lot was empty, save for his car, and out front the street was quiet. Earlier he'd spoken to the police chief and been told they'd determined George Fowler must have driven from the town early Sunday morning before the roadblocks were set up. Now, with the warning having been broadcasted, it was unlikely he would come back.

"You can tell your congregation what happened next Sunday if you like," the chief had told the minister. And Reverend Edwards had been contemplating this.

Throughout the day, the minister's anxiety had settled on the responsibility of delivering the sermon on Saturday at the town's memorial service and his nervousness over revealing George's visit to his congregation. As he walked into his building, he focused on these concerns, but when he opened his officer door, all he saw was a cloud of smoke.

"Get in quick and shut the door." Like an apparition, George sat on the couch, hunched over with a cigarette.

The minister hesitated, one hand still on the doorknob, the other in his pocket grasping his car keys. "Hurry up. Get the door shut and lock it." He lifted a pistol, using it to gesture.

The minister reached behind him uncertainly and pulled the door shut, turning the small lock.

"Good," George said. "Now quick, go over to the windows and close the curtains."

The minister walked to the windows. At the meeting, Reverend Dodd, the other minister, had said, "George Fowler attended your church, didn't he?"

"Yes, a couple of years ago," Reverend Edwards had answered. Afterward, no one had commented on it, and there had been a stillness in the room.

Looking out the window before pulling the curtain shut, the minister saw the empty parking lot. The sun had dropped below a line of clouds at the horizon, and a deep purple color, similar to the cloth he sometimes laid on the altar, pooled beneath it. Everything felt clear, whatever he should have done and whatever he needed to do. In his head, he heard the words from the parable of the prodigal son—"And he would gladly have fed on the pods that the swine ate, and no one gave him anything." Then George spoke and everything felt confused again.

"What are you standing there for? Hurry up," George said in a harsh whisper, and the minister closed the curtains and turned back to the room. The office had darkened, and the red glow of George's cigarette floated above the couch.

"All right, now sit down in the chair," George told him, gesturing at the small armchair where George himself had sat two nights ago. As the minister walked toward it, he bumped against the edge of a table, his eyes not adjusted to the change in the light. He knew where everything was in this room, but now the room felt foreign. Then he reached the chair, and as he slid down onto the upholstery, there was an odd comfort to its familiarity.

"I got in through the basement window at the back," George said. He put the cigarette to his mouth and sucked on it. "I could have waited and come to your house, but I came here instead. Everything just keeps happening and I can't get any of it to stop."

The minister recalled the basement windows which he'd opened last week to let the stale basement air out. They were small, barely large enough for a man to squeeze through. "Bring quickly the best robe, and put it on him; and put a ring on his hand, and shoes on his feet." He felt as if he were floating somewhere high above his body.

"I heard on the radio what you said," George told him. "And now there's a warning out. What am I supposed to do? What do you think I'm supposed to do?"

The minister didn't answer. When he glanced down, he saw that his hands were trembling, but they didn't look like they were his.

"You swore on the Bible you wouldn't say anything. And you're a minister."

There was a long silence as George dropped his cigarette on the floor and stepped on it.

"I didn't know what else to do," the minister said.

"Bullshit. I'll bet you told everyone. I'll bet you told the whole congregation, not more than two hours after I left."

The minister shook his head. "I didn't, George. I only. . . ."

"I can just hear what they're saying. 'We knew he was a nutcase. We always felt sorry for his wife.'"

The high-pitched sound in his voice was more frightening than the mocking sound or the threatening one. "They're not saying that," the minister wanted to explain, but he couldn't get the words out.

"You say you welcome everyone, but there's those you invite and those you shun."

"I don't, George. I welcome. . . ."

"You shut me out."

With the hand that had held the cigarette, he began patting his thigh with the quick, motion of his flat palm. "Now what choice do I have? What can I do? I don't know what to do."

He stared at the minister, the hand still going. The minister tried to make himself say something, but he couldn't. George kept staring at him, waiting. "There are always choices," the minister said, and even though his voice was barely audible, it felt loud.

"There aren't, not really," George said. "I don't know where to go. There's this place out at Crowfoot Lake, at the far end with a white sand beach, which you can't believe until you see it. I took Joyce out there. It's where I proposed. But now I can't go anywhere. I have to disappear completely."

George glanced up at the ceiling. "The moon was huge that night when I proposed. We lay outside and watched it."

Just then the telephone rang, and the minister shifted in his chair. "Stay where you are," George said. "Don't answer it."

The minister slid back against the cushions, and the telephone went on ringing, harsh and rhythmical. Earlier, he'd received phone calls from parishioners asking about the memorial service or volunteering to help, but this call would be from Nancy. He'd told her he'd be home straight after the meeting, and whenever he was late she telephoned, letting the phone ring numerous times in case he'd stepped out of the office.

"That's your wife looking for you," George said as if it were a fact as the phone rang several more times. In the past, when he hadn't answered, especially if it was at night, his wife had driven the few miles to the church to check on him. Tonight she would be especially likely to do this. He could picture her opening the door to the building, then calling his name. If he didn't answer, she would walk down the hall and into his office.

"Your wife," George repeated, louder, and because the phone stopped ringing at that moment, it sounded as though he were shouting.

The minister looked at the floor, focusing on one thing: his intent for Nancy to not enter his office. If I see headlights from her car through the curtains, I'll run toward the door, he told himself. If George shoots me, it'll give her a warning before she reaches the building.

George perched on the edge of the couch, and the minister could smell the pungent odor of his sweat. He could see the growth of a beard on George's face. The man's hair looked oily, his eyes too large. The minister hardly recognized him.

"Remember all you said—God is here for you?" George watched him, expectantly. The minister nodded. "Well, where is he?" There was a pause, the minister holding tight to his plan, George gazing at him. "Where is he?" George repeated.

"God's here for all of us," the minister said softly.

"He didn't stop you from lying, did he?"

George moved closer, and his smell was overwhelming. The minister squeezed his eyes shut. Without realizing it, he shook his head. There was a trap, and he had fallen into it.

"Answer me."

"No," he said, saying what he sensed George wanted to hear.

"So God is dead in this world we're living in, is that right? I could shoot you, and he wouldn't stop me."

The minister didn't answer.

"Right?" George demanded. "God won't stop me. Will he?" He picked up the gun and pointed it.

The minister shook his head. If there was a God, there was righteousness. If there was righteousness, there was judgment.

"Answer me."

"No," he said.

"No," George repeated, smiling pleasantly. "Because he doesn't exist."

The minister stared down at his hands. In the Gospel of John it was written, "No man has seen God."

"No," he told George, glancing up.

"No, he won't stop me, or no he doesn't exist? What are you telling me?"

"No, He *does* exist."

"Where is he then?" George glanced around the room.

"He is here even though He can't be seen."

"Then how can you prove it?" George demanded.

"The proof is everywhere. He is evidence of Himself."

George glared at him, but his next words were a moan. "Why doesn't he *do* anything?"

The minister didn't answer right away, and for a moment, the moan hung over them. "I don't know," he said finally.

George settled back in the chair. He lowered the gun to his lap. "You don't know anything, do you?"

In the distance, a dog was barking, and every few minutes when a car drove past on the road out front, there was the sound of tires against the pavement.

"You don't know anything about me," George added. "I built a bomb. Do you get what that requires?"

Slowly, the minister shook his head. He felt that George was right, and that he didn't know a single thing.

"One day I'm married to Joyce, and the next I'm building a bomb," George said. There was a tone of wonder in his voice, underneath the darker, more deliberate tone, as if he was thinking about the disparity of those two things himself.

How could that have happened, the minister asked himself in that silence.

"I got a song. You want to hear it, Reverend?"

The minister glanced up and saw George's face. They were, both of them, caught in some sort of trap. Nothing was what it seemed to be. "All right," he told George.

George laid the gun down next to him on the couch and cleared his throat. He straightened his back, and his body changed, uncurling so that his chest widened and his hands opened at his sides.

Then he began to sing. The hymn was an old German one, "Lo, How a Rose E'er Blooming," usually sung in winter, sometimes during the Christmas season. George's voice was a tenor, resonant and clear, and as it rose out of the darkness, the minister felt something break apart inside of him. There was a sense of soaring that came with the higher notes, pulled taut like a wire. Toward the end of the song, George paused, and then he sang the final verses, describing the fragrance of a flower.

The notes hovered over them. The minister could sense the flower, which was fragile and transitory, inside the lingering notes. George stared across at him. "My mother used to sing that hymn in the morning while she was cooking breakfast," he said softly.

The minister shut his eyes, still hearing the notes. He couldn't carry a tune. Many ministers led their congregations in singing and participated in the choir, but when he sang, he did it softly, sometimes only mouthing the words. His voice was raspy, and his ear was good enough to tell that he was usually off-pitch. But he knew music, especially hymns, which he loved. On Thursday evenings when the choir practiced, he sat in the back of the church and listened. George had one of the best voices the minister had ever heard, a voice that made him feel the intent of the hymn. Even now in the silence, that intention felt like a physical presence in his body. There was the possibility of the flower blossoming. Had George sung when he came to church services in the past and the minister hadn't heard the man's voice above the others?

"I repent," George said softly. "Tell me I'm absolved."

Reverend Edwards opened his eyes. It took a minute for George's face to come back into view, and when it did, the minister saw that the whites of his eyes were bloodshot, his skin soiled with dirt. A wave of nausea swept through him. "You would need to turn your-self in first," he said.

"No, you can do it," George told him, insistently. "You're a minister. I repent everything."

The minister looked down at the floor. The moment could tip in either direction. George might decide not to harm him or even to turn himself in, or he might pick up the gun again. "I can't, George, not unless it's sincere, not unless—"

"It's sincere," George said, growing more insistent. "I want communion. Give me communion."

"I don't have the necessary things here," he told George, floundering.

"Don't have what?" George shifted forward, and the minister saw his face up close.

"The elements. The bread or the wine."

"Where are they? Where do you keep them?"

The minister had no idea what he should do. It was a sacrilege to give George communion without his clear repentance, and yet the minister's wife might arrive shortly, and if George got what he wanted, he might leave.

"There's grape juice and some communion wafers in the kitchen down the hall," he said. There was another feeling besides self-protection underneath the decision—I can turn this around, that feeling declared. The desire for communion is the desire for connection. I can convince this man to turn himself in.

"Get them." George stood up, waving the gun at the door. "Just move slow. I'll be right behind you."

The minister stood up, his legs wobbling a little as he began to walk on them. One minute his mind felt sharp, reasoning the amount of time it would take to get the elements and administer some facsimile of communion, but the next minute he couldn't think anything at all.

"Turn it slow," George said as the minister reached for the doorknob. "Look into the hallway before you step out."

He opened the door and peered into the murky hallway. At the end of it, a square of light from the outside lamp by the entrance marked the floor.

"Do you see anything?" George asked, and he felt the tip of George's gun against his pastor's shirt.

"No."

"Go ahead then. Don't turn on any lights."

He was trembling all over now, as if electricity buzzed under his skin, and the trembling made him stumble. Feeling his way, he walked to the entrance of the kitchen, and standing in the doorway, he saw that the shade on the window was drawn, making the room darker than the hallway.

"Don't turn on any lights," George said. "Open the refrigerator."

The minister moved across the room. He made his way to the refrigerator, and when he opened its door, a yellow light spilled across the floor. The kitchen was old with a wooden countertop that a church member had recently covered with a piece of white-speckled linoleum left over from his own kitchen. The refrigerator was another member's castoff.

"Hurry up and get the things," George said from behind him.

The minister removed the grape juice and set it on the counter. Then, leaving the refrigerator open, he went to a cabinet, and took out a tray he used for giving communion in his office. He found the package of wafers, slid one out, and placed it on the tray. He took a small communion flask from the cabinet, but before he could open the bottle of juice and lift it, he had to press his hands against his legs to steady them. Grasping the bottle, he rested its lip against the glass, and poured a thimbleful of the dark juice. Quickly, he recapped the bottle and returned it to the refrigerator. As soon as he shut the refrigerator door, the room went black.

"Pick up the tray and carry it back to your office," George told him. He lifted the tray from the counter and stepped toward the hallway. The room felt totally unfamiliar. It wouldn't have surprised him to run into a wall or a piece of furniture he had forgotten was there. Just then, he heard a car on the road in front of the building, and he glanced back toward the window to see if it was turning into the parking lot. He waited, but there was no sign of headlights, and the room was so dark that he couldn't even make out the window. Turning back, he took another step, walking more quickly now. Then, as he reached the doorway, he felt the tray tip. He tried to straighten it, shifting his weight, but there was the sound of shattering glass as the flask fell to the floor.

"Shit." George's voice came from behind him in the dark. "You did that on purpose. You could have carried the glass, but instead you left it on the damn tray."

Seconds later, light washed the room again as George opened the refrigerator. "Quick, clean it up."

"I wasn't thinking," the minister told him, his apology automatic.

George gestured with the gun, pointing toward the floor. "Just hurry and clean it up."

The minister went to the sink. As if in a dream, he knelt down on the floor with a dishrag, gathered the pieces of glass in one hand, and wiped the juice away. That accomplished, he stood and dropped the rag and the glass into a trash can.

"Pour another one. Hurry up." George spoke louder now, more insistently.

Working as quickly as his hands would allow, the minister took out a second flask and filled it with juice. A bead of blood formed on one of his fingers, and he hurriedly wiped it.

"I'll close the refrigerator after you reach the doorway," George said. "Just make sure you have hold of everything."

The minister picked up the flask separately from the tray this time and carried them toward the hallway. He tried not to think about anything else except not dropping what he was carrying, but the harder he tried to still his hands, the more they trembled, and he felt a little of the grape juice slosh onto his fingers.

"Go on back to your office," George said as he stepped over behind him.

It was only a few steps down the hallway before they reached Reverend Edwards's office, and as they entered it, the minister felt relief, so that when George came toward him, he held out the tray, setting the flask on it, thinking that George might simply eat the wafer and drink the juice, and then the ordeal would be finished.

"No, don't just give it to me. Do the whole thing." George glanced up at the minister, and the minister read something like hope in his face. They were standing not far from the doorway, and a dim light from hallway came into the room. Beneath them lay the rug, worn thin from the years of church members who had entered and left. With a clumsy effort George got down on his knees, setting the gun next to him on the floor. "Say whatever it is you say first."

Across the room was the window where Reverend Edwards had stood earlier, and where he would look to know that his wife had arrived.

"Almighty God," he said, making the general confession and praying for the deliverance from sin.

George glanced up when he paused after the prayer. "Keep going. Don't stop."

Reverend Edwards swallowed hard. The words slipped away from him, and his throat felt tight and dry. His lungs ached from the smoke-filled air. But then he looked down at George's bowed head, and it seemed as if all the other times he had performed the sacrament flowed through him so his voice when he spoke the words of communion was clear and deep.

He bent to place the wafer between George's lips, his hand hovering for a moment in front of George's face, as George opened his mouth. Help me, he prayed silently, oh Lord my God, oh Father. He set the wafer between George's dried lips and watched George take it into his mouth, then he straightened back up still holding the tray before him, his hands a little steadier. He took in the dim light of the room and the quiet of the building, and it was as if his prayer was answered, and his body flooded with a sensation of lightness and well-being, even though he knew this situation held no possibility of redemption.

"Drink," he said, his voice full of import as he recalled Christ's blood.

George reached up and took the flask. The minister watched as he tipped it toward his mouth and drank, and in that moment the minister thought—this man will be saved.

He laid his hand lightly on George's head, touching the crown, blessing him. They stayed that way for a second or two, George's head bowed and the minister's hand on it, and everything in those seconds felt transcended by the act, even the fact that George had created a sacrilege by forcing the minister to perform it.

Then George reached up and set the flask back on the tray. "That was it?" he asked.

The minister nodded. He held onto the tray, unsure of what to say or do next. His hands were shaking again, and the flask clattered as it moved against the metal of the tray. Just then a pair of headlights shone through the curtains, and tires crunched gravel in the parking lot.

"Who's that?" George pocketed the gun, got quickly to his feet, and stepped toward the doorway.

The minister didn't say anything. The plan he made earlier to run out into the hallway sped through his mind, but he couldn't grab hold of it. He felt as though he were inside several different worlds at once—one in which he was terrified, one in which he only desired to protect his wife, and one in which he was hopeful because he believed absolutely in the power of the sacrament. Swimming through the different worlds inside him, he couldn't move. He didn't know what to do.

George swung the gun toward the minister, his other hand on the doorknob. "Who is that?" he said louder.

"I think it's my wife," the minister told him.

George stood staring at him, as if undecided, and then he stepped toward the open door. "Get rid of her," he whispered. "I'll wait nearby. Make sure she drives away, then come back." He glanced at the hallway then back at the minister. "Just make sure you come back."

The minister felt himself nod. A car door slammed, and there were footsteps as George closed the door to his office and someone almost simultaneously opened the door to the building.

"William?" Nancy's voice rang in the darkness. "Are you here?"

It took him several seconds to set the communion tray on his desk and turn on the lamp. "I'm in my office," he called back, hearing his voice fill the empty room.

He walked to the door of his office, opened it, and glanced up and down the hallway. The building's front door was open, and Nancy stood in the doorway in the wedge of light. The minister didn't see George anywhere.

"I'm in here, Nancy," he said, turning on the light switch in the hall as she closed the door to the building.

Her loafers treaded softly as she came down the hall to his office. Everything felt full of danger and full of relief. George could have already run from the building, or he could be lurking in another room or outside.

"Why are you still here?" Nancy asked as she walked toward him. "Why was the building so dark?"

As soon as she stepped inside his office and he shut the door, he wished he hadn't frozen and had instead been able to run and force George to chase him. Now there was no way to know how close or far away George was. "The planning meeting for the memorial service went on past seven-thirty. Afterwards I went to get a sandwich with John Scott," he told her, trying to think of the best way to get her out of the building quickly and back into her car.

"It's nearly nine o'clock," Nancy told him. "The building was dark when I drove up. What were you doing here?"

He walked toward his desk and made an attempt at straightening a few papers. He needed to say something that was ordinary and reassuring. "I came back in to get some papers to bring home, and I guess I closed my eyes. I was so tired, I must have dozed off."

"Well, come home now. You should go to bed. This has been too much the past few days. You don't look yourself at all." She glanced around. "This room is full of smoke."

"I'll come home in a few minutes. You go on back. I've got my car. I'll walk you to the door. Then I'll gather my things and be along."

He stepped toward her, reaching for her arm, and when she pulled away, he went to the door, opened it. Nancy stood staring at him.

"Why can't you leave now? I would rather wait a few minutes while you get your things, and then we can go out together."

He leaned back against the door, shutting it again, listening for sounds from the hallway. Whereas earlier he'd felt not inside his body, now he felt too much inside it. His heart bumped up against the wall of his ribs and his breath caught there.

"It will take me a bit to get ready," he said, keeping his voice steady. "I need to sort out my notes for this memorial service. You go ahead. I'll be home in twenty minutes."

"You're acting so strange," she said, backing away, as if he were the one she should be frightened of. "Something's going on."

"There's nothing going on," he said, but his voice sounded too forceful. "I just have a lot to do right now."

"I don't believe you," she said more loudly. "Why is the communion tray on your desk? Who else was here? Tell me what's going on."

"There's nothing to tell you. Sometimes I need to give communion in my office. You know that. It's not something I can talk about. I'd appreciate your giving me a few more minutes here undisturbed so I can gather my thoughts and my notes for this service."

She stood where she was another minute, watching him. "I don't know who you are," she said finally. Her face was pinched looking, her eyes filmed with something else—hurt, he wondered.

"I just want you to go out to the car and drive home," he told her, and there was a shift in his voice. "Is Sandi there?"

"I think she's up in her room."

"I want you to go back home and get Sandi and wait for me."

"What do you mean? Why?"

"Just do what I say."

She nodded then, and he saw he had frightened her. As she walked to the door, he opened it, and they both stepped into the hallway. They moved quickly, but to the minister their movements felt slow. The minister opened the front door to the building and stood

144

holding it as Nancy stepped through. She paused for a second, and they were standing so close under the bright light that hung above them that he could have put his arms around her, but he didn't. Then she stepped away from him and walked down the front steps out onto the sidewalk.

"If you're not home in ten minutes, I'm coming back," she said as he followed her, stopping at the bottom of the steps.

"You won't need to," he whispered because he knew what he would do. He wouldn't go back into the building after she was gone, even though just a minute ago, he had believed that was his duty. "I'll be right behind you."

Nancy kept walking, and the minister stayed at the bottom of the steps watching her. Even though it was dark, he saw the quickness of her movements and the slimness of her hips under her pedal pushers. Her hair, which fell almost to her shoulders, swayed as she walked. When she reached her car, there was a sliver of light as she got inside it and shut the door. He heard the engine turn over and saw the burn of the headlights as she pulled out of the parking space and rotated the vehicle before driving toward the road.

For another minute or so, he stood by the steps. Behind him, his office building was silent. He walked back, moving quickly, and pulled the front door shut, not allowing himself to glance inside. There was no way to say what would happen as he did this. George could be watching him from inside the building, or he might have fled already, disappearing into the woods behind the church. The minister stepped down to the sidewalk and walked the way Nancy had walked toward the parking lot. He didn't notice the other vehicles on the road out front, including the police car slowly rounding the corner a block away. He didn't hear the far-off bark of a dog or the voice of the man who was calling it. He was breathing without effort, as if he lived in someone else's body, and there was a prayer moving through him. It wasn't a specific prayer, but it was the feeling of prayer. This. Now, it seemed to say. Forgive me, Father. Help me. Keep me.

One hand dug into his pocket, gripping his keys, as he reached down with the other hand and grasped the car-door handle and swung the door open. He bent and slid onto the seat. When he shut the door next to him, he didn't stop to press the lock. He pushed the key into the ignition and turned it.

As he backed the car up, he glanced at the building. He had left his office light on—he was almost sure of that, because until he'd stood in the doorway to the building with Nancy, he'd planned on reentering. But now the building was dark, as if all of the lights had been turned out. He marked this, staring at it for a moment, even though later he wouldn't be sure what he'd seen. Then he angled his car around as his wife had done and drove toward the road, heading home.

Chapter 14

As the minister pulled into his driveway, he saw lights inside his house, pouring out the windows. He walked quickly to the front door, which stood open with Nancy just inside.

"Are you all right?" she asked.

He closed the door behind him. "Is Sandi upstairs?"

"I don't know. I just called her but she didn't answer."

"Why not? Where could she have gone?"

Nancy shook her head. "She was here when I left. Maybe she fell asleep."

"Sandi!" the minister called. "Sandi, are you here?"

If George had watched the minister driving away in his car, George wouldn't have reached the minister's house before Nancy returned. The minister told himself this, but the logic didn't penetrate.

"What's going on?" his wife asked as he pushed past her and took the stairs two at time. Upstairs, he opened the door to Sandi's bedroom. Quickly, he surveyed the empty room, then turned and went back down the stairs too fast, stumbling.

"Wasn't she up there?" Nancy asked.

"No." Without stopping, he walked past her to the kitchen, scanned the room, then did it again. He couldn't trust what he saw—an ordinary kitchen, neatly cleaned, the table freshly wiped. While driving home, he'd hardly felt the steering wheel under his hands, as if the car were carrying him of its own volition through the dark streets of Centerville. Pulling into his driveway, he'd had no clear memory of how he'd gotten there.

Nancy came up beside him, and when she touched his shoulder, he turned so abruptly he knocked into her. "William, you're frightening me. Tell me what's going on. What was happening at the church?"

He stared past her at the kitchen table where Sandi often left a note if she went somewhere. "George Fowler came to see me at my office," he said. "I need to telephone the police."

"Do you think he could have taken Sandi? Do you think he came here?"

The minister shook his head. "I don't know."

Their telephone sat on the kitchen counter, and he reached for it, dialing the operator. When she connected him, he told the officer that George Fowler had come again to his church office. He described his wife's arrival and how he had followed her back to his house where they found their daughter missing.

"They're sending someone out to the church and here as well," he told Nancy when he hung up. "They said to wait at the house. A police car should arrive in a few minutes."

"What about Sandi? Do they think he took her?"

Turning away, Reverend Edwards gave no answer. He walked through the downstairs rooms, searching them again, then went back upstairs. Once there, he walked through the bedrooms, opening closets and checking the bathroom. He stood in the middle of Sandi's room, taking apart her desk with his eyes and staring at the American history book on her bed, open to an illustration of a Revolutionary War soldier. Her slippers sat on the floor as if she'd just taken them off. He could still make out the impression of her body on the bedspread.

"Did you find her?" Nancy called up. Her voice was shrill and faraway sounding as she came into the front hallway.

"No," he called back.

"Why did that man come to the church? What did he want from you?"

The minister came back down the stairs where she stood by the front door, but as he brushed past her and stepped outside, he hardly saw her. The light over the door gave him a clear view of the front yard. Sandi's bike leaned up against the house. "Put it inside the garage when you're done with it," he was always saying to her, but she never listened. He stepped toward the garage where the sudden glare of headlights from a vehicle turning onto his driveway startled him.

"Reverend?" someone called as he stepped out of the garage's shadow. "Is that you?"

"Yes," he called back, registering that the vehicle was the police car.

"Just making sure." Officer Beckley moved from behind the door of the patrol car, as Jack Turnbow opened the door next to him and pushed himself slowly to standing. Beckley had just picked Jack up, and they had been on their way over to the station when the call came through.

"I can't find my daughter," Reverend Edwards said as he approached them. Although he had called to report what had happened with George, now his missing daughter seemed the main thing.

"We'll help you locate her, sir," Officer Beckley told the minister, who noted that he was the young, black officer written about in the newspaper several months ago.

"George Fowler came to your office again at the church?" Jack asked him.

The minister nodded. "He was sitting there when I walked in."

"What time was that at?"

"Between seven and eight. I don't know exactly. My wife drove out to check on me, and he went into the hallway after he told me to get rid of her. My wife and I were in my office for several minutes, and then I got her to drive back here. I left just afterwards."

"And there was no sign of him as you were leaving?"

He shook his head. "I don't know if he was still around by then or if he'd fled. I got back here to the house, and my daughter was missing."

"Could she have gone anywhere?" Officer Beckley asked him. "Was she planning to go out?"

"No," he told the young officer. The questions felt like a delay, and with each one he grew more impatient. "My wife said Sandi was here when she left to drive over to the church, and it's not like Sandi to go out without telling someone. Usually she would leave a note telling us, and her homework is still on her bed."

"We'll search the house for you," the officer said.

Jack turned to the minister as they walked to the front door. "Do you have any idea where he was going or what he was driving?"

"There was nothing in the parking lot except my car. A church member had dropped me off. We'd gone out to get sandwiches after a meeting. He must have come in then. John dropped me off, and I walked into my office and saw him there."

Officer Beckley bent over a notepad, writing down the minister's answers. "They're setting up the roadblocks again on the highway," he reassured the minister. "They'll stop and search any vehicle they see."

"He seems to just slip away. He's there and then—"

"And then he just disappears," Jack whispered, finishing the minister's statement.

Nancy stood next to the staircase. "Our fourteen-year-old daughter is missing, did you hear that?"

Jack nodded. "We'll search the house," he told her.

"We've already done that," Nancy said. "She's not here."

"We'll make sure everything looks normal. Her bedroom's upstairs?"

Nancy nodded. "The first one on the left."

As Jack went up the steps, the minister told the younger officer, "He had a gun. He said he could have come to my house instead. He must know where it is. He said he had no idea what he should do next. He kept repeating that."

"Did he talk about where he might go or where he'd been staying?"

Jack stepped out from one of the bedrooms into the upstairs hallway. The minister heard his footsteps just above them. "He talked about a place out at the far side of Crowfoot Lake. He said the cottage was abandoned with a white sand beach. He mentioned that he'd taken Joyce there. It's where he proposed to her."

"Do you think that's where he's staying?" Beckley asked him.

For a minute there was just silence. "I don't know," the minister said. "He told me there was nowhere he could go."

Officer Beckley made a few more notes. "We'll report all this to the police chief," he said, glancing up from the pad. "They're setting up roadblocks on the major roads. There are alerts out."

"What about the roads around the church? Are they checking those?"

Officer Beckley paged through his notes and Jack treaded down the stairs. "Two other officers are over there now," Beckley said, still looking at the notepad. "Does your daughter know Bert Greenly?"

"Yes," Nancy answered. "They're good friends."

"Why?" the minister asked him.

"She's missing also," Officer Beckley said, as he made another note. "Mrs. Greenly called earlier to report it. Maybe they're together."

"Missing when?" the minister asked. "After George Fowler came to my office?"

Jack walked past them and through the dining room and kitchen. The minister heard him go out the back door, leaving it open. He pictured the darkened yard, with its row of pines at the back.

"I'd like to talk to Chief Reynolds myself," he told Officer Beckley. "I need some assurances."

Beckley nodded. Behind them, Jack stepped back in the house, closing the door. "Did you find anything?" Beckley asked as Jack came into the entryway.

Jack shook his head.

"We can take you and your wife over to the station if you like, then bring you back," Beckley told the minister.

"Thank you."

"Be sure to lock the house up first."

The minister went immediately to the back and side doors, securing them. Then he and Nancy followed the officers to the patrol car. Jack walked past them toward the side of the house, while Officer Beckley got into the driver's seat and Reverend Edwards squeezed into the back next to Nancy.

"You married that man," she said. "I remember the wedding."

The minister stared out the window, watching Jack disappear around the side of the house.

"What happened?" she asked. "Everyone thought he was dead."

"He came to my office at the church late Saturday night. I was asleep on the couch."

"Why didn't you tell me?"

He shrugged. Earlier his main thought had been to protect her. Now he wished she wasn't sitting next to him. "I don't know."

As Jack walked around the corner of the garage, another car pulled up behind them. Reverend Edwards noted the rounded lines of the front end and roof. An older model. He felt the officer in front of him stiffen, and out of the corner of his eye, he saw Jack Turnbow reach for his gun. Then the passenger door opened, and Sandi stepped out. Immediately his wife opened the car door and ran to their daughter.

"Where were you?" he called as he got out and walked over to the spot where they stood. His chest tightened and his heart was beating too hard. Like a car with a blown tire, it lurched toward one thud after another, and his whole chest hurt.

"I went with Harry to look for Bert," Sandi told him, her voice sullen and defensive.

"Is everything all right?" Harry asked through the car's opened window.

"Yeah," Sandi told him. "It's fine. I'll see you around."

Harry sat there for another few minutes. Then, as Sandi walked toward the house, he pulled slowly out of the driveway. The minister turned to watch him, and their eyes met just before he drove away.

"You didn't even leave a note," the minister shouted after his daughter once the boy was gone.

She glanced at him over her shoulder. "Mom wasn't here, and I was just going to be gone for a few minutes. I didn't think you would call the police."

"Do we need to watch you every minute?"

Nancy followed their daughter, walking toward the house. "The man who bombed the drugstore came to your father's office. We were scared."

Sandi turned around and looked at them. "You had everybody worried," Jack told her. "Your parents were about to go over to the police station and request a search for you."

Sandi glanced at him, disbelieving.

Jack turned to the minister. "We'll contact you if we have any more questions."

"I want to make sure you'll watch the house and the church tonight," the minister said.

"The building you were in was searched right after you called. We'll be watching the entire area, and we'll check on your house."

Reverend Edwards nodded, hardly hearing what was said. Sandi was back and unharmed, but nothing felt safe. It didn't feel like anything would ever feel safe again. "I want to know what will happen," he said.

At first, Jack didn't respond, and Reverend Edwards felt the ache deep in his chest. "I can't say, sir," Jack answered finally.

Jack climbed awkwardly into the patrol car, and Reverend Edwards watched them pull out onto the road. He stood there silently as Nancy followed Sandi into the house and the taillights diminished to two red points in the dark. His anger ballooned inside him. He had never known the terror he'd felt tonight, and it seemed like no matter what, that feeling wouldn't go away. The worst part was he knew he couldn't ever fully explain what had happened to anyone.

He stood in the dark, going back over the moments with George in his mind—each moment when George had looked as if he was ready to give in and each moment when his expression had hardened. While giving George communion, the minister had been filled with a feeling of the sacred, and now he didn't understand how he could have felt that way, nor comprehend his nagging guilt that he should have returned after his wife had driven away.

The difference between what was right and what was wrong blurred together. This week's *Life* magazine had shown the president on vacation at his ranch in Texas, standing next to his large new boat, side by side with shadowy images, taken at dusk, of the Detroit projects. Storefront windows had been broken, and a woman killed by the National Guard lay on the pavement.

Standing in his yard, the minister gazed at his own comfortable street and felt the unmooring of his moral compass. Behind him, light from his house puddled on the front steps. Inside lay familiarity and comfort, but he walked out onto the street and glanced up and down it. What was a man like George Fowler capable of?

By the time he went inside, Sandi and his wife had gone upstairs. He spent another thirty minutes or so walking through the empty rooms, checking the locked doors, and turning off the lights.

One night he and Joyce made love over half a dozen times. The more times he had her, the more he wanted her. He was nowhere and everywhere at once. It was as if he had no center.

It is like a game of marbles, where his shooter is stuck in the ring, and he's waiting for the next player to aim at him. Joyce said, "If you loved me, you wouldn't act this way."

Chapter 15

Upstairs, Sandi was lying on her bed, her history book face down on the floor where she'd dropped it. She lay on her side, staring at a page from *Tiger Beat* magazine that she'd just taped to her wall, which showed Herman of Herman's Hermits riding a bicycle with a girl sitting on the handlebars. The girl had blond hair, the color of Bert's, and she wore a short skirt with a crisp-looking blouse. A dark beret perched on her head. Her arms stretched toward the sky, and she was laughing. In the background, a fountain sprayed into the air so that it looked like drops were falling on them. It was the kind of thing Bert would do—ride on a pair of handlebars without holding on, showing off with a dramatic gesture. Sandi wondered how the beret would stay put.

"Don't tape things to your walls. The adhesive will be impossible to get off," her mother had told her. Sandi had come upstairs a few minutes earlier and torn the page from the magazine on her desk and taped it up where she could lie on the bed and stare at it.

Earlier that evening, just after her mother had left to go to the church, Harry had phoned and said they couldn't find Bert, and Carl thought she might have gone to the bus station downtown.

Since Sandi was Bert's friend, he wanted to see if Sandi could go down there with him. Sandi had said yes, and ten minutes later Harry was waiting out front in an old Plymouth, barely giving Sandi time to pull off her pajamas and put on her jeans and a T-shirt.

Sandi had climbed quickly onto the wide front seat that smelled of old cigarettes. She hadn't known what to say to Harry, and everything she thought of was canceled by something else. Then Harry had started asking her about Bert.

"You're good friends with her, right? What's she like? Carl says she's a little nuts."

"Well, not exactly," Sandi told him.

Harry glanced sideways at her, still focusing on the road. "She came over to the high school this afternoon after school was out. Did you see her?"

Sandi said no. She tried to think if there had been any sign of Bert that she could have missed.

"She was hanging out with Johnny Lander and Gil Hess. They're the kind of guys she should stay away from. You should tell her that. They'll take advantage, and they won't care that her father just died."

Sandi didn't know what to say to that. She couldn't imagine that Bert would hang around with guys like that, and she didn't know how to feel about Harry saying it to her.

When they reached the bus station, they went inside together, and Harry asked the woman at the window selling tickets if she had seen a teenage girl with long blond hair who might have come in and bought one. The woman told them a girl like that had come in earlier and asked for a ticket. She hadn't had enough money for it, but the guy who came in behind her had given her the dollars she was short.

"What bus did she get on?" Harry asked her.

"The seven-o'clock."

Harry thanked her. As they walked back out to his car, he said he would drive Sandi home, then stop over at Carl's house and tell him. When they were driving again, Harry asked where she thought Bert was going. Sandi said she had no idea. "Maybe she just wanted to ride on the bus," she said.

"Carl says there might not be a funeral," Harry told her as they turned onto Sandi and Bert's street. "The only service might be the group memorial on Saturday."

Now as Sandi sifted through the conversation, she didn't know what to think or feel. A year ago she never could have imagined that the drugstore could blow up, killing her best friend's father, or that Bert would get on a bus without telling anyone, or that she, Sandi, would sit next to a boy in his car and that it would make her so upset.

One summer when they were younger, Bert and she had formed a club with just the two of them as members. They had held their meetings in a tree house that Bert talked her father into helping them build, a single piece of plywood stretched between two large branches and nailed down. They tied a rope ladder to reach it, and the two girls would scramble up into the branches and pull the ladder up behind them.

Sandi had felt brave climbing that ladder. She had felt like someone special because of the club, and she loved lying on the rough plywood board and looking up through the crisscrossing pattern of branches, leaves, and sky.

"I could lie here all day," she'd told Bert once. "I could live up in this tree."

Once they'd tried spending the night in the tree house. Bert's mother had found sleeping bags and given them sound warnings about not placing them too close to the edge of the plywood. Sandi hadn't slept much that night. She'd lain awake even after Bert was asleep and stared at the nest of stars deep inside the dark lines of the branches. She'd felt as if she were caught inside that nest, spinning within their patterns.

Now, she felt trapped inside her own self. There were so many things she knew she should have been doing, such as talking to her parents about what had happened and phoning Bert's house to see if they had found her, but she was lying in her bed crying and she didn't know why. Her father had advised her to calm down when she was upset so that she could think clearly. "God is always there for you," he'd said, but now it didn't seem as if God or anyone else was there, and any advice her father had given her fell flat.

Suddenly, she thought about something Joyce had once said. "You know you're in love when you lose all perspective and you're willing to risk anything."

Joyce had said this less than a month ago, Sandi guessed, and now Sandi questioned if Joyce had been talking about her husband or someone else. Joyce was somebody who was careful to think things through. A few months ago when the store was doing inventory, Sandi had seen the neatly written lists Joyce had tacked up in the storage area. Joyce knew where each item in the store was kept, and Sandi had heard Bert's father praise her organization. But at some point Joyce hadn't been thinking. She had lost all perspective, and her husband had ended up killing her.

Someone knocked on Sandi's door, and she heard her mother's voice. "Sandi, can I come in?"

"No," Sandi answered, reaching up and turning off the lamp next to her bed.

"All right," her mother said, and Sandi heard her hesitation. "I'll see you in the morning then."

Sandi looked at her clock. It had green neon hands so that she could read them in the dark, and she saw that it was nearly eleven. She shut her eyes and tried to visualize the fire. She tried to call back what George Fowler had done, but she saw only darkness. Maybe some of them would never get over this, she told herself—not Bert or Bert's mom or her parents or herself.

George Fowler had come to her father's church and threatened him. A part of her felt like he deserved that. What Marge had said about even small actions connecting to other actions was true. Everything you did touched everything else, which ultimately made her father, who had married Joyce and George, culpable.

A minister was supposed to be able to see inside people and know them. She knew her father met with couples several times before he agreed to perform a marriage, in order to make sure he was confident of their intentions. "Don't make careless decisions," her father was always telling her. And yet he had married George Fowler to Joyce without any thought as to what might happen.

She opened her eyes, and for a long time she lay in the dark staring at the place on the wall where she'd taped the magazine page, something hardening inside her. "I'm glad he scared you," she thought, staring at that page. "I'm glad he came to the church. Maybe now you'll be more careful."

Chapter 16

Elizabeth was sitting cross-legged on her kitchen table examining her wall. It was just past midnight. A while ago, Carl had come downstairs to see Harry out. "Thank you, Harry, for finding out where Bert was," she had called out when she heard them in the front hallway.

After Carl had told her about the woman at the bus station, she'd telephoned the police. They'd been able to stop the bus a few hours north of the town, and Bert was being driven back home by a state officer. Elizabeth didn't know where Bert had been going.

"I know this has been very hard for all of us," she'd said earlier to Carl. "But why do you think Bert did this?"

"Because she's certifiable," Carl had said without hesitation.

She'd given him a steady, quiet look. "I would appreciate a serious answer."

"I am serious," he'd told her. "Yeah, this is really hard for all of us. Now we have to worry about Bert on top of it. You need to find her a shrink."

Now, sitting in front of the wall, she traced one of the paths she'd made with the glass. This morning she'd broken her favorite mixing bowl, a large, ceramic one, glazed brown on the outside and cream-colored on the inside, with a design of small ridges worked into the border around the top. She'd arranged the pieces next to one another in a line that wound from the center of the wall toward the ceiling. On some of the pieces, the soft brown color showed, and on others the creamy white. It was a fragmented path, one that could be read two different ways depending on how you looked at it. The white path, the brown path. The girl who was transparent, the girl who turned her back. There was something painful in that path which Elizabeth understood, and something spectacular as well.

"By the time the state police get her home, it'll be after midnight," the officer had told her on the phone. "Do you want him to ring the doorbell?"

"Tell him to just knock," she'd told the officer. "I'll still be up."

When Bert was little, she had followed her mother everywhere, imitating whatever her mother did, and Elizabeth had called her "my little shadow." She had paid Carl and Bert a kind of attention that she had never paid to Izzy. Each morning she had planned out their day together. There were always meals and naptimes, but also at least one outing. She took them to parks and to the library downtown. Sometimes she took them out to eat. And she drove them to see things she would have wanted to see when she was little, such as a field of corn or a grove thick with cedars or the paint display at the hardware store with its tiny swatches of different colors. She would stop the car at the side of the road next to a cornfield, lift them from their seats and set them on the ground in front of the forest of stalks.

"They're higher than humans," she might point out. "And they're growing so fast you can hear them if you really listen."

Carl grew easily bored. He might run down a row or reach up and grab an ear and ask her to peel back the husk for him. But Bert always became rapt as Elizabeth talked. She squeezed her eyes shut and listened.

"I hear them, Mommy," she said, her voice full of amazement. "It's a tap, tap sound, whoosh, whoosh. They're growing into the sky."

She could remember bending over and picking Bert up and carrying her through the corn rows, whispering, "whoosh, whoosh" and holding her out as they walked so that she could run her fingers along the leaves.

"They feel that way when you touch them too. They feel like their sound."

It was as if Bert had climbed down inside of Elizabeth and seen everything through her mother's eyes, and in doing that, she had made Elizabeth more aware also. That was a way in which you were instructed by your children, she'd realized. They could make you more of who you were supposed to be just by being so much themselves.

She hadn't thought of Bert as her shadow in a long time. Now, as she followed the brown and white path with her finger, she thought that Bert was so foreign that she was scared by her. "She needs a firm hand," she'd said recently to Carlton. "She shouldn't be allowed to dress inappropriately or talk back or go out without asking permission."

The last few years, Bert thundered up the stairs and slammed her door if Elizabeth questioned her. She agreed to rules, then turned around and broke them. When Elizabeth had told Carlton what she'd done, Bert had always found a way to appease him, so that what was supposed to be a serious conversation about insisting on curfews or groundings ended with the two of them watching a TV show together.

The brown and cream-colored path led both everywhere and no

place. It didn't touch any other pieces, and she couldn't imagine placing other colors next to it. Carlton had been the center of everything, and now that he was gone, the rest of them were unraveling. Her children were spinning off, in their own directions, and she couldn't hold onto them. Soon an officer would bring Bert to the door, and she had no idea what she would say to her.

Come inside—those were the only words she could think of. They'd have no choice. They would be thrown together in a new way without Carlton, and they would collide against one another. Elizabeth could sense this. She could feel the current of emotion that lay just beneath the surface of Bert's actions. Carl and Izzy would have their grief too, but it would be a quieter grief—they were, both of them, more like Carlton.

She got off the table and walked to the kitchen cabinet where she found a delicate dish Carlton had given her from Japan. A small black bowl, it had a gold rim around it with a picture of a red crane, hand painted on the bottom. She had been so pleased with the design and with the fact that he had seen it and known she would love it. She used it whenever she served small delicacies, like stuffed olives or a special sauce or jam.

She took the bowl, wrapped it in a piece of newspaper and cracked it apart with the hammer. When she opened the paper, she saw that it had shattered into dozens of tiny pieces, many of them too small to work with. Sliding the pieces onto a tray, she carried them over to the wall where she applied a layer of adhesive and began to set the larger ones in place. After some time, a black sky with swaths of red and pricks of gold swam in front of her. The path led here, to a place of darkness with the delicate possibilities of color. She was tired, but she didn't feel her exhaustion. She kept working until the knock came at the front door a little before two that morning.

Chapter 17

After Jack and Beckley left the minister's house, they stopped in at the station and then patrolled the area around the church and Reverend Edwards's neighborhood, driving slowly up and down the streets. Jack was so tired he hardly saw anything.

On Saturday when Beckley had picked him up at the hospital, he'd been relieved to see his partner, and Beckley had been solicitous, helping Jack to his front door. But now, tension crawled between them.

"You should have radioed in the report before agreeing to take them with us to the station," Jack said, referring to the minister and his wife.

"I can't see why the department would say no to that."

"There might have been another call they needed us to answer. Point is, ask before you make a decision like that."

Beckley drove, focusing on the road.

"And next time spend more time investigating."

"That's what you were doing. I handled the interview."

"You need to do both. Use your eyes and ears. I was listening even when I was upstairs searching the bedrooms. I heard everything the minister told you."

Pain medication churned in Jack's stomach. If he'd answered the officer who had trained him with a defensive remark, he'd have risked being written up. He wouldn't have argued with his training officer the way Beckley had, and his resentment piled on top of other resentments—his injury, his mother's death, the elusiveness of George Fowler.

"What about that car over there?" Beckley asked pointing out an older station wagon parked away from the houses next to a field.

"What about it?"

"It wasn't there earlier, and it's a weird place to leave a car."

Jack shrugged. "Probably somebody walking a dog."

A few seconds later, as Jack had expected, they passed a man standing at the roadside holding a dog leash. Jack knew where George Fowler had gone. His instinct unwound like a ball of string inside him. He could grab hold of the end of the string, and at the center of the ball, George would be waiting.

As they turned onto a deserted street, he told Beckley. "We won't find George Fowler anywhere near town. He's out at Crowfoot Lake, that's the only thing that makes sense. His parents' house is there, and he knows the area. It's remote, and several of those summer cottages are abandoned. Twenty years ago, people built those places when the lake was first made and they thought it would be something. But it turned out there were too many trees, too much shade. The public beach out there shut down ten years ago. I know that place. There's an abandoned cottage out there, off Buehler Road with white sand on the lakefront. I could find that cottage he talked about in the dark."

"They put a roadblock up on the highway immediately after the minister called," Beckley told him. "They would have caught him if he tried to drive out there."

"How fast was immediate?" Jack asked, pissed that Beckley would challenge him.

"It was quick. I know that area also. There's acre upon acre of pine trees. You go up there in the dark, and it'd be like looking for a needle in a haystack."

"If he's there, it has to be done."

Jack fumed and for a few minutes neither spoke. Then Beckley said, "He wouldn't talk about a place if he'd been staying there. Besides we were given these streets around the church to patrol."

"I'm not disputing that."

They had reached the church parking lot. They got out of the patrol car and walked around the churchyard not speaking. Stumbling in the dark with flashlights, they searched for places around the building next to the church where someone breaking and entering might have left clues. They traced a path back into the trees toward the minister's neighborhood. Jack shone his flashlight on some impressions in the dirt, but there was nothing definitive about them. When they reached the road at the end of the path, there were no tire tracks. Nothing had been dropped, not even a coin or a slip of paper.

"I'm tired of wasting time," Jack said when they stood in the church parking lot again.

"We haven't done a thorough search of the church," Beckley told him.

"We can do that in the morning. The shift ended more than an hour ago. Take me home."

Jack started for the patrol car, not waiting for a response. Beckley followed behind him. "Whatever you say, boss." Jack heard the edge in the other man's articulation of the word "boss."

"You think you have all the answers," Jack said.

"What are you talking about?"

"Sergeant Beckley."

Beckley picked up his stride and walked ahead, not responding. In their six months of working together, he hadn't talked about his service in the army. Jack had missed the Korean War by a year, serving in the National Guard instead. The older officers referred to World War II, their comrades, their actions. He was shut out.

"You think you know more than anyone else. Just because of whatever it was you went through over there, gunning down Vietcong."

They had reached their vehicle, and Beckley stood with his hand on the car's door. "You have no business talking about what I went through."

"Maybe not."

Jack waited for him to say something else, but instead, the other officer threw the door open, and slid into the driver's seat. He stuck the key in the ignition, leaving his door open and one foot on the pavement. Jack leaned against the open passenger door, peering in.

"You don't want to admit to anything I know, but I've got ten years on you. What I said about George Fowler will be proven when that place gets searched." When Beckley didn't respond he pressed on. "There might be others who see you as different because you're black. But I don't. I'm not willing to give you breaks because of it."

Their first week of working together, Beckley had said, "You must love being assigned to work with the first Negro in the department." He'd drawn out the word "Negro" so it sounded like an obscenity. The animosity behind the remark felt like it had come out of nowhere. From the start, Beckley's race had lain between them, but neither of them had brought it up again until now.

Beckley started the patrol car. "A break is the last thing I've asked for," he said. "And you have no idea what it's like to be me."

Jack lowered himself onto the passenger seat. Beckley had been driving all evening, because of Jack's injury. He thinks I'm treating him like a damn chauffeur, Jack told himself now. He slammed the passenger side door. Beckley drove slowly through town, staring straight ahead as they turned onto Main Street and passed the police station. Jack glimpsed the dark hole where the three buildings had burned down. When they were stopped at the traffic light, he said, "I didn't mean to insult you." But Beckley's expression only hardened.

Several minutes later, when they pulled up in front of the bungalow Jack had bought several years ago, he prepared to get out. He told himself he could play the silent game just as well. Beckley shifted the car into neutral, and it idled roughly. As Jack opened the door, a groan escaped him.

"You want help?" Beckley asked.

"No," Jack told him. "I'll manage."

"Well, don't feel like you have to start back too soon because of me."

"Thanks, but I'm fine. Besides, we're understaffed. There's no one to partner with you if I don't. Pick me up tomorrow. I'll be ready." He used his hands to pivot his legs toward the door.

"Maybe you think I didn't perform well enough on Saturday. Maybe you think I should have rushed in to the area of the fire like you did, since we were the first ones on the scene and the firefighters hadn't arrived," Beckley told him. "But I've seen the result of those kinds of impulses. I've seen what happens. The important thing was to secure the area, move bystanders away."

Jack jerked around to look at Beckley and his back seized. "Are you telling me I don't know how to do my job?"

Beckley shrugged. "I'm saying a man's instincts aren't always right."

"Anything else you want to say?"

Beckley glared at the windshield. "I know you weren't thrilled to have me assigned to you."

"I get that what you did over in Vietnam was harder than anything that could happen here. I understand that. The rest of us didn't take a bullet for our country."

Beckley shrugged. "If you don't want to work with me, I'll request a reassignment or a transfer."

"That's not what I'm saying." Suddenly Jack didn't know what he was saying, and he couldn't acknowledge that the animosity that had slipped up around them had anything to do with him. Beckley stared ahead, not speaking.

"Look," Jack said. "I was glad when the chief hired you. I admired your record. But the *Amos 'n' Andy* routine gets old, the yeah sir, boss, when you don't always treat me as your superior."

"Well, I'll make more of a point to deprecate myself."

Jack shot him a sideways glance. "Just be here at nine."

As he worked his way toward standing, Beckley tipped his hat. "Yah sir." Jack heard the soft reply as he turned and slammed the door shut.

As Beckley drove off, Jack lumbered into his house. In the bathroom, he swallowed another painkiller with a glass of water. Then he picked up his keys from the kitchen table, dragged himself back outside to his car, and forced himself into the driver's seat. As he started the engine, he told himself that once the additional painkiller took effect he wouldn't be feeling anything.

He could still see the skepticism on Beckley's face, but that wasn't the only reason he was bent on driving to Crowfoot Lake late at night to search the area in the dark alone. Crowfoot Lake had gotten its name years ago, before the dam was built in an attempt to convert it into a place for recreation. Before then, several wide streams fed into the body of water causing it to look like a crow's foot. When Jack was growing up, his mother had planned weekend picnics, and on several Sundays, he and his parents and sister had driven to the lake's public beach. As he got older, those trips had become less frequent, and if they spent the afternoon at a lake, they tended to go to Silver Lake, which was closer. But one afternoon at Crowfoot Lake when the weather hadn't been great, his mother had convinced his father to take them on a drive around the lake's perimeter. That was when they'd seen the small, private, white-sand beach. The trees around it had been cut down, so they had a good view of it from the road. Jack had thought the sand was snow.

His father had remarked on the ridiculousness of the impulse to truck in sand, while his mother had argued for the beauty of it, which for Jack summed up the differences between them. All this had happened twenty years ago, but the moments felt as close as the argument he'd just had with Beckley. He trusted himself to find the place the same way he trusted his gut feeling that he would open the door to the cottage and find George Fowler inside it.

Not far outside of town, he came upon the roadblock, but they waved him through when they saw his uniform. The roads that led to the far side of the lake were more confusing than he remembered, and after he got off the highway, he made a couple of wrong turns and had to back track. His back throbbed, despite the medication. He thought about Elizabeth Greenly's wall with the glass, and how she looked when she saw her husband's ring. He thought about her little girl with the cut foot, and then he thought about his mother. At the hospital, just before the nurse had come to bring him to see her body, the other driver who had been speeding when he hit his mother's car had walked out.

"Just a few scrapes, I got lucky," he'd heard the guy telling his wife who met him at the hospital's entrance.

Now as the road narrowed and he was forced to slow down, his rage felt fresh, as if his mother's death had just happened. Lakeview Road, which meandered around the lake, intersected with Buehler Road at the far end, and several smaller drives peeled off of Buehler, heading toward the water. Jack was sure one of them led to the cottage.

He drove a while longer before he found anything. Several of the dirt roads off Buehler simply ended at the lake, and the one cottage he found, a more recently built structure, was locked and showed no signs of having been disturbed.

Then as soon as he turned onto the final drive off Buehler, he noticed recent tire tracks. Everything inside him quickened, and before he reached the lake, he pulled over and got out, sliding his gun from its holster. Trees encroached on both sides of the drive, creating the effect of a tunnel, but the moon that was directly overhead kept him from having to use his flashlight. His exhaustion and the effects of the medication made the gun feel strange in his hand, as he stumbled on the uneven ground.

After a few more minutes, he knew he had reached the lake before he saw it. The air smelled moister, and the space around him breathed differently. As he stepped into a clearing, he could hear the water.

He stopped and took a few minutes to turn in all directions. Nearby was a small, low structure. Slowly, he crept toward it. Cracking open the door, he peered inside. It took a minute for his eyes to adjust, and his finger moved nervously across the gun's trigger. The one-room building was a small hunter's cabin with a neatly made-up cot, a table with a photograph on it, a large container of water, and a few kitchen items. He snapped on his flashlight, walked over, and lifted the photo to get a closer look. The foursome reminded him of his own family when he was growing up.

Outside, he checked the area more thoroughly, shining his flashlight into the trees along the edges of the clearing. Nothing added up, but the whole thing had him spooked. He'd been certain of George's location, but now he couldn't find a reliable clue. With an unexpected impulse, he wished Beckley were with him.

He lumbered over the uneven ground down to the water and stared at it. The blackness of the lake ate into him—mysterious and unyielding. Switching off his flashlight, he took a last look. Then something stopped him. He stepped closer to the water. Around the bend in the shore, under a patch of water that he had thought was lit by the moon, he saw an area of white sand. He bent forward, palms on his thighs, and stared hard at the shore above it. Behind a stand of pine trees, he could see the outline of a building.

The pain in his back felt suddenly nonexistent, and he didn't feel the grip of his muscles as he spun around and ran back stumbling to his car. He drove too fast on the dirt drive, scraping the car's bottom against ruts and potholes, and after several minutes, he'd driven far enough to know he'd gone too far. Back tracking, he retraced his steps, certain, but not certain, the web of roads like a maze with no outlets. He forced himself to slow down and scan the sides of the road. This time he spotted the overgrown drive that was really no more than a path a hundred feet or so before the drive's entrance.

He turned and pulled off into the weeds and got out, noting that the weeds looked trampled, evidence that another vehicle had recently driven on them. One of his hands rested on the grip of his gun. He moved quickly, breathing heavily and ignoring anything but the path. As he crept closer to the lake, he could smell water again, and overhead he spotted bats flapping above the trees. He squeezed behind a tree. The old cottage was less than fifty feet away. The wind was still, and from nearby came the sound of water splashing as a fish leapt into the air. From where he stood, he could see the glint of light where the moon shone on the white sand.

He stayed there for a few minutes before scrambling toward the cottage. Once he reached it, he took a deep breath, held his gun in front of him, turned on the flashlight, and kicked open the door. The circle of light from his flashlight picked up the inside of the room in pieces. He noticed an old table, the walls with their holes, a small stone fireplace, and animal droppings on the wooden floor. Moving carefully, he made his way into the kitchen where his flashlight revealed a sink with a countertop piled high with old bottles and cans. There was no sign of George or anyone else.

After several minutes, he went back to the front door and stepped outside again, walking down to the lake. The water stretched out in front of him, still and dark, like the pool inside of him. He aimed his flashlight at it, and there was the white sand, which over the years had washed into the water. Beckley had been right about the futility of searching the cottage and the area of the lake. There was no evidence George Fowler had been here, and the lake was so large and forested that it would take a massive search to look for him.

Turning back toward the cottage, Jack decided he would check the upstairs of the cottage to make sure there was no evidence of recent habitation, and then he would drive back. He wouldn't embarrass himself by telling anyone what he'd done. If other officers searched the area around the cottage in the morning, they probably wouldn't see any signs that he'd been here.

Deftly, he strode across the old porch and back inside. He noticed the rot in the steps of the staircase and let his weight settle onto them gingerly. "Get this last piece over with so that you can drive home," he told himself.

Suddenly, as he stepped on the next to last step, he heard a loud crack and his balance was instantly gone. It took him a second to realize that the board under him had split, and by then he was in freefall, a quick slide that dumped him into the enclosed area of the stairwell. A piercing pain ping-ponged off his foot and ricocheted back up to his hip. He groped the darkness, realizing he'd dropped both his flashlight and his gun.

He couldn't see anything, but the taste of dust and the smell of animal dung was everywhere. He inhaled the sticky cotton of a spider web that clung to his face, then clawed at his nose and mouth, trying to remove it. The air was warm and stifling, as if it had been closed into this small space for years. He tried to move his legs, cautiously at first, then with greater urgency, painfully twisting his torso. Feeling down along his body with his hands, he realized he'd been pinned by the fallen boards and what felt like a two-by-four.

As the pain traveled up and down his leg, he lay still. All around him was darkness and silence. He tried to touch his leg to find out if he was bleeding, but he couldn't reach down far enough to tell. Beckley would see that his car was gone in the morning, and when he didn't answer the door, Beckley would report his absence, and eventually someone would find him. He told himself this in an effort to calm himself, but his mind spun out questions. Would Beckley remember his mention of Buehler Road? And after their exchange that night, how eager would his partner be to try to assist in a search for him?

He lay in the dark with the spider webs, not knowing what would happen. After his mother died, he'd felt encased in a kind of protection, as if the worst had already happened, and nothing else could hurt him. That feeling had allowed him to take risks and not feel afraid. Now he was crying for the first time in years. He told himself it was because of the pain in his leg and being trapped, but he felt as though he were ten years old again and his mother had left him.

He'd found George Fowler's picture in his yearbook, included with Jack's graduating class. Looking at the picture, Jack had had the nagging sense that he'd known the man, but he couldn't remember how. Now, suddenly he remembered. They had been in homeroom together the year he'd started junior high. One morning when Jack had come to school late, he'd walked through the empty hallway and spotted George by the lockers. As Jack came up alongside him, George pulled a few dollar bills and some change from a coat hanging in one that was open. Then, seeing Jack, he handed Jack one of the bills.

"Hey, thanks," Jack had said, pocketing the money. The locker belonged to a new kid at school, who had been the object of constant ribbing, and Jack wouldn't risk being put on the other side of the bullying. The following year he and George had been in different homerooms, and by high school, George had disappeared from his awareness.

Shortly after Beckley had been hired, he'd asked if Jack wanted to grab a bite to eat with him at the end of their shift, but Jack had refused. He'd imagined the looks they would get sitting across from each other in a public place.

"Fine. I get it," Beckley had said.

"I don't go out with anyone," Jack told him, which was mostly true. Except for the few women he'd briefly dated over the years and the friendly but superficial relationships he had with other officers, he kept to himself. "Antisocial."

"Right."

Sometimes at the police station in the locker room, Jack overheard whispered jokes and racial slurs. He knew Beckley heard them also, but still he hadn't said anything to the men making them. He'd acted as if he hadn't heard anything.

Now, Jack didn't know why he hadn't stood up to the couple of officers who'd made those remarks. Recently when he and Beckley had searched the town's movie theater, a man had challenged Beckley, refusing to let him enter the men's room. Hearing the challenge, Jack had walked over, ordering the man out of Beckley's way.

"You think I can't handle situations myself?" Beckley had asked later when they were in the patrol car. "I was a goddamn MP."

In instances where he should have stood up for his partner, he hadn't, and in instances where he should have trusted Beckley to handle himself, he'd interfered. He'd told himself his disagreements with Beckley had nothing to do with his attitudes about Beckley's race, but now he wasn't sure where the tension had come from. It seemed understandable, suddenly, that Beckley wouldn't like him. Prior to this assignment several months ago, Jack had spent his time at work driving alone in a patrol car, then gone home to sit in his quiet house. He'd told himself he wanted it that way, and his disdain for the human race had felt justified. Lying in the stairwell, Jack saw himself for what he was—a solitary, middle-aged white man, uncertain of his own competence, who couldn't stand up for what he knew was right, or relate to the younger, knowledgeable black officer assigned to work with him.

The pain in his leg settled into his ankle and shin. The stairwell smelled of rot, and he heard the sounds of small animals, but he was too exhausted to feel afraid. He missed his mother, he realized, and he'd been missing her for years. Each summer, his mother had grown a flower garden full of zinnias, marigolds, phlox, and

Echinacea. When he was really young, an age that lay at the edge of his memory, he used to carry the weeds she pulled to a pile at the garden's border or hold the flowers as she cut them, grasping the stems between his loose fingers so that he wouldn't bend them. By midsummer, the garden filled with butterflies. Some were orange, others were blue and yellow. Whole clouds of small white butterflies flitted about like tiny moons, landing on the blossoms, opening and closing their wings. Now in the darkness, he saw bits of color that reminded him of those butterflies. As he closed his eyes and drifted into a light sleep, he felt as if they were flying all around him.

The county sheriff and his deputy found him the next morning. As soon as Jack heard a vehicle, he started shouting, and several minutes later, boards were lifted and knocked away, and the stairwell flooded with light. Looking up, he saw the county sheriff staring down at him, his gun drawn. "What the hell? How did you end up down there?" he wanted to know.

Jack didn't answer at first. He felt as though he were waking up from the dead.

"Are you hurt? Do we need to get an ambulance up here?"

"No, I don't need an ambulance. Just help me up," Jack told him. The emotions that had been so powerful the night before vanished with his embarrassment and relief at being found. He'd been trapped in the dark for so long, he had no idea how late in the day it was.

The sheriff called to his deputy for help. "Your leg could be broken," he told Jack. "There's two of us. We better lift you carefully. Your police chief asked us to help search this area when you turned up missing this morning. How did you end up down there?"

"I drove up here last night after hearing that George Fowler mentioned the place," Jack admitted. "I wanted to search the area. The staircase didn't hold my weight."

"Find anything?"

"No," Jack told him.

It took a while for the sheriff and his deputy to remove the heavy boards. Then, they hauled Jack out of the stairwell, and helped him to the porch. As soon as Jack was vertical, his ankle throbbed. The pain he'd felt in his back the day before felt nonexistent next to it.

After they set him down on the porch, the sheriff removed Jack's boot, revealing the swollen ankle and foot. "Rest up for a minute," he told Jack. "Then we better drive you back to town to get your ankle looked at."

"I guess you'll have to explain where you found me."

The sheriff nodded. "Can't get around that, but you're not the first officer to do something stupid. I'll try to radio your station in a few minutes, after we get you to the car. There's a few officers searching the other side of the lake. They need to know you've been found."

Jack nodded, staring out at the water. Beckley had obviously reported his absence and had guessed where he'd gone. He wondered if his partner was one of the officers searching for him.

As the sheriff and his deputy walked down to the water to have a quick look before they drove back to town, Jack sat alone. The sun was high above the lake, the water shimmering. A few years ago Jack's father had sold the house where he had grown up and moved in with his sister and her husband. They lived about thirty minutes away from Jack, and for a while his sister had called each week, inviting Jack to Sunday dinner. He had accepted the invitation only a couple of times. Now she just called twice a year before holidays.

He shut his eyes and saw the sunlight through his closed lids. The pain in his ankle reduced to a dull and constant throb. He wanted to be a different person. Someone more honorable, someone less driven by impulse and less closed-up inside himself. He heard the sheriff and his deputy walking back to the cottage to take him to their patrol car. Beyond him, what was left of the white sand glittered in the water.

Once when his nephew fell and skinned his knee, he was the one to bandage it. The small boy sat in his lap while he brushed the stones out and washed it with a clean cloth. He applied iodine to keep away infection, and when the cut began to sting, he blew on it—long, slow, cooling breaths. The boy acted as if it didn't hurt, sniffing back any tears. He bandaged the cut, laying down a piece of gauze and taping it to the boy's knee.

Chapter 18

Long after the minister had gone inside and the officers had left, he lay awake, aware of Nancy also lying wakeful next to him. Prior to going to bed he'd walked through the house, checking the locks on the windows and doors. Then he'd spent twenty minutes or more at the front window, watching to see if the police were driving past the house as they'd promised. He'd done these things, even though he felt they didn't matter. George Fowler was a member of his congregation, but the man was also a killer, and it startled him to think he'd spent all those hours with such a person.

As he was readying for bed, Nancy tried to get him to talk to her. "Why won't you tell me what happened?" she asked him. "What did he do? Did he have a gun? Did he threaten you?"

While he'd always kept things from her in his position as a minister, they had never been this personally affecting. He told her he couldn't talk about it, and then he lay awake in bed, falling asleep a few hours later. But at six-thirty, just a half hour past dawn, he was wide-awake again. Nancy stirred, and he rubbed her back until he was convinced she was asleep, then he went downstairs and made himself coffee. When Sandi came down dressed for school, he encouraged her to stay home.

"You can take a day off after everything that happened last night," he said, but she insisted she was ready to go.

"I'll drive you," he told her, as he went outside to wait, nervous about her leaving the house. Several minutes later she got into the car sullenly with her books and lunch, perching on the seat next to him without fastening her seat belt, as if she might bolt.

The sun was still close to the horizon, and when he glanced over to look at her, he couldn't see her face in the glare. He expected her to ask about what had happened the night before, but she didn't ask anything.

"What happened with Bert last night? Did you and Harry find her?" he said.

"No," Sandi answered.

He turned toward her, feeling a prick of alarm. "Does anyone know where she is?"

"She walked over to the bus station and got a ticket."

"Why?" He waited a second for her to answer, but she didn't. "Does her mother know about it? Are they going to be able to find her?"

"Harry went over to tell her mother after he dropped me off last night. He said they would probably be able to get the police to bring her back." She turned away from him to face the window.

He wanted to ask more questions, but they had reached the high school, and as soon as he stopped the car, she jumped out. Feeling aimless, he drove back to his house and drank the coffee he'd made. He paged through the magazine that lay on the counter, thinking about last night. Johnson's smiling face in the photos taken at his Texas ranch now struck the minister as oblivious. The president's face didn't acknowledge anything that had happened that summer—the weeks of rioting or the escalating war that played nightly on the television screen with images of body bags and American soldiers plodding through rice fields, lighting the thatched roofs of villagers' huts.

Finishing his coffee, the minister turned the magazine face down, rinsed his cup in the sink, and put it away. A few minutes later, he found himself in his car headed toward the church.

It didn't occur to him that last night had been traumatic and he should stay home. Instead, he told himself he had work to do. He wanted to be at the church in case there were questions from the police, and he needed to write the sermon he would give on Saturday at the large memorial service. He was caught up inside of his own mind, split off from anything he was feeling. The last thing he could imagine was talking to anyone, so when he turned into the parking lot, he was irritated to see one of the officers from last night standing next to his patrol car.

"Reverend," Officer Beckley called out minutes later, walking toward him. "Everything looked fine last night. I've just been inside your office building again, which looks unchanged, and I'm about to search the church more thoroughly. We closed that window in the basement for you last night. From now on, you might think about locking the doors to both buildings when you're not here." The officer had dark brown eyes, almost black in the bright sun, and he was smiling. "How are you?" he asked. "Were you able to sleep?"

The minister nodded, and it took a minute before he answered. "I lay awake a long time, and then it seems I slept soundly, but I woke early. It makes no sense."

He wasn't sure what he was referring to—his sleeping soundly or everything else. They stood next to each other in the strained silence.

"I feel foolish that I alarmed everyone about my daughter," he added.

"It might take you a while to get your bearings," the officer said.

Reverend Edwards shrugged. A moment ago, he'd felt irritated at the thought of having a conversation, but now he was embarrassingly close to tears. "I'm fine. I just need to get to work on the memorial service I'm supposed to be helping with."

"Don't push yourself," the officer told him. "You went through a lot."

"I still can't put it together. I married the man, and I never could have believed he would do anything like carry a bomb into a store."

Officer Beckley glanced at the church. "You can't predict what a man like that will do. People are capable of anything."

"Maybe." The minister followed his gaze, uncertainly. "Weren't you in the service over in Vietnam? I think I read about that in the newspaper. You were decorated."

The officer nodded. "I took some mortar fire. Ended my tour."

"How did it happen?"

"I was with a convoy transporting supplies. It was sudden, out of nowhere. I didn't have a chance to think. I just acted."

The minister shut his eyes. He saw mortar lightning and foggy darkness. Human forms. "I can't imagine that."

"I saw some bombings over there, mostly from a distance. One was close enough you could hear rocks whirring through the air like boomerangs. But the drugstore in the middle of town—you don't expect that. I came back and thought I would never see another bombing."

"I'm glad we have you as an officer," the minister told him.

"There's respect that comes with a badge."

"Is it difficult being the first black officer in the town?"

The officer shrugged. "People think the only problems are in places like a Detroit ghetto, but segregation is everywhere. I bet you have some nigger haters in your church."

The minister looked away, close to tears again. He saw himself in front of his white congregation, never considering that.

"George sang a hymn," he said, speaking of what he thought he wouldn't say to anyone. "One second he was going to kill me, and the next he was singing. A few minutes later he convinced me to give him communion. He set his gun on the floor and knelt in front of me. The communion felt genuine, the way it should feel, even though he was forcing me. I was terrified, but I still felt close to him, and as if we were close to God."

Officer Beckley was quiet. "My faith isn't strong enough," the minister added. "I married George Fowler, but I didn't see him. I have a feeling I don't see anything."

"I've done that. Gone back in my mind, chastised myself." The officer glanced at the church. "My grandfather was a minister. He used to say the evidence of God was everywhere. 'That's the meaning of the covenant of Noah,' he would say. 'It's a rainbow, and within the circle of the rainbow is all of creation.' I argued with him. 'There's all of this racism and nigger this and nigger that. How can you say we're all together inside some covenant? Maybe there's one rainbow for us, and another for them.' 'You can choose to remain outside it,' my grandfather said. 'But we're meant to be in it.'

"One night I sat alone on duty and yelled at him. He had died shortly after I enlisted, and I called him every name I could think of. Then I heard him say, 'We doubt God when we doubt ourselves.' That stopped me."

"You sound more like a minister than I do," Reverend Edwards said. "I don't know if I can stand in front of a congregation again."

The officer glanced at him. "Once when I was on guard duty, I came across an old man, a Vietcong. We brought him back and tied him in a chair so he wouldn't escape. It was late at night, and he started screaming and crying out, so we taped his mouth shut. But that old man kept trying to make noise, moaning, so then the MP I was working with starts pouring water over the guy's head to shut him up. Lasted an hour or more."

"Did the man die?"

"Yeah. I went back on patrol. I didn't want to see it. When I came back he was still tied in the chair, not breathing anymore."

"Was the old man a threat? Did he do something?"

The officer shrugged. "Sometimes one of them would have a weapon, but this guy didn't. He had these thin arms that felt like they could break under my hands." The officer glanced down at his hands. "I enlisted thinking to get myself respect," he added.

"Was there that? Camaraderie?"

"Yeah. There was that. I heard of guys in some of the barracks who hung up Confederate flags. But not where I was."

The minister watched the officer struggle with his feelings. He said, "I think despite anything that happened over there, you understand faith better than I do."

Officer Beckley shrugged. "I don't," he said. But a second later he smiled, a sudden, quick smile. "I try to dance with my eyes closed." He took a step back, gave a slight wave, and the minister could imagine the officer's agility, dancing. "I better let you get to your work. Call the station again if you notice anything else or get nervous. And like I said, you should lock both buildings when you're not here. I know people don't like to lock a church, but you should consider it."

The minister nodded. "Where's your partner?"

"I don't know. He didn't report in this morning, and his car was gone. If they haven't found him by the time I'm finished here, I'll take a drive out and look for him. I have a pretty good idea where he might have gone."

They turned away from one another then. It was the last the minister saw of Officer Beckley, who left a note before he drove away under the door of the building next to the church that the minister would find much later. *Everything checked out fine. No evidence of anything disturbed.*

As Officer Beckley went into the church, the minister walked back into his office and reviewed the papers on his desk outlining the memorial service scheduled for Saturday. He took out a blank sheet to compose his sermon, and for a long while he sat staring at it, unable to write. There was the sound of an engine turning over, but when he glanced out the window, the lot was empty, save for his own car. The only living thing seemed to be the maple tree with its dark green canopy of leaves. The sun's white ball looked caught within its grasp.

Returning to his blank paper, he wrote down a phrase from St. Augustine. Should he mention George Fowler in his sermon?

He stood and walked to the place on the carpet where George had knelt. He went to the couch, noting the impression in the cushion and the cigarette ash on the rug. George had sat here and the minister had argued for George's soul, but now it felt like the soul he'd fought for had been his own.

Outside, the parking lot was empty. No one was in the building besides him, and yet he thought he heard a door moving on its hinges. He walked out into the hallway and glanced inside the nearby meeting rooms. Nothing amiss. Listening intently, he heard a slight creak, the building settling into its foundation. He stepped into the kitchen. If he'd refused to give George communion, would the outcome have been different? Now morning sunlight poured into the small room through the open window. He found the broken glass from the communion flask in the trash can. Drops of juice stained a few spots on the linoleum floor. He wet the sponge, knelt, and tried to scrub them away. He worked hard at it, but the stains only darkened with the moisture.

Outside, the sun was nearly overhead, and when he peered up behind him at the window he saw the steeple of his church, the tip of its bell tower gleaming black against the sky. He hunched over, scrubbed some more, then gave up and began to push himself to standing. The edge of the counter was there, just in front of him. As he stood suspended between crouching and standing, he wavered. His heart rate picked up, and he couldn't lift his head. Seconds later, as his chest tightened, the floor dropped away.

He came to in bits and pieces. His chest was being squeezed, and his head where he'd struck it on the edge of the countertop felt as if he'd been bludgeoned. George was in the room, but not in the room. There were white faces among black ones. The whole country was threatened.

He didn't hear his wife enter the building, but he heard her voice when she called from the hallway. "William? Are you here?"

Seconds later, she crouched next to him. "What happened?"

"I fell," he whispered, the wheeze from his chest unmistakable now.

"I'm calling for an ambulance," she said before she left the room.

The minister closed his eyes. Maybe George Fowler would always be in this building, absorbed by the walls, making the air unbreathable. He gave way to whatever was making it hard for him to stay conscious, as the sound of a siren drilled into his awareness.

Minutes later, Nancy sat down on the floor next to him. "Breathe," she said. He felt the whisper of her voice move through him, and then there was nothing.

Chapter 19

Sandi had waited until her father drove away from the high school and the parking lot was empty of teachers before walking away from the school and toward the downtown. She wasn't sure where she was headed or what she was going to do. All she knew was that she was furious, and the feeling made her want to be somebody completely different than she was—the girl who skipped school, the girl who wasn't afraid, the girl who could get on a bus headed to a place no one knew of.

She walked fast, feeling warm already in her short-sleeved T-shirt and bell-bottomed jeans. Her mother had told her the outfit did not qualify as school clothing, but her father hadn't taken note of it. Last night when she'd sat next to Harry on the front seat of his car, she'd been wearing the same clothes. He had commented on the shirt, which was tie-dyed, asking if she'd made it. When she'd said yes, that she and Bert had tie-dyed T-shirts during the summer, he'd said it looked good, and she had worried he was saying that just to humor her because she was younger than him. She knew the worry was trivial, compared to everything else, but still this morning it was the main thing on her mind—how did Harry see her, as a kid sister or as an actual teenager?

After walking three quick blocks, she turned onto Main Street. The stores and businesses that lined the downtown were mostly still closed, and the streets were empty and still. For a few minutes she stood in front of the bakery, and then she walked across the street and stood in front of the hole where the drugstore had been. Yellow warning tape marked off the ash and rubble, and the sides of the buildings left standing were black.

She stared at the rubble and tried to distinguish what the pieces had once been. Several chunks of burnt metal lay in a heap, including what looked like a light fixture. Not far away, she spotted a metallic piece of glass from a mirror. She tried to picture where in the store the people she knew would have been standing. Bert's father, she'd heard, was at the back of the building. Billy and Davy had been thrown through the store's front window onto the sidewalk, possibly onto the same spot where she was standing now. The soda fountain, where she and Bert sat so often paging through magazines, was halfway back on the left side. She thought about the silver handles Debra had pulled to fill glasses. Bert had called Debra snooty once, but Sandi had loved watching Debra make an ice cream float or a milkshake. Debra knew just how much to pour into the glass so that it was full to the top, but never overflowed, and she poured all at once, with the quick, assured turn of her hand.

Sandi scanned the area where the soda fountain would have been, but she couldn't find any remnant of it. Then, closer to where she stood, near the yellow warning tape, she noticed a square-shaped piece of burnt metal. One side was slanted with holes across its surface, and suddenly she realized it was a cash register. As soon as she recognized it, the shape took definition, and she saw the drawer where the cash had gone hanging out with its slots for dollars and coins. Staring at it, she could picture Joyce's fingers pressing the keys and reaching into the different slots in the drawer.

She shivered in the stillness of the morning heat. Glancing down at the sidewalk, she saw where someone had written the word *BOOM* in ash next to her feet. Slowly and deliberately, she dragged her foot across it, smearing the letters. When they could still be read, she reached under the yellow tape, picked up a piece of something charred, and rubbed the black from it into the concrete until the word was one dark stain.

By now cars had begun to fill the street as people headed to work, and she noticed a police car as it drove past her. Not far away, she heard an awning being unfurled, and several streets over, the paint factory's whistle blew. She walked on, still not sure where she would end up, and came to Fearing Street and turned onto it.

This time, walking along Fearing, she peered down the side streets and alleys. The neighborhood, with its narrow row houses and apartments, was so different from the one where she lived. There was a realness to this world, she told herself as she peered down a side alley. It contained love, betrayal, and even murder.

She turned down one of the alleys, thinking it would lead to Marge's street, but as she reached the end of it, she saw that instead it led to another alley which ran behind two more sets of the row houses. Behind her, a cat jumped onto a trash barrel, knocking it over, and when a glass bottle shattered next to her, she smelled the sour odor of curdled milk. "Who are you? What the hell are you doing?" a man shouted at her from an open window.

Sandi turned and started running. As she skidded around a corner, she heard a door slam, and a car drove past her going slow as someone whistled. A woman slipped out from behind one of the front doors and picked up a newspaper left on her step. "Shouldn't you be in school?" she called out.

Sandi kept running. The streets wound into each other, so that it felt like no matter which way she went, she would end up back where she started. Finally she rounded a corner, and recognizing Marge's duplex, she ran up to it, still not really considering what she was about to do. She climbed the steps to Marge's door and knocked.

A few minutes later, Marge cracked the door and stood in the opening, glaring at her. "What are you doing here?" She wore a plain skirt and blouse, and unlike yesterday her hair lay flatter against her head. Instead of the pink slippers, she had on solid-looking white shoes. She looked older and not at all like somebody who could be Joyce's sister.

"George Fowler was at my father's church last night." Sandi stepped back a little from the open door. Suddenly she felt as if she needed to catch her breath, and the words tumbled out in a rush. "The police came out and searched our house and the whole area, but they didn't find him."

"Why are you telling me this?"

Marge's face was pasty with powder. She glared at Sandi, and Sandi felt nervous and a little afraid. She didn't know who she was anymore, and she didn't know why she was on Marge's step except that somehow it was the only thing she had left. "I wanted to tell you because of Joyce."

"Do you think I need to hear that from you?" Marge demanded. "Don't you think I can find out what I need to know from the police?"

The question jerked her awake. What *was* she doing here, and why did she think Marge needed to hear anything from her? Abashed, she shrugged a little.

"Stay away from here," Marge said, leaning toward her.

Sandi stepped back as the screen door slammed shut, sudden and definitive. She turned around, feeling stung. She had wanted to tell Marge what she hadn't said yesterday, that her father had been the one to marry George and Joyce. She wanted to say that she knew her father was partially guilty, not for what he had known, but precisely for what he hadn't known.

Next to Marge's house was a row of yellow flowers, which she realized, as she stepped off the porch, weren't real. She'd seen artificial flowers at the store once and had begged her mother to buy some, but her mother had refused. The flowers in the store had seemed so real to Sandi, but these looked worn and certainly fake. One of their heads had come off and lay next to its stem in the dirt. She wondered if they would be gathered up in the fall or left out all winter, surrounded by frost and snow.

Whenever Sandi had seen Joyce at the store, Joyce had stopped working for a few minutes to tell her a funny story about a customer or interesting facts she'd read in a magazine about how to keep a man. Bert's father had called Joyce a dreamer. "She spends all her spare time reading those magazines and romance novels," he'd said with a sad smile. Sandi had wondered later what could be sad about that because, to her, Joyce always seemed full of fun and excitement.

Joyce was dead and Sandi would never see her again. She'd been killed by her husband who had blown up almost everyone in the drugstore, a man who was dangerous enough that the whole town was afraid of him. Debra Gregory was gone, as well as her younger brother and his friends, boys who had been just ten years old. And Bert's father was gone also.

Sandi felt older suddenly, but instead of that feeling good, as she'd always anticipated, it felt burdensome and scary. For the first time she knew that she would not always live in a house with her parents. From now on, her own world would be different, not so neat or careful or predictable. She didn't know yet what it would be instead, and not knowing felt like a hole she had fallen into inside of herself.

"Your father could have been killed," her mother had told her last night, but Sandi was still too angry to be worried about him. She thought of the careful life he had built, following the yearly liturgical seasons where the right prayers were said at supper, and the right words were spoken to each person after church. There was no room in that world for what George Fowler had done, and she felt as if her father was at fault for making a life that was so careful it denied reality.

She knew her father would have told her to stay out of Marge's neighborhood. He would have said it wasn't safe. As she walked toward Main Street, she thought of other things he would have told her—that she should be grateful she lived in a nice house, that if she skipped school, she would only be cheating herself. If her father found out what she'd done after he dropped her off, he would be worried, and he would wait patiently for her to explain where she'd been and why she'd gone there, and his silence would feel like a penance.

She walked back to the downtown and meandered, wandering through the Five and Dime, glancing at the shelves, not really noticing the merchandise. In the back, bolts of fabric stood on a table next to drawers filled with patterns and a shelf with row after row of different colored spools of thread. She ran her hand over the fabrics and sat on a stool paging through a catalogue of patterns. Normally, she would have concentrated on the dress patterns and tried to find one for the next home ec. project, but instead she found herself just turning the pages.

"Can I help you?" a saleswoman asked her at one point.

"No," Sandi said without pausing to worry about what the woman thought of her.

She investigated the spools of thread, the zippers, and the packages of elastic and binding. She liked the objects—the feeling of the fabric, the colors of the thread, and the mechanics of the zippers visible through their clear plastic sleeves.

After a while, she left the Five and Dime and walked down to the bakery, not particularly caring that Mr. Bradley attended her father's church and would probably mention to him that he saw her on a school morning. It was nearly ten o'clock, and she was wondering if she should go back to the high school for lunch and attend her afternoon classes. Trays of cookies, donuts, and breads already filled the glass cases in the bakery, and two cakes sat on top, one chocolate and one vanilla, both laced with curly icing. Last year, Sandi's mother had bought her a vanilla cake with a yellow flower in the center for her fourteenth birthday. "I could make cupcakes again," her mother had said. "They're easier for a party." But Sandi had begged for the bakery cake, which had made her feel more adult.

Shortly after she opened the door, Mr. Bradley came out from the back where the ovens were. "Sandi, what are you doing here?" he asked.

"I just came in to get a donut," she told him, focusing on the cases, ignoring his implication. She felt invincible, like she could do anything she wanted, and no one would try to stop or help her.

"Is your father okay?" he asked, peering at her strangely.

Sandy glanced up. "What do you mean?"

"Mrs. Bradley called just a few minutes ago. She said an ambulance was called to the church for him. They took him over to the hospital. I assumed you knew. When I saw you, I thought that's why you weren't in school."

Before Mr. Bradley could say anything else to her, Sandi turned around and ran out of the store. He called after her, but she didn't hear him. She didn't pause at the stop sign, but instead ran out in front of a car, unaware that the driver was honking at her. As she sprinted down the six long blocks, she didn't feel the short bursts of her breath or notice the way her book bag bounced, smacking the side of her hip, sliding from her shoulder so that she had to reach up and hitch it back into place.

Several minutes later, as she ran past the church, she saw her father's dark blue Falcon in the parking lot. She kept going, heading for the hospital. She didn't feel the concrete under her shoes or the way her lungs were aching. She felt as if she could run forever.

Rounding the corner to the hospital, she spotted an ambulance by the emergency entrance and sprinted across the parking area, up to the large glass doors where she stepped inside, panting. Suddenly she felt the sense of power and locomotion that had carried her drop away.

The receptionist was talking with a woman and small child. "I need to find my dad," Sandi blurted out.

"You'll have to wait a minute," the woman told her. "You can have a seat." She pointed to the row of chairs by the wall.

A seat was the last thing she could comprehend, and instead she walked to the door and back, pacing. She peered outside and tried to see who was in the ambulance, and she stopped in front of a door that led to a hallway, considering walking straight through it.

The receptionist finished with the woman and her child and left the room. Sandi walked over to the desk and waited. When the woman came back, Sandi spoke loudly. "I need to find my dad."

"Who is your dad?" The woman's gaze was calm.

"Reverend Edwards," Sandi said, hardly hearing herself. "I heard an ambulance brought him here."

"That was twenty minutes ago. I'll try to find out for you." The woman turned, and as Sandi started to follow her, she pointed to the row of chairs against the wall. "Sit down until I get back."

Sandi still couldn't sit, but she forced herself to go back to the chairs and stand waiting. There was a clock on the wall, and she stared at its hands. The minute hand moved in tiny but noticeable increments, shifting a notch at the end of each minute.

"Hurry up. Please hurry up," she whispered. She couldn't let in other thoughts—Save him. Let him be okay.

Finally, the woman came back, and Sandi walked immediately to the desk. "He's here," the woman told her. "I couldn't get any details about his condition because the doctor is with him, but I'll try again in a few minutes."

Sandi moved toward the door to the hallway where the examining rooms were. "I want to go back and see him," she said.

The woman shook her head. "I'm sorry, but no one under eighteen can go back there."

"That's not fair!" Sandi whined, raising her voice as the woman tried to wave her aside in order to speak to someone else. "He's my dad and I ran all the way here."

"I'll find out how he is for you in a minute," the woman told her firmly, pointing to the chairs. "Until then, sit down."

She shuffled back to the chairs, kicking at the floor and stood next to them, crossing and uncrossing her arms over her chest, her foot jiggling nervously up and down so that her whole body rocked a little, jostling the book bag on her shoulder. Suddenly she felt so much younger. The bravado she had felt before was gone.

The woman and her child were taken back, and eventually Sandi was the only one left in the emergency waiting room. She was staring at the empty desk, waiting for the receptionist, when her mother came through the door that led to the hallway. For a second Sandi stared at her, startled.

"Is Dad okay?" she asked.

Her mother nodded. "You can come back with me if you want. The doctor said he would make an exception."

Sandi followed her mother through the door and down the hall to a curtained room. Inside, her father was lying on a bed. He had become conscious earlier when they gave him an injection. Since then, he'd been lying wakeful, breathing but not speaking. A few minutes ago, he'd overheard the raised voice of Jack Turnbow when he was brought back into the triage area. From the conversation, the minister was able to piece together that an empty patrol car had been spotted just outside town, pulled off to the side of the highway.

"I'll kill that bastard," he heard Jack yelling.

"We don't have clear evidence yet of who did it," another voice spoke.

"Officer Beckley?" the minister asked, but the doctor who was listening to his lungs had told him to be quiet.

"Just breathe for me," he'd said, leaning over the minister.

Now his wife was explaining to Sandi what had happened. "They think it was his asthma, brought on by everything that happened. He hit his head when he fell, and they want to keep him for a few days to get the asthma under control and for observation."

Sandi sat down on the bed next to him. Reverend Edwards stared at her and his wife, but he didn't say anything. They were all motionless, as if none of them knew what to do. Then Sandi reached out and held her father close.

There's a place somewhere inside him. He pictures it like a string of tiny lights, electrical. It takes lying next to those lights. It takes risking that. When he was a teenager he stood next to the tracks when a train was coming, just to feel the wind blow through him. That bit of brilliance, like a web thrown across the dark.

lizabeth had slept soundly that night, for the first time since the fire, and she woke up late, a little before lunchtime, when her friend, Maryanne, telephoned her.

"They had to send an ambulance over to the church for Reverend Edwards," Maryanne told her.

"Why? Is he all right?"

"I don't know. I called the hospital, and they said he was being treated. They wouldn't tell me anything else. Also, there was a police officer found shot. Can you believe it? His empty patrol car was on the side of the highway. Ron called me about it. The county sheriff found his body in the bushes."

"Do they think George Fowler did it?'

"They don't know. It was that Negro officer, the one they put on the force several months ago. We need to learn to watch out. I remember when Joyce and her husband came to the church a few years ago, and I thought, here is trouble waiting to happen."

"How did you know?" Elizabeth asked her.

"I knew, just looking at them," Maryanne said.

As she hung up, Elizabeth felt a brittle needling that worked its way through her. "You were so damn careful," she told Carlton in her mind. "You refused to take risks, but you didn't see this."

Carlton had given Joyce a job a couple of years ago to help her out. On a few occasions before that, he'd made up the difference when she was short the money for her insulin. It was something he'd done once in a while for a customer, a generosity Elizabeth had admired. But she had objected when he said he was going to give Joyce a job. "Does she have any experience?" she'd asked him.

He'd refused to answer her, and she had kept bringing it up. "Are you trying to tell me I shouldn't hire her?" he'd said finally, looking confused and tired.

"I don't trust her," she'd told him.

"But you don't even know her."

"I know of her. I've heard about her from you. And it doesn't sound as if she's ever held much of a job."

"People can learn this sort of work. You did," he'd said pointedly. Elizabeth had been working as a cashier when they'd first met. "She really wants the job. I think she'll work hard."

Carlton had given Joyce the job, and Joyce had seemed happy at the store, moving from one task to the next with efficiency. "What's her husband like?" Elizabeth had asked Carlton once after noticing George when he was picking Joyce up. "He doesn't look too friendly."

Carlton had merely shrugged, not answering.

Now she remembered the afternoon when George had given Carlton a ride home from work. She'd glanced up from her flowers, surprised to see his truck pulling into their driveway. Izzy had been smaller then, and Elizabeth had been cutting flowers while watching her toddle about on her newly found legs.

"Something about him makes me nervous. I wonder what their marriage is like," she'd commented as the car pulled away.

"That's a strange thing to say," Carlton had told her. "Who knows what any marriage is like?"

Now that comment seemed obtuse. Had he been referring to their marriage? Over the summer Carlton had mentioned that Joyce had moved in with her sister and had even voiced his concern that George might come in the store and cause a scene, but Elizabeth guessed that he never brought the matter up with Joyce or let it affect how he acted toward her.

Last night, Julie, another friend, had insisted on taking Izzy to sleep at her house to allow Elizabeth to sleep late. Now Elizabeth went outside to meet her friend's car. Julie waved at her as she lifted Izzy out of the car. Yesterday Elizabeth had explained to Izzy what happened to her father, but Izzy hadn't understood. She'd kept returning to the same questions: "Where is Daddy? What happened?" Elizabeth had found her questions exhausting, and she'd dreaded Izzy's coming back home. But now, when she saw her daughter, she picked her up and didn't put her down again.

Julie left her own two children in her car. She stayed only long enough to hand Elizabeth a bottle of milk she'd picked up for her at the store.

"They're saying George Fowler must have been some kind of nut case. People felt sorry for his wife, and when she left him, he just lost it." She set the cold milk bottle in Elizabeth's hands. "I'm glad I never met him."

Elizabeth nodded her acknowledgement, and after Julie was gone, Elizabeth stayed outside sitting on the grass in front of the flowerbed with Izzy in her lap. She could smell the pungent odor of the marigolds that always made her eyes water if she cut them and brought them inside. Izzy's body felt compact and contained inside her arms. This younger daughter was so simple and direct, as if she would never be capable of the extreme emotions that Bert felt.

She nuzzled Izzy, dropping her chin onto the small head and breathing in the faint smell of baby shampoo. Izzy didn't say anything. She curled up inside of Elizabeth's lap, until Elizabeth decided to take her inside and coax her upstairs for a nap.

At three Carl came downstairs and announced that he was going to be picked up for a driving lesson. She wanted him to cancel it, but he argued that it was the final lesson before he got his license, which now was even more important.

"You don't have to grow up all of a sudden because of this," she told him. "I'm not asking you to become the man of the house."

He didn't answer her, but his demeanor said everything—the stiff way he carried himself and the determined set of his jaw. He was gone by three-thirty, which was why she was alone in the quiet of the kitchen when Bert came downstairs to get a bowl of cereal.

The kitchen wall she'd been covering with glass was ten feet by seven, and already the surface was over half filled. When Bert had been dropped off early that morning, she'd refused to talk. Elizabeth had grabbed her arm. "We *have* to talk about this. I'm not giving you any choice," she'd said.

"I don't have to say anything to you," Bert had replied.

She'd wanted to shake Bert or slap her. She could feel Bert's skin under her hand, and she knew she was gripping her arm hard enough that there could be small bruises later.

"Let go of me," Bert had said, evenly.

Elizabeth had done it. She had opened her hand and stepped away, watching as Bert turned around and walked up the stairs to her bedroom. Now she watched as Bert went over to the counter and found a bowl and poured cereal into it. Rice Krispies were her favorite, and Elizabeth had always made sure there was a box in the cabinet. "She's a snappy, crackly sort of girl," Carlton used to say, rubbing Bert's head affectionately.

"Mrs. Warren brought by a bottle of fresh milk when she dropped Izzy off earlier," Elizabeth told her. "It's in the refrigerator."

Bert took out the bottle without saying anything back. "Are you ever going to talk to me again?" Elizabeth asked her.

Bert shrugged, and suddenly Elizabeth noticed the tears that were just underneath. Elizabeth got up and stepped toward her, reaching out and touching her shoulder. It was a motion meant to draw Bert into her, but Bert pulled away so abruptly the milk lapped up over the bowl's rim, dribbling onto the floor. "Don't," she said fiercely, and Elizabeth felt as if Bert had struck her.

"You're making all this worse," she told Bert. "You're making me wish I had been in the store with him."

"You think I don't wish that?" Bert glared back at her.

"You wish both your parents were dead? I guess then there would be no one to stop you from doing what you wanted."

"I wish *I* had been in the store when it happened, not you," she snapped, spitting the words out over her cereal bowl.

Elizabeth held onto the back of a chair, feeling a wave of weakness and rage. "How could you say that?" she said, knowing even as she spoke that she had felt the same way late at night in the kitchen when she was breaking dishes in the sink. If George Fowler had entered the store twenty minutes later, she and Izzy would have been killed also. Dying suddenly would have been easier than all this grief.

Seconds later Bert was gone, taking the cereal back upstairs to her room. Elizabeth stood by the chair, still gripping its back and thinking of all the things she could have said instead, words that might have been right or helped. "Your father loved you so much.

He wouldn't have wanted that. He would want you to be strong and get over this and have a wonderful life." But she also knew she couldn't say any of those words, and it didn't matter how right they would be, or even that those words could save her daughter's life. She couldn't bring herself to say them. *I loved him as much as you did*, Bert seemed to be saying.

She sat down in front of the wall she'd been covering and looked at it. The mosaic was an extravagance. Because of Carlton's death, she would probably have to sell the house, which would mean removing it and replacing the sheetrock. The areas that were finished looked like stained glass, even though the surface was uneven and there weren't any clear pictures in it. She could sense the place where she had grown up in the corner, blue of ocean meeting off-white of land, and the pieces that made up her children and her life with Carlton, a spiraling path of changing colors. Joy and sorrow, love and loss. One moment you were filled, and the next you were emptied out.

Eighteen years ago, when she and Carlton were first dating, they'd ridden a Ferris wheel together. Standing in line for it, Carlton hadn't said anything about his fear of heights, and once they were buckled into a car and the wheel started to turn, she'd been too excited to notice how strangely quiet he was. Up at the top, looking down over the crowds with their tiny balloons and cones of cotton candy, she'd started to rock the car back and forth, and she hadn't stopped until she'd felt his hand slide out of hers.

The operator had brought them down immediately, and Carlton had come to as soon as it stopped by the ground, embarrassed and apologetic. "You're everything I'm not," he'd said afterward when they were sitting together on a bench. "I wish I had your spirit."

Now it all came back to her—it was later that night after they'd gone to the fair when she'd asked to go up to his room, then taken off her clothes and made love with him for the first time. They'd done it again in the middle of the night, waking and reaching for one another, awkward at first, and then more certain.

Now she picked up her empty coffee mug, still sitting on the table from earlier, and threw it against the wall. Carlton and she had been so different from one another. That was what drew her to him, but now she felt as though she had never really known him. Had George made threats toward Joyce that Carlton never told her about? The past few weeks Joyce had started going out with a man who worked at the paint factory with her brother-in-law. Once when Elizabeth stopped in at the store, the man was there, talking with Joyce.

"It doesn't seem right that he comes by to see her when she's working," Elizabeth had told Carlton.

"Why not?" Carlton had asked.

"Because she's still married."

He had refused to talk about it any further, making it clear that Joyce's actions were none of her business. Others had noticed that there were problems with Joyce's marriage. What had made Carlton so resistant to seeing the dangerous conflict being played out under his nose?

She picked up a couple of the larger pieces of the cup and flung them at the wall, splitting them again. Carlton had left her, that was the worst of it. They wouldn't ever go to Florida. They wouldn't even argue about it again. She couldn't remember the last time they had made love. It hadn't been Saturday morning, so it must have been earlier that week. She tried to call back the details, but she couldn't even remember the touch of his arms around her.

Just then, as she stood glaring at the wall, Bert came back into the kitchen with her bowl and spoon. She looked at the floor where the pieces of the broken cup had landed. "Jesus, Mom," she said. "I think you've gone off the deep end."

Bert walked to the sink and rinsed out her dishes.

"Maybe I have," Elizabeth said.

Chapter 21

On Saturday Sandi attended the memorial service for the victims of the fire with her mother, and then they drove to the hospital to bring her father home. By now it was known what had happened to the young black officer who had helped her and Bert the afternoon of the fire. On Tuesday morning, after leaving the church, he'd driven out on the highway, headed toward Crowfoot Lake. At nine o'clock, he'd radioed in a sighting of a vehicle pulled off to the roadside. The driver looked distressed and he'd given the license plate number and description of the car and driver, before leaving his vehicle. While the vehicle was a 1965 Dodge Polara instead of a pick-up truck, the description of the man inside the car could have been George Fowler. Soon after, the county sheriff, driving back into town, had discovered the empty patrol car and Officer Beckley's body in the brush nearby.

Saturday afternoon, when Sandi carried a bowl of soup to her father in his bedroom, she wanted to ask him about what had happened. She wanted him to say something about the officer's death and about the bombing and the people who had been memorialized at the service. And she wanted to tell him what had happened

Tuesday morning, that she hadn't gone to school, that she'd walked around downtown and gone into neighborhoods she'd never been in before. The memorial service had felt strange, and the words spoken had glided past her as if they didn't mean anything. She wanted to know what they did mean, and before she carried him the tray, she lined up her questions, one on top of another.

While her father ate the soup, Sandi sat next to his bed and named the hymns sung at the service and said who had delivered the sermon. Her father asked a few more questions about it, and when the soup was gone, she took the tray back downstairs without asking her own.

She lay on her bed turning the pages of a magazine, unable to sleep, recalling what people had said about Joyce and Bert's father and the others. All week her mother had picked her up at school, and at night the doors were locked with deadbolts. Nothing was what it had been.

As she read the caption beneath a photograph in her magazine, she heard the thump of a dirt clod hit her window. She dropped the magazine and sat absolutely still. Another clod hit the window, and this time she heard Harry and Carl's voices. When she looked outside, she saw them below on the driveway, waving at her to come down.

She pulled on a pair of jeans and grabbed a sweatshirt, then crept downstairs. Her parents were in their bedroom, and the front hallway was dark and silent. A week ago, she would have breathed relief at this, but now as she unlocked and slipped out the front door, she wished her mother would call after her. She eased the door shut, and then shoved her feet into her sneakers before she walked around to the driveway. Harry's car was parked on the road, just past her house.

"What are you guys doing?" she whispered as soon as she saw the two boys.

"Bert ran off. Can you come with us?" Carl said as they walked toward her in the gray light. "She's on top of the water tower. Johnny Lander drove over to tell me. She climbed up to the top, and now she's just sitting there, and they can't get her to come down."

The water tower sat at the edge of town, a turquoise monstrosity that rose above all the nearby houses, buildings, and newly established pine groves like an odd, giant mushroom. A dirt road led back to it, and that and the pine tree plantings, which provided good coverage, made it a frequented hangout for high-school kids who drove there and parked. Beer bottles littered the bushes, and at least once a year some teenager ended up trying to climb the metal ladder on the tower. Usually, they only had to go up partway to realize the foolishness of trying to make it up the narrow, vertical ladder, but occasionally one of them reached the top. Earlier that summer, someone had hung a flag with a peace symbol from a pole above the top rung, and several years ago a drunk high schooler had fallen after reaching the top.

Sandi followed the boys to Harry's car. The air felt cooler now, and she jerked her sweatshirt over her head as she slid onto the backseat. "What happened?" she asked as Harry started the engine.

"I have an insane sister, that's what happened," Carl answered. "On the night after our father's memorial service, she decides to disappear."

Harry glanced back at Sandi as he pulled out onto the road. "We think Johnny Lander and his friends talked her into going out there."

"Does your mom know?" she asked Carl.

Without turning around, he shook his head. "Thankfully, she's upstairs, asleep for a change."

After that, they drove in silence. Carl lit a cigarette, but the night air blew through the car's open windows, and Sandi hardly noticed the smell of the smoke. This was the way she had envisioned high school in her best dreams—riding in a car through the dark of the night with a couple of high-school boys. She'd wanted it badly, but in her dreams she had seemed so unlike herself that she'd never expected it to happen, and if it did, she'd assumed Bert would be sitting on the seat next to her. Now, as she watched Harry over the back of the seat, she wasn't thinking about whether or not he liked her. Instead, she watched the lights of the town slide away.

Sandi had never been out to the tower. She'd been aware of its presence every time she rode to the grocery store with her mother, where it was clearly visible, but after the first few times of seeing it, you glanced in its direction, and you hardly saw its turquoise color ballooning against the sky.

They parked on the side of the dirt road, and Harry rummaged in the glove compartment for a flashlight. Its beam was pale and small, and they ended up stumbling on the uneven ground as they walked single-file. Above them, the water tower loomed. Even in the dark, Sandi could trace its outline, hovering like a spacecraft.

They staggered through the brush, pushing away the undergrowth until they entered a wide clearing that surrounded the tower. As they stepped out into it, Sandi noticed that the sky was filled with stars. When she was younger, she would have wanted to lie down on the ground and name the constellations. Her parents had done that with her on summer nights, allowing her stay up late and spreading a blanket on the front lawn. The Big and Little Dippers with Polaris—she could find the major ones, and her father would point out the others such as Cassiopeia.

Now she only glanced up, and the patterns she'd found on those nights seemed like they must have been superimposed. The stars wove above her in an indecipherable matrix.

She lowered her gaze and peered at the water tower. Next to its base stood a cluster of boys, and up at the top of the ladder in front of the enormous bubble was the crouching, hunched shape of a girl.

"It's about time," one of the boys called out. "She's just sitting up there. We've been standing here for an hour, trying to get her to come down."

Sandi tilted her head back again and followed the long, straight line of the ladder. Above Bert hung the tattered flag with the peace symbol on it that had been the talk of the high school the first couple of days of classes.

"Hey Bert, your brother's here! You better get the hell down!" one of the boys yelled.

"See?" the first one said when nothing happened. "She doesn't even respond."

"Maybe one of you is going to have to climb up there and help her," Harry told them.

"One of us? Are you nuts?"

Carl took a few steps toward them. "You're the reason she's up there," he said.

"Hey, we just drove out here to drink a few beers. We're all hanging out, and suddenly we look up and she's climbing the goddamn ladder. Next thing we know, she's up at the top and won't come down. No way one of us is going up after her. She asked Johnny if she could drive out here with us."

"You took advantage," Carl said.

"We did what she asked."

"Doesn't matter that our father's service was today." Carl shoved the kid hard enough that he fell backwards, sprawling on the ground.

"Hey, what the hell?"

"Too bad that maniac didn't blow you up," Carl hissed lunging toward him.

But before he could throw himself on the boy, Harry grabbed him and held him back. "Not worth it," he said.

Carl stepped away, but Sandi saw how he was shaking. The tension crawled between them as though a fight might begin.

"I'll go up," she said.

Harry spun around to look at her, and even in the dark, she could read the surprise on his face. "You can't do that," he said. There was a sudden hole inside the tension, nobody talking.

"That's why you brought me out here, right?" she asked them. "I'll climb up as far as I can and try to talk to her." She glanced up, her eyes following the ladder. From the nearby brush, came the sound of a breeze blowing through the branches. Was there someone out there, Sandi wondered, but then she shoved the thought away. "I'll go, that is unless someone else is volunteering."

"She's smaller than us, so she stands a better chance on that ladder," one of the guys said.

Carl crammed his hands into his pockets. Harry turned to look at her. "If one of us goes, she might not listen."

They stood there silently, considering. "I don't like being out here," Carl said. "Get her down quick. We need to get out of here."

"Are you sure about climbing up?" Harry asked her.

She nodded. "I'll try it. If it's too hard I'll come back down."

She walked over to the base of the tower where the ladder hung, and the others followed, clumping around her. Gripping the ladder's handles, she accepted the boost that Carl and Harry gave her so she could more easily swing up to the first rung.

"You all right?" Harry asked her.

She nodded.

The ladder went straight up, making it harder to climb. It reminded her of the rope ladder she and Bert had hung from the tree house. Placing one foot, then the other on the successive rungs, she moved slowly. A half moon squatted at the top of the tower. She kept her eyes on it and didn't look down. The climb was scary enough that it made her stop thinking about George Fowler. All she could think about was not falling.

When she was partway up, she stopped and focused on Bert. She could make out her friend more clearly now, sitting on the top rung, hunched over with her chin on her fist, a smaller version of Rodin's *Thinker*. In the moonlight, her hair looked white.

"Hey Bert, it's me," Sandi called up.

Bert didn't say anything.

Sandi tilted her head back a little to get a better view, but then felt dizzy and had to straighten it. She waited another minute, steadying herself. Bert called down, "What are you doing?"

"Trying to help you."

"Why?"

"So that you can come down." She picked up her foot and took another step. Her heart pounded, shifting up into her throat, and she was shivering. She noticed her leg shaking as she brought up her foot and placed it on the next rung, which suddenly felt the width of a drinking straw. Her body swayed, and the ladder seemed to jerk a little. The weight of the massive tank loomed above her. When she stared up at it, she could see the dark shadows that marked its underbelly.

"This is hilarious," Bert called down. "You climbing up the water tower."

"Really funny," Sandi told her. She moved faster, trying to get to the top where Bert was as quickly as she could, as if getting there faster would end the danger. As she took the last several steps, she said, "I'm gonna need to sit down. But I'll be too scared to turn around like you did."

"You have to sort of let go for a second to swing your butt around," Bert told her. "It makes you feel like you're already falling." She was staring down past Sandi at the ground. "So none of those assholes would come up. They sent you instead."

"I volunteered." Sandi locked her eyes on Bert's face. Her hands were just below Bert's sneakers, and she was shivering hard enough that her teeth chattered.

"They're leaving." Bert pointed at the ground where the group of boys she'd come to the tower with appeared to be slumping off toward the bushes. "Afraid they'll catch hell when we fall and kill ourselves."

Sandi squinted, still gazing up. Seen from this angle, the water tank looked like its own planet, wearing the moon like a hat. "Is that what will happen?" she asked Bert.

"Maybe." Bert tilted her head back and looked up also. The moon seemed to roll a little across the edge of the tower. For a few minutes, neither girl spoke. Sandi tried to think of what she could say to get Bert to climb back down again. Then Bert said, "I keep thinking about the drugstore. I can't stop."

Sandi tightened her grip on the ladder. "Me too."

"We were going in there, and then you said, 'Let's go down to the bowling alley.'"

"I know."

"Then, *kabang*. The whole place goes up without us." Bert spread her hands out, and for a second it looked as if she would fall forward, rolling through the sky. Sandi felt her stomach turn over, but

Bert settled back onto the top rung, hunching over again. "I was mad at you. Like I wanted to be in there because of my father, and it was your fault I wasn't. I keep thinking about it, especially at night before I fall asleep, like if I can picture it good enough, being inside the store when it happened, then I won't wake up in the morning, like I can reverse time or some such crap." She stared down at Sandi. "Why the hell did you stop us from going in?"

"I don't know," Sandi said. "I keep trying to figure out what happened, but I can't. I just turned around. It's not like I knew what was going to happen or anything."

"Jesus, I could have said something else or not turned around, and it all would have been different. What are we supposed to think about that? What are we supposed to do now?"

They stayed where they were for several minutes, not saying anything. Sandi looked straight ahead, trying to steady herself. She didn't know how to answer Bert, and she felt the weight of the tower and even the moon on top of her. She thought she heard Carl or Harry calling up to them.

"Bert, I'm scared," she said finally. "I want to go down."

"You're the world's worst climber, and you expect me to go down with you in front of me?"

Sandi tightened her hands, feeling as if the side rails of the ladder were permanently embedded in her palms. "I'm not turning around just so you can go down first," she said, taking a shaky step, feeling with her foot for the rung under it.

Bert hadn't moved from the top rung where she still sat with her chin propped on her fist. "Are you coming?" Sandi asked her.

Bert sighed. "I guess." Then in one smooth motion that seemed to require no forethought, she grabbed hold of the ladder and pivoted her body as she swung around and took the first step down in front of Sandi. "Hang on," she advised, glancing down at her. "It's a long way to the ground."

They spent the next several minutes moving awkwardly in tandem, gripping the side rails of the ladder. Bert's sneaker sometimes brushed against Sandi's forehead, as they made slow, shaky progress. Then, partway down, Sandi started crying, and she didn't know why. The doctor had assured them that her father was going to be all right, and Sandi had successfully climbed the water tower and convinced Bert to come back down. She knew all this, and that the closer they got to the ground, the less likely it was that they would fall, but the tears wouldn't stop. She paused for a minute on a rung, and Bert moved down in front of her. She knew that she had to keep moving, but she stayed like that, with Bert's weight leaning into her.

"Were you thinking about jumping?" she asked Bert finally.

Above her, Bert shrugged. "Not really. I just liked it up there. At the edge of the world and all, at the edge of the sky. Then I thought about my dad. He had this thing about heights. It suddenly made me scared to climb down, and I got stuck."

Something in the air shifted, and for a few minutes, it was completely dark. The moon had moved behind a cloud or the tower. They were almost halfway to the ground, but Sandi felt as though they were hanging so far above earth they would never reach it. "Just before you guys came through the bushes, I felt my dad up there," Bert said. "I was thinking about him, and I really felt him, like he was right there."

Sandi nodded. She tilted her head back a little to look up at Bert, but then she got scared again and leaned in close, resting her forehead on Bert's calves.

"I just wanted to tell you that," Bert said.

They started to descend again, stepping down a little faster one rung at a time. Sandi reached one foot down after another, hardly daring to breathe. She'd heard what Bert had said, but she couldn't allow herself to think about it, not really. Instead, she concentrated on reaching the ground beneath them. She told herself that Bert would be okay after this, and maybe in a week or two they would do something together, like go and get french fries and Cokes at the new McDonald's, or sleep over at each other's houses and wake early enough to watch the sunrise.

As they drove home in Harry's car, Sandi felt exhausted. A cool breeze blew through the open windows and no one spoke. When the others dropped Sandi off, she slid through the front door she'd left unlocked and soundlessly made her way through the sleeping house.

She slipped between the cool sheets on her bed. She'd been so angry at her father, she almost felt like she'd brought on what had happened to him. That was something else she couldn't contain now, along with what had happened to Bert's father and the others.

As she curled up in bed, her thoughts went elsewhere. There would be school on Monday, and because the class periods rotated each day, she would have home ec., her favorite class, first. Bert hadn't said whether or not she was coming back to school next week, but Sandi told herself she might. She dropped toward sleep, these thoughts settling.

Once while they were still dating, Joyce called him on the telephone and said she didn't want to see him anymore. That night he drove out to her apartment and pounded on the door for two hours. He did it again the next night and the night after, and at some point, he convinced her to give him a second chance. They went for a drive that night, and he took her across the flat farmland outside of town where they came upon a carnival of spinning lights that glowed like a city in the darkness. He pulled off the road, and they sat staring at the lights, ephemeral.

"I would build this for you each night, if I could," he said. "I would make it for you over and over again."

Chapter 22

On the day of Officer Beckley's funeral, Reverend Edwards woke early and drove to the other side of town, to a small church where the funeral would be held. His doctor had warned against his going anywhere, but he was determined. He had missed the memorial service, and he would not miss this. Dressed in a suit with his pastor's collar, he made his way across town.

It was hot again, and for the third week in a row the sun seemed too large in the sky. It reminded him of the verse from John that he sometimes used to begin communion, "I am the living bread which came down from heaven; if anyone eats of this bread, he will live forever; and the bread which I shall give for the life of the world is my flesh." Those words had the same feeling of certainty, as if you would never have to stop counting on them.

There wasn't much he was counting on as he parked his car and walked toward the brick building that housed the church. While he was in the hospital, the staff psychiatrist had explained that asthma attacks like his had psychological origins. They'd discussed a possible stay at a sanitarium, but Saturday morning the minister had insisted on returning home.

His doctor had advised him to spend time with his wife and to visit with those in his congregation who stopped by his house, but what he wanted was to be left alone. The events of the past week had fallen on top of him, it seemed, from some great height, and when he recalled them, they still felt alive, as if they were happening over and over again.

Groups of people were gathered outside the small church, wearing suits and dark Sunday dresses and hats. Reverend Edwards walked among them, but, as the only white person approaching the church, he was aware that he was not one of them. He passed the black-robed minister who was grasping the hands of a congregation member, talking with her. Then he went inside, despite feeling out of place, and saw Jack Turnbow sitting in the last pew. Nodding at the officer, he sat down next to him. In a pew closer to the front, the police chief and other officers from the town were seated together in a row, wearing their uniforms.

The inside of the church, with two rows of pews, was larger than it looked from the outside. The altar had been covered with a white cloth, strewn with flowers. A purple clematis vine draped across the front, and behind it were piles of white and yellow roses and blue hydrangea blossoms. Vases filled with more roses had been set on the floor in front of the altar around a closed casket that was draped with an American flag. Long lengths of honeysuckle were wound around the wooden prayer rail. Even from where he sat in the back pew, Reverend Edwards could smell the honeysuckle and the roses.

Next to him, Jack Turnbow sat silently staring at the front of the church. He had arrived some twenty minutes ago, wearing his uniform like the others, but he'd chosen to sit by himself in the back. He'd learned that on Tuesday morning, Beckley had called in to ask if he had been found, several minutes before radioing in the license plate number of the vehicle he had stopped behind. Hearing this, Jack had felt as if he might descend into madness from self-rage.

"I'm sorry you lost your partner," Reverend Edwards told him.

Jack had nothing to say to anyone. Next to him, a pair of crutches leaned against the pew, and his sprained ankle was wrapped in a bandage that wouldn't allow his left shoe to be laced. He noted who in the department was present and who was missing. The chief had said he wanted everyone in attendance, but Jack saw that the couple of officers who had made comments in the locker room had managed to get out of being there.

Others were filing in now, filling the pews, talking and crying, as Reverend Thomas swept to the front of the sanctuary, his hands stretched high in the air. "Brethren, let us sing out, let us praise the Lord, let us sing our brother to the Promised Land!"

A woman near the front stood and began to sing, "Swing Low, Sweet Chariot." Her voice was both high and deep, and she sang the first few lines alone before others in the chorus stood and joined her.

"That chariot is here, Brethren," Reverend Thomas called out when the song was finished. "It has arrived in all its glory, for Martin Beckley has been called home wearing his uniform. The chariot has come to carry him to the gates of Heaven."

"Hallelujah," someone called out. "Praise the Lord."

Reverend Edwards listened to the words of the Scripture: "He has risen, he is not here; see the place where they laid him." He heard the hymns and the hallelujahs. "Martin Saul Beckley," Reverend Thomas shouted. "We give you over to God's hands."

The sweetness from the flowers filled the room. The voices rolled down the aisles and among the pews. Then relatives and friends began to come to the front to speak.

"Martin was a good son. He always went to school, then came home and helped his mother."

"Just after high school, Martin joined the army. He planned to get his college degree with his G.I. bill."

"He was decorated for saving the crew on that boat."

They talked on until the essence of Martin Beckley was palpable. When it was all done, and the police chief had stood to talk about the promise Officer Beckley held as an officer, Jack forced himself up to standing, using his crutches to maneuver himself out of the pew. He hadn't planned on getting up, but moments later, he stood staring out at the mourners.

"Martin Beckley was a fine officer," he began. "I was assigned to train him, something I'd never done before, and I won't pretend I was good at it." He looked down at the woman in the front whom he recognized as Beckley's mother. "He was driving out on the highway Tuesday morning looking for me when he came upon that car."

He stopped, unable to continue. "He was honorable, I just want to say that," he added. "He was more honorable than most." For a moment longer he stood there, and then he made his way back to his seat, his eyes tearing up so that he couldn't see what he looked at.

After the service ended, he stood out in the parking lot next to Reverend Edwards. "He asked me once to get a bite to eat with him when our shift ended, but I wouldn't do it. I wouldn't sit across from him in a public place." He had no idea why he was telling the minister this, except that he had to tell somebody. "There was talk sometimes in the station house—racial remarks, all under the guise of kidding, only they weren't. I could have tried to stop it, but I just figured, that was the way it was." Jack waited a moment, but the minister didn't say anything.

"What did Beckley say when you saw him Tuesday morning?" Jack asked. "Did he say anything about me?"

"Just that you weren't at your house when he stopped by, but he had an idea of where you went. He mentioned going out to find you."

Jack stared down at the pavement. "What else?"

The minister glanced at the church. "We talked about faith. His grandfather was a minister. He experienced some difficult things, but he had that."

Jack nodded. "Accounts for why he quoted the Bible."

Their eyes met, and then the two men looked away from one another. "You know, I might have convinced George Fowler to turn himself in, but I didn't," the minister said.

"You can't take the blame for that," Jack told him. "No one can take the blame for that."

It was all he could say, and it wasn't much. He opened his car door and threw his crutches onto the back seat, then got into the car and drove away, not saying goodbye, or waving, or looking back. The police chief had found the name of the hunter who owned the cabin Jack had discovered at Crowfoot Lake. When questioned, the man had reported seeing someone matching George's description on Monday morning, in a canoe near the hunter's cabin. Unused to seeing anyone at that end of the lake, the hunter had called out and asked where the other man was staying. The man in the canoe hadn't replied. He had pushed his paddle against the silt-covered bottom, then glided out into deeper water.

Jack's instinct about George Fowler had been right, but he hadn't figured on the impossibility of locating a man in an area as large and remote as Crowfoot Lake. It had amounted to exactly what Beckley had said it would amount to—finding a needle in a haystack. The roadblock set up by the state police Monday night had been discontinued Tuesday morning. If George had been somewhere else in the vast area of brush and pines around the lake on Monday night, he could have been driving back toward town Tuesday morning, when Beckley noticed him pulled off to the side of the highway looking distressed and crossed over to turn around and find out why. The bullet fired into Beckley had belonged to a .38 gun, a common weapon. The detective who investigated had commented that it looked as if the body had been kicked toward the bank, then rolled down into the bushes. There had been no other evidence except for tire tracks. Without something more substantial, it was mostly speculation.

Jack drove the short distance to his house, and minutes later, hobbled into his kitchen, slammed the door, then kicked it, forgetting about his bad foot. Seconds later, he lay on the floor cursing, his foot held high. Outside, the air was shifting. A cool breeze blew through the open windows, but he hardly noticed it as he crawled over to a chair and used it to help pull himself up. Hopping over to the doorway, careful not to put any weight on his foot, he leaned down and grasped his crutches.

Earlier, the air had been hot and humid, and sitting in the church, he'd felt drenched in sweat. "It's supposed to rain later," he'd heard someone say as he walked through the church parking lot, but he hadn't believed it. Now, his shirt clung damply to his back, and he shivered a little, feeling the breeze and the slight drop in temperature, as he made his way over to the door of his basement. He tossed his crutches down the stairs, and then started down the steps, leaning heavily against the rail.

Above him, the wind blew audibly through the opened windows, but in the cool cave of the basement, the house was quiet. Five years ago when his father had moved out of his parents' home, Jack had stored the boxes of things he'd wanted to keep. In one of them was his mother's set of good dishes, diminished over the years. His father had wanted to give them to his mother's church for a bazaar, but Jack had taken them instead. He'd known he might never use them, but he'd wanted them, even if they only sat in his basement, in a box among other boxes.

They were the dishes his mother had used on Sundays, holidays, and for company. The last time he remembered eating off them had been the night of his high-school graduation. His mother had cooked lamb, his favorite, and served it with mint jelly. There had been purple irises in a vase on the table.

He couldn't remember what the dishes looked like. His mother had told him once that she'd chosen the pattern herself, and that it had taken her weeks to pick out the one she wanted. Jack had sensed the pleasure she'd taken in picking them out. The set had been a wedding present from her parents.

Instinctively, he went for the largest of the boxes on the bottom, lifting the others from it, and there inside, wrapped in old pieces of browned newsprint, he found the dishes. He slid a dinner plate out from the paper. Hairline cracks marked the surface, and it was edged with a pale green vine and small, blue flowers.

He peeled the newsprint from more of the plates, along with cups and saucers, and with each dish came more memories of the meals he'd eaten off them. He could remember the linen tablecloths she'd used, and the heavy silver on the folded napkins. When he was small, he'd been both excited to eat off those dishes and a little afraid he would break something.

His mother had set a store by anything pretty. Occasionally his father had complained about the hours she spent working in her flower garden. "Can't you grow tomatoes or something useful?" he'd asked her. But in the end it hadn't been a serious complaint. Both Jack and his father had appreciated what the flowers meant to her.

Now he fit the dishes back into the box and began to drag it across the basement floor. Normally he could have carried it easily, but he was forced to climb the steps on his knees one at a time, gritting his teeth as he lifted the box and set it on the next step in front of him. When he reached the top, he shoved the box across his kitchen floor toward the door to his driveway.

The clouds that had ridden the horizon all week without amounting to anything had lifted higher by now, and one of them slid in front of the sun. He limped over to the door, opened it, and dragged the box outside to his car. Once he got the back door open, he knelt down next to the box and lifted it with a loud grunt. Then he squeezed inside, and backed the car toward the road.

It was darker now, and he could imagine that the rain might come. The streets were curiously empty as he drove his car through town toward Elizabeth Greenly's house. He had no idea how she would react when she saw him at her door, whether she would be glad for the dishes or would think he was weird for hauling them to her house, when he hardly knew her. When he reached her driveway, he sat there for a few minutes before getting out of his car. Then he bent and pulled the box out, leaving his crutches behind. His back was hurting, and he felt his muscles grind as he hunched over the box and limped to the front door.

He had to ring the bell twice before it opened. "My goodness," Elizabeth said when she saw him. "What are you carrying? It looks heavy. Come inside."

Her hair was hastily tied back, and loose strands hung in her face. She had been sitting in her kitchen, staring out the window, watching the clouds gather. Izzy was asleep on the couch in the living room.

Painfully, Jack lowered the box, setting it on her floor. "I'm the officer who was here earlier in the week."

She nodded.

"I just wanted to give you something for your kitchen wall. Just a few old dishes I had in my basement. I don't know if you can use them, but I thought. . . . "

He leaned over and shoved the box toward her; she knelt down and pried it open. Reaching her hands into the newspaper, she pulled out a teacup.

"Oh, these are too lovely," she said, looking up at him. "I can't accept them."

"They were my mother's years ago, but she's been dead for a long time, and they've just been sitting in my basement. I'll never use them. Truthfully, I'd like you to take them. It would help me out."

"Help you out?"

He faltered, trying to think of a way to make light of what he was doing. "They'll end up in a yard sale someday if you don't take them, and I think my mother would appreciate my giving them to you."

"Are you sure?" Elizabeth asked, carefully lifting a plate, holding it to the light. "There are quite a few here. You might want to use them yourself."

"I won't," he told her. "My father wanted to give them away five years ago. I'm just finally doing it."

"Well, thank you." She stood up, still holding the plate and cup. "You know I've just realized that it's my birthday. I'd forgotten about it until now, but there you go," she said.

Jack grinned, feeling lucky in the midst of everything. "Well, happy birthday, then."

She thanked him again, and he went back out to his car, even though she asked him if he would like to come in and rest first.

The clouds were massing swiftly now, and the air felt damp. He wanted to drive home and be alone in his own house when the rain started, but he found himself sitting in Elizabeth's driveway. In the strange light from the clouds, the walkway and her flowers looked like a painting.

Eventually, he started the engine and turned on his headlights. His partner's death lay on his shoulders. No one had said that to him, but he felt it was true. Jack had simply been told to take a sick leave until he was able to walk without the crutches.

The Wednesday before, as he'd left the police chief's office, he'd passed one of the officers in the hallway who had made the racist comments. "You had no right to treat Officer Beckley the way you did," Jack told him, but the other officer kept walking, ignoring him. Now Jack wished he had punched him instead of saying anything.

"I'm sorry," he said out loud, as he pulled out of Elizabeth's driveway, something inside him cracking open. The words were drowned out by the sudden sound of the rain as he turned toward home.

Chapter 23

After Jack had gone back out to his car, Elizabeth carried the box of dishes into her kitchen, still feeling surprised by what had happened. She set the box on the kitchen table. The rain was coming soon, and it was badly needed. Patches of grass had gone brown, and her flowers, which she'd neglected, were beginning to wilt. If there wasn't a good bit of rain, the leaves on the trees wouldn't turn orange and yellow and red, and summer would only fade into winter.

She slipped a dinner plate from the box, handling the other woman's dishes carefully, holding them up to the light. In the past few days, she'd broken close to half the plates she and Carlton and the children had used over the years. There had been more dinners on those dishes than she could count, more evenings than she could remember spent together at this table.

First it had been just she and Carlton. "What are we going to do with a whole big set like that?" Carlton had asked when she'd said she wanted to purchase eight settings. Neither of them had been able to imagine the family they would end up creating, but over the years, those dishes had covered the table, then filled the sink each evening.

As the rain began to fall outside, she wrapped a plate from Jack's box in newsprint and tapped it gently with her hammer. It cracked easily. She took the adhesive and spread it over an area of the wall and began to arrange the pieces. One fit against another, never perfectly, but with jagged edges that would have to be smoothed later with grout. There was something in the action of fitting together irregular pieces, in the nesting of them, that she found so satisfying. There might be a protrusion or a crevice, but even the oddly shaped pieces could be blended with the rest, and sometimes they were the ones that made the pattern distinctive.

The rain fell harder, insulating her, and as she worked, she noticed a small section of the mosaic that she didn't recognize. Someone had taken the rest of the pieces from the coffee cup she'd broken a few days earlier and fit them together in a circular pattern in the far corner of the wall. The coffee cup had been a deep, transparent blue, and the circle alternated that color with the white grout. From where she stood it looked like a small, spinning Ferris wheel.

There was a noise behind her, and she turned to see Bert had come into the room, newly showered, her wet hair wrapped turban-style in a towel. "I'm going back to school tomorrow," Bert announced, as she opened the refrigerator and filled a glass with iced tea.

"Are you ready?" Elizabeth asked her.

"I don't know," Bert said after a long drink. "But I want to try."

They both turned then and looked out the kitchen window. The sky was dark, thick with rain. It was difficult to make out Carlton's grill in the yard or the small dogwood tree.

Elizabeth turned back to look at the wall. "Someone added a circle," she said. "There in the corner."

"I did," Bert told her.

Elizabeth walked up and passed her hand over the blue and white pattern. "I think it's perfect."

Bert smiled and walked to the front hallway. "Carl's home. Maybe we can all eat supper together tonight," she said, turning.

Elizabeth nodded. "I'll clear the table."

She put the box of dishes Jack had given her in the pantry and began to clean up the various small piles of glass, sweeping them into mixing bowls. At first it felt like a monumental task, but she warmed to it, moving more swiftly as the rain drummed against the house.

Carlton was gone. Here were his shoes, which he'd left by the front door, and there were his rubber boots in the mudroom, which he would have worn on an afternoon like today. His work shirt hung on a peg next to his hat with the wide brim he wore for shade. He had disappeared in an instant, but here were all his things, as if he would be returning at any minute.

Now she put on his blue work shirt, rolling up the sleeves. Rain streamed down the windows and pummeled the roof as she carried the box to the mudroom and set it there. Silently, she began to cry. It would never make any sense. There had been no body to bury. All that was left was his ring.

She wet a dishcloth and wiped the dust from the powdered grout off the table. She counted out four plates and felt fortunate she hadn't broken them all. Her friends and neighbors had dropped off food daily all week, including a ham that morning. She had always loved a good storm, and in the distance she could hear the rumble of thunder as she worked.

As she was warming the ham, Izzy awoke and wandered sleepily into the kitchen, rubbing her eyes. She wanted a kitty, she'd said just before falling asleep. If her daddy wasn't coming back again, that was what she wanted. Bert came downstairs, Carl close behind her. They both looked subdued, but Elizabeth could sense an eagerness about the dinner underneath. The heart of the storm was moving closer, and she stood in front of the window watching the sky brighten, so that all things glistened, with a streak of lightning.

"Bert, get out some glasses and pour the milk," she said. "Izzy, count out four napkins and four sets of silverware. Carl, you can help me get the plates and lay out the food on the table."

Chapter 24

After Jack left the funeral service, the minister sat in the parking lot of Reverend Thomas's church. The final hymn of the funeral service had been "Will the Circle Be Unbroken," and it played on in the minister's head. Everything felt broken, and he couldn't imagine being whole again.

The interior of his car was hot, and he found himself sweating even though he'd taken off his jacket. He didn't want to go home. Nancy had argued with him that morning when she'd come into the bedroom and seen him dressing for the funeral. Then realizing how determined he was, she'd said she would go also, and drive them. But he hadn't wanted her there.

"Promise me you won't stay long," she'd said before he left the house. The minister knew he shouldn't worry her, but part of him felt like sitting in his car until nightfall.

The hearse was waiting at the door of the church, and Reverend Edwards watched as the coffin was brought to it. Officer Beckley had talked about his grandfather who had believed in the covenant of the rainbow. One rainbow for us, another for them. Was that how they saw it?

He watched the gathering of mourners disperse as the back of the hearse was closed up. Someone was wailing and the sound made him shudder. A few minutes later the hearse began to pull away, hesitated, and then drove slowly as the mourners came for their cars and formed a line that stretched to the road with their headlights gleaming. The minister watched them crawl along the drive, and when there were only a few left, he started up his own car. His own church was several miles away. He had driven past it on his way here, but he'd hardly looked at it. Now, as he followed the roads toward Maple Street, he told himself he was finished with the ministry. He would compose a letter to his congregation, announcing his decision.

Fifteen minutes later, he was parked next to the church. Above him the clouds were gathering, full of purpose, the way they must have looked when Noah watched for the flood. He thought of the mourners who would just now be arriving at the cemetery. The rain when it fell would drench everything—all those gathered at the burial ground and the ruins of the drugstore.

He stepped out of his car and stood in front of his church. A week ago he'd felt nestled in the small town, protected, but now the earth seemed too large to comprehend.

The rain was beginning to fall. Within minutes, it came down in such thick sheets that it looked solid. It pounded the ground and coursed down his arms and legs and streamed down his face.

"Thou preparest a table before me in the presence of mine enemies: thou anointest my head with oil; my cup runneth over." He repeated those words from the Psalms in his head, words he had planned to use in the sermon for the memorial service he'd never delivered, but he didn't feel anything.

In the cemetery across town, the coffin was being lowered into the ground. He told himself this, and he thought of the mourners huddled under their umbrellas with their loss. One afternoon, as he lay in the hospital bed, he'd dreamt of Officer Beckley. In the dream, he'd seen the officer lying in a field of fire. The fire had been widespread, and the minister felt as though he'd walked through miles of it before spotting another human being. He'd knelt down, reaching out, intending to help the other man stand, but when he touched the officer, he found the man was made of light. There was no substance, only an image. Above the officer's head, a white cone emanated. The minister reached out and touched the cone, and the light went straight through him. It was wide and narrow all at once, and full of nothing and the world and grace.

He knew the dream wasn't real, but it felt as real to him as his memory of their conversation. It felt as real to him as the loss of Carlton Greenly and Stella McNeese, and as real as George Fowler's appearance in his office.

Rivulets of water poured down his face, and through the curtain of heavy rain, he couldn't see anything clearly. When a car pulled into the parking lot, he could barely make out its shape. The vehicle stopped next to his, and John Scott got out and opened an umbrella. The man hurried over to the minister, his umbrella bending with the force of the rain.

"Reverend," John called out, attempting to hold the umbrella over both their heads. "What are you doing standing here?"

"I feel like this is the end," the minister said.

"It's not. Come inside the church out of this downpour."

The minister shook his head. He felt like he couldn't move. "It will all come to light eventually, John. George Fowler came to my office at the church. That's why the warnings were issued. He came there because I married him several years ago, and he'd come to services here."

They stood not speaking, and there was just the sound of the rain. Then John said, "Let's go inside where we can talk."

"I can't. I can't imagine standing there again. I can't see myself writing another sermon."

John was squeezed in close to him under the umbrella. "You'll preach again," he said. "You will."

From a distance came the sound of thunder, and a line of lightning etched the sky. The minister thought of Officer Beckley, Carlton Greenly, Joyce Fowler, Stella McNeese, and the others. Once George was dead, his soul would enter Hell. Reverend Edwards had little doubt about that. He rarely spoke of Hell in his sermons, but he believed absolutely in its existence, just as he believed in Heaven.

"I married that man," he said, but the words were drowned out.

While he was in the hospital, Chief Reynolds had brought by a recent photograph of George Fowler. "I just want to be certain this was the man who came to see you," he'd said.

The police hadn't been able to find fingerprints on the envelope opener, which meant they had no hard evidence.

"That was him," the minister had said.

"The lightning is getting closer. We should go inside or get in our cars," John told him.

The minister nodded. "I should go home."

John took the minister's arm, and they waded through the water. Rain penetrated the umbrella, and it sloshed up onto their pants and into their shoes as they walked. John stopped by the minister's car and opened the door for him. "Will you be all right?" he asked, shouting over the sound.

The minister nodded. "I'm just a few minutes away."

He got into his car as a pool of water spread across the floorboards.

"There's a lot of us thinking about you," John told him. Rain pounded the car's roof. "I'm praying for you."

Reverend Edwards reached out and gripped his hand. "Thank you, John."

In the past few days, several of those in his congregation had phoned his house or stopped by with food. After the funeral, Reverend Thomas had shaken his hand and said, "Go home, heal yourself."

Reverend Edwards had never thought about the Baptist church on the other side of town. He had known of its existence, but he hadn't really considered it. During the service, Reverend Thomas had said that even Martin Luther King recognized the reality of evil in the world and demanded that we recognize it. He had recalled those killed in the riots and in crimes of bigotry. Now, sitting in his car, the minister saw images of men wielding clubs. Last night, lying on the couch watching the evening news, he'd felt the reality of the caskets being carried off the plane. In several months Charlie Bourne, the young man he'd counseled, would be shipped out. Would the minister end up responsible for his death?

Rain pounded the windshield, and in front of that curtain, one picture after another flashed past, so quickly they blended together—Marines fishing with villagers in a faraway country, armed National Guard soldiers patrolling dark streets, helicopters hovering, and stacks of body bags waiting to be airlifted. The thunder moved closer. Suddenly he wanted to be at home, and it didn't matter that getting there would mean driving through the downpour. He was soaked through and shivering, and he could barely see the outline of his church or of John's car, still sitting next to his own. Staring at the rain, he felt the crushing weight of all that water falling toward earth. This storm marked the end of the world he knew and the beginning of an unknown one, a world he didn't understand. The quiet sleepiness of a small town didn't exist anymore.

Starting up his car, he flipped on his headlights and the windshield wipers. They worked back and forth furiously, but made no difference. He eased his foot against the pedal and drove toward home.

Once, on a Saturday, he took Joyce to see the Indian mounds. They visited the museum first. The Indians had built the mounds more than a thousand years ago, using sticks and clamshells to dig the earth. They'd carried dirt in large baskets. An exhibit case showed a preserved skull, obsidian blades, and the prints of human feet embedded in rock.

When he and Joyce left the museum, they climbed up one of the mounds, which was large enough to hold several houses. From the top, they could see out into the distance, across the flat earth where other mounds rose like the backs of gentle, humped creatures.

Joyce said she could feel the spirits of the people who had built them. She said standing there made them part of the ancient civilization, if just for a few minutes. The slope on one side was fairly steep, and on an impulse, he lay down on the ground and rolled all the way to the bottom. Joyce came tumbling after him, her body colliding against his. They lay like that, next to each other, under the earth's roof, looking at the clouds.

Now it's morning. The light is silver, birds chatter, and the streets are speckled with lights from houses where people stand brewing coffee or frying up breakfast. Someone pours milk into a bowl. Someone butters bread for toast. The sun rises fiery and whole. Across the surface of the earth, the leaves and tree trunks are glazed with rain-water.

Whatever happens next—a car engine turning over, the sound of laughter on a sidewalk—the earth never hesitates in its great, thundering spin.

Far above, the clouds move in wisps. They drift across the expanse of blue-gray, changing their shapes. Beyond them, the sky's dome extends for miles. It appears solid but it is permeable, a membrane of light and darkness surrounding the world beneath it.

Author's Note

The characters, the town, the references to Methodism, and the events of *Centerville* are fictional, but the novel's impetus is a childhood memory. In 1967, I witnessed the bombing of a drugstore in a small Midwest town. Like Sandi, I had made a sudden, inexplicable decision not to enter the store moments before the bomb exploded.

I would like to thank Hilary Attfield for her insightful direction, Rachel King for her close and astute attention to the manuscript, and everyone else at West Virginia University Press for their hard work on the novel. Also, thank you to all those who read early drafts of the book, especially those who spent many hours on it, including Janet Osborn, Linda Osborn, Evie Reda, Erin Malone, Jane Gelfman, and Lorraine Glennon. Thanks to Linda Shockley for her humor, her knowledge, and her love of books. Finally, thank you to the Virginia Center for the Creative Arts for their residency and to the Cushman Writers Group. Community means everything. As always, I am grateful to Mike Jenkins for his encouragement, his sound technical advice, and his support.

Questions for Discussion

1. Sandi turns away from the drugstore at the last minute, a decision that saves both her and Bert's lives. Later, she doesn't know why she didn't enter. Discuss how this lack of understanding haunts her. As a fourteen-year-old, how does she cope with the unexplainable?

2. At the beginning of the novel, Jack Turnbow is a self-assured police officer and volunteer fire fighter. After the bombing, he ends up questioning his abilities and performance. How do the bombing and the events that it triggers force him to change?

3. During the first third or so of the novel, the fire exists at the center of the action, and the four main characters move around it. Later, when the fire has been extinguished, George Fowler moves to the center, as the others respond to his actions. In what ways is George Fowler similar to the explosion and the fire?

4. Following the sudden loss of her husband, Elizabeth begins breaking the family's dishes. Discuss the motives and the effects of using her dishes to make a mosaic. How does the destruction of the dishes lead her both into and out of her grief? How does it help her to connect with her daughter and with others, such as Jack Turnbow, the police officer who delivers the proof of her husband's death?

5. Reverend Edwards's crisis of faith is multifold. How is George able to unhinge the minister's beliefs in such a short period of time? Do you think Reverend Edwards will be able to continue his work as a minister?

6. Sandi comes of age quickly during the days following the explosion. What are the trials she must pass? Which characters act as guides in her journey toward growing up? Which characters present challenges?

7. While lying in the dark stairwell of an abandoned house, Jack Turnbow has several realizations about his behavior toward his partner, Martin Beckley. Discuss the causes of racial prejudice. What makes Jack blind to the prejudices inherent in his actions? What enables him to wake up to them?

8. Martin Beckley carries his own ghosts. How do these ghosts affect his relationship with his partner? How do they affect his exchange with the minister when he talks with him in the church parking lot, shortly before Beckley is killed?

9. *Centerville* takes place in the few days following a large and unexpected tragedy that affects an entire town. Before the town existed, others lived in this place, including the mound builders, who left clear evidence of themselves. How is a sense of place important in the novel? Discuss how place affects your view of the tragedy.

10. The novel takes place in 1967, during the Vietnam War and a summer of racial riots in many American cities. Discuss the importance of the time period in the novel. How are the events in the novel relevant to more recent events, such as 9/11?

About the Author

Karen Osborn is the author of three previous novels, *Patchwork* (a *New York Times* Notable Book of the Year) *Between Earth and Sky*, and *The River Road*. She lives in Amherst, Massachusetts with her husband and teaches fiction writing at Mt. Holyoke College and for Fairfield University's low residency M.F.A. program.